WHAT PEOPLE ARE SAYING ABOUT

VOICES OF ANGELS

"Out of this world. Touching. Magical. *Voices of Angels* whisks readers into a mystical gift. Unwrap it and watch your universe ignite."
Keidi Keating, author of *The Light* featuring Marci Shimoff from *The Secret*.

"Take a fascinating journey with Lizzie and her angel...lose yourself in this magical tale as I did myself...I loved it."
Jacky Newcomb, Sunday Times Best Selling author of *An Angel Saved My Life*

'Voices of Angels takes the spiritual and angelic to the young masses, dolls it up, spins it in the familiar and gives it full on sexy guts. A mesmerizing story that is well written and addictive. A fantastic first novel."
Alice Grist, Author and Publisher

"I've read hundreds of books over the years, so it takes a lot for me to sit up and take notice. But I loved this so much, I stayed up late into the night reading it. The story moved along at a cracking pace and it just got better and better. Not many writers can pull off such a feat, least of all first-time authors. This was impressive."
Stephanie Hale, founder of RichWriterPoorWriter.com

"Voices of Angels is a real page-turner that effortlessly captures the sensual, transforming secrets of first love."
Alison Bond, author of *Ho*
Valentine and *A Reluctant C*

"When coming of age everything hurts more, means more and promises more. In this immaculately crafted novel, brimming with real wisdom – Hannah's ability to capture the depth of the passionate highs and lows of the teenage years is beyond good. It's magical. I had tears streaming down my face by the end. It's just delicious. As soon as it comes out, I'll be giving to everyone I know – not just teenagers!"
Dr Joanna Martin, Founder of Shift Lifestyle, international speaker and author of *The Lifestyle Shift*

Voices of Angels

Voices of Angels

Hannah M Davis

Winchester, UK
Washington, USA

First published by Soul Rocks Books, 2012
Soul Rocks Books is an imprint of John Hunt Publishing Ltd., Laurel House, Station Approach,
Alresford, Hants, SO24 9JH, UK
office1@o-books.net
www.o-books.com

For distributor details and how to order please visit the 'Ordering' section on our website.

ISBN: 978 1 84694 869 5

A CIP catalogue record for this book is available from the British Library.

Design: Lee Nash

Printed and bound by CPI Group (UK) Ltd, Croydon, CR0 4YY
Printed in the USA by Offset Paperback Mfrs, Inc

CONTENTS

'Baby, you're a firework
Come on let your colors burst'
- Katy Perry

"I know I got angels watchin' me from the other side."
- Kanye West

Acknowledgements & Gratitude

When I was about seven, blond haired and with pig-tails, I remember asking my mum what 'infinity' meant and when she said it meant forever I decided there and then it was one of my favourite ever words. It still is. How magical that something could never end?

I can't remember when I first decided I wanted to be an author. Was it before I knew about infinity or after? But in some form the urge to write has always inside of me – my very own eternity.

However, this book has been a long time coming. So my thanks span three different countries, two continents and about five years. If you're reading this, please forgive me if I have not mentioned you by name. In truth almost everyone I have ever met has played a part in getting this book to where it is today and it would be quite impossible to mention you all!

But we have to start somewhere and I'm going to travel backwards in time to a boutique hotel in Potts Point, Sydney where I was a writer in residence for 2 months writing the first draft of this novel and where I fell head over heels in love with the writer's life.

My first visit to Australia was so much fun - from ginger to skin, to crazy nights out, from federal agents to lots of Jacob's Creek. So a huge thank you to everyone from that trip. What a whirlwind and the start of a lifelong love affair with that country.

More recently, I'd like to give my gratitude to my Shift family, Joey, Greg, Jo, Donna, Colleen, Andie, Daniel, Stu, Tam and H. Thank you for giving me the space to be my own star.

To my ever present writing group in Spain, Albert, Maggie, Mike, Wendy, Jan and David, thanks for allowing Slasher Davis time to talk about her own book! And hey, if I can do it so can you! And that especially includes you, Mike.

To all my individual writing clients over the past few years in my guise as Book Doctor. You will never know how much you taught me. Really.

To living in Spain and for being such a rich, colourful and passionate place to live. You provided the inspiration for most of this book and in particular, a white mountain town with beautiful sea views of the Med and Morocco.And to all my lovely friends who live there and on the coast.

To my virtual friends on authonomy where I once nervously posted the first 10,000 words of this book and found out people might actually like it. I got the number one spot and the gold star but the real reward was meeting you.

To Lee for being so proud of me.

To my publishers, Soul Rocks Books and O-Books, for coming along at the perfect time. I do love a bit of synchronicity. And to the gorgeous Alice Grist for believing in me and believing in the book. Thanks also to Lisa Clark for her sassy edits.

A very special thank you goes to my best mate, Ali, for being the one person over the past few years who never let me give up on my dream of being an author. You've played such a key role in my life and I'm always grateful for you. And you make me laugh. BFF.

To my brother, and my mum and dad without whose willingness to support my dreams has helped me more than you can know and because you've always allowed me the space to be different. Or in dad's eyes – hocus pocus!

And lastly, thank you to my very own angel who will hopefully let this book fly into your hands. Because my friend the reader, ultimately I wrote this book for you.

Hannah

Chapter One

'Infinity.'

'What?'

'Lizzie, I asked you what the meaning of infinity was. The answer is not 'what''.

The class sniggered.

Mrs Froust pushed an impatient hand through her hair. 'What's wrong with you today?'

What's wrong? Lizzie thought. *What's wrong?*

What's wrong was the *thing* above her teacher's head. It had appeared from nowhere. One moment the day was like any other and the next Lizzie had looked up and all the breath left her body in one big whoosh. Why? Because an ominous dark shadow the shape of a crow's wing hung above Mrs Froust's hair and Lizzie had no idea what it was. Goose bumps scuttled up her arms. There was something so unworldly to it. As though the skin to this world had been pierced and this *thing* thrust through it.

Mrs Froust frowned. 'Speak up, I can't hear you.'

Dear God. Had she spoken out loud? Lizzie never spoke in class, not since the first day of term when she said her name and got it wrong so everyone had laughed at her. She swallowed but it didn't help. The words reared up like a stallion, as if they had an untameable spirit all of their own.

'You have a black mark above your head.'

Mrs Froust touched the air above her head, as if playing an invisible piano. There was nothing there so she let her hand drop to her side. It hung limply.

Inky and yet see-through, shapeless and yet tangible. It reminded Lizzie of the shadow a cloud makes on the pavement.

Never had she seen such a thing before.

Never.

From the back of class she heard someone filing their nails. She didn't need to turn round to know who it was.

'*I* know what infinity means.'

'Yes, Belinda?' Mrs Froust said warily.

'Infinity means to continue with no end.'

Lizzie peeked behind her. Bee sat in a cloud of caramel and honey-colored locks at the back of class with a nail file in one hand and the open textbook in the other.

'Well answered.' Mrs Froust smiled thinly at Bee. 'But I was actually speaking to Lizzie. So? What does it mean?'

Lizzie gulped. 'I… I don't know.'

Mrs Froust raised her eyebrows. 'You surprise me, Lizzie. Surely a girl like you so interested in astronomy would know the answer to such a simple question?'

Prickles of sweat formed between Lizzie's shoulder blades. Too late, she realized that Mrs Froust had been asking about infinity and not about the black mark. She had a sudden sharp yearning for a wormhole to take her far away from here. As she mumbled something incoherent in reply, she blushed bright red when she caught Nathan Parks' cool gaze. She had been staring at *it*.

The rest of the class looked from Lizzie to Mrs Froust and back to her again. Lizzie gulped and the black mark fizzed momentarily, like a dying light bulb.

There was a deafening silence until Bee chirped up. 'I think Lizzie is seeing things because *I* can't see it.' She gazed around her, inviting the others to answer. 'Can anyone else?'

One by one her classmates shook their heads. As far as their faces revealed, there was nothing extraordinary about Mrs Froust today. She was dressed in her normal overly-colorful clothes with her auburn hair sat loose on her shoulders and bracelets jangling on her wrists. In a different life she could have been a folk singer.

There was no black mark.

Bee opened her mouth to speak again but was cut off.

'Enough of this nonsense,' Mrs Froust snapped. 'Everyone turn to page 111.'

For once, Lizzie was glad of her thick mane of hair as she tucked it around her ears. It didn't matter though; she still felt the curious eyes of her classmates boring into her back. She ended up staring so hard at the textbook she actually couldn't see anything at all.

Three, two, one. She counted the minutes until the classroom bell rang, then slammed her maths book shut and flung it into her bag, deliberately keeping her eyes downward as the rest of class filed out.

She smelled, rather than saw her. The sweet tang of mint chewing gum mingled with drizzled honey.

'Are you seeing things, Frizzo?' Bee leant over her desk, splaying her filed finger-nails like a fan. Her blue eyes were full of bemusement. 'What do you think, Nath?'

Lizzie looked up. With tousled blond hair, a chiselled jaw and a body he'd sculpted into angelic perfection, Nathan stood in front of her desk.

'Well, I suppose anything's better than looking in a mirror.'

Lizzie opened her mouth to retort but nothing came out. It never did.

Bee snorted. 'Frizzo can't help looking the way she does. She was *born* with a face like that.' She cackled as she thrust her bag into Nathan's arms. 'Here. Carry this for me.'

Nathan slung Bee's bag over his right shoulder and wrapped his other arm around Bee. As they left the room arm in arm, Lizzie cradled her own arms around herself for warmth.

She shivered anyway.

Because *it* was still there. Like crow's wings. Flapping in the still dank air of the classroom. It moved when Mrs Froust moved. It stilled when Mrs Froust stilled. In its own unique way, it was beautiful. In the way that stark, empty deserts were beautiful.

It was beautiful but it was also menacing.

And for someone who had never been afraid of the dark, it scared her.

It scared her a lot.

Chapter Two

Thank God maths class meant the end of the day.

The red double-decker bus sat outside the school gates, swelling in size as her classmates boarded. She took one look and turned the other way, picking her way through disused back streets. A painful knot sat in her stomach, like gut-ache, and stayed like this until she turned into the cul-de-sac and spotted Joopy's face waiting for her in the bay window of number thirty-four.

He barked excitedly as she fumbled with the door-key.

'Joopy!' He bounded up and pressed his paws against her thighs. 'Calm down, silly.'

Nevertheless, she took his paws into her hands and held them tightly. She'd had Joopy since she was four years old and she loved him in a way that made her heart hurt. He was a marmalade colored crossbred mongrel, and his eyes were squinty. But who cared? She loved him. And he loved her.

The narrow hallway smelt of lavender air freshener and Lizzie tried not to choke. She kicked off her shoes and raced upstairs to her room. Then ignoring all the clothes her mum had bought her in the past year, she got dressed in a pair of dark combat trousers and a loose fitting black T-shirt that she'd bought herself from Camden market. She shoved her feet into a pair of grubby trainers and wrote a curt note for her mum saying she'd be back for dinner.

Joopy hovered by the front door with an expectant look on his face. The skies were bruised with a brewing storm.

She grabbed his lead. 'C'mon then!'

The pair of them stepped out of the door. She took a sidelong glance at the adjoining semi-detached house. The lights were off and she let go of the breath she'd been holding.

Of all the neighbours to have.

'Let's go, Joops.'

She'd only found the graveyard by accident a few months ago and since then she'd been drawn back at least twice a week. The day Joopy found it had been gray but it was strange how the graveyard had actually added color to her life. Joopy had sneaked down the side street and wormed his way through the hole in the fence. When he barked in excitement she thought he must have found a bone or something. In a sense, he had found bones. Lots of them. But bones of a different kind.

It was a proper, old-fashioned graveyard, not one of those modern manicured cemeteries with polished tombstones and fake flowers. Milton Graveyard was straight out of a gothic movie with dark grey gravestones standing up at odd,perpendicular angles, and dewy tentacles of ivy clawing their way over the inscriptions. Moss covered broken statues completed the scene.

There was something eerie and yet compelling about it.

It held some kind of spell over her. One of London's many forgotten corners, she'd never seen another soul here and even though it was dark and creepy, she felt at home here in a way she never felt at home in her real home. She didn't feel quite so compressed.

The narrow path was overgrown with thick ivy. She wound her way past the neglected gravestones, past elaborate gothic tombs, past statues of resting lions guarding their owner's graves, to the heart of the cemetery. A clearing. It smelt clean and pure.

'Hello,' she murmured and felt the tension drain off her. 'I'm back.'

The marble statue stood in a grass circle all of its own. This clearing was one of the few places where the sun could penetrate the vines and actually make its journey all the way down to earth. She felt safe here. Protected. She finally felt the knot unravel and disappear.

'My angel.' She whispered and pressed her cheek against the base of his wing.

He must have been about six foot tall and was cool to the touch. She reached upward and lightly stroked the tips of her fingers across his face. How many times had she done this? She had memorized every groove: the full lower lip, the hollows in his cheeks, the high curve of his cheekbones and then the deep sockets of his eyes. Although he was just a statue, she always had the feeling he was looking at her. He had eyes that could see straight into her soul.

This was why she came back here, especially when she felt down. He felt like *her* angel. As if he could take away all her pain and hurt. As if he could take away the jibes and the comments. When she was around him, it didn't matter so much that she was different and didn't fit in.

And for an angel, he sure was good looking.

Were angels supposed to be sexy? She smothered a smile. Surely angels were supposed to be *angelic*? With blond hair and serene faces? Even Nathan Parks looked more like an angel than this one. This angel was a different breed. It was as if he couldn't quite believe he was an angel at all. Maybe he'd really wanted to be something more rebellious, something wilder, something dangerous. And as such there was a sense of pain about him. Somebody in the wrong skin.

He reminded Lizzie of herself.

It was crazy to have a crush on a statue. *Crazy*. But at least the statue couldn't hurt her.

And then she remembered. The image of Mrs Froust's black mark popped back into her mind. Clear and stark, as if she could see it now. She shuddered.

'What was it?' she whispered.

It wasn't as if she expected an answer. But it felt good to talk to someone. It wasn't like she could tell mum. No way. That's why she came here, time and time again, because the angel was the only person who understood her. Apart from Joopy, of course. But he didn't count.

'What does it mean?'

She listened for anything other than the leaves on the breeze and the distant sound of traffic. Nothing came. The statue felt cool and lifeless. So she didn't even articulate the next question. The question that fascinated her the most: What happens after you die?

Was there anything?

The wind sifted through the trees with a loud murmur and if there was an answer, it drifted away through the branches like a ghost. Thunder cracked suddenly and the skies opened. She stepped back tilting her face upward as she did.

Lizzie had always loved thunderstorms.

She didn't even flinch when lightening splintered the clouds.

'Bye,' she whispered and touched the angel's face once more, letting her fingers linger on his lips, before reluctantly pulling away.

She wanted to walk away without seeing it. Just for once. But it caught her eye anyway. The dull grey slab of a tombstone that the angel had guarded for over a hundred years. Rain sloshed down it making the inscription even less legible. She licked her lips and looked at it briefly. She knew why it got under her skin. Of course it would. The girl had the same name as her, Elizabeth *and* she'd died aged fifteen. The same age as Lizzie was now. She stared at the gravestone for a long, hard time even though her clothes clung to her and the skies raged overhead.

Was there anything after you died?

Or nothing.

Chapter Three

'Elizabeth, I have some terrible news for you.'

Lizzie's mum stood by the counter and waited for the kettle to boil. It was exactly seven days after she'd first seen the black mark above Mrs Froust's head. Rather than disappearing, like she'd hoped, it had grown stronger and more intense each passing day.

'What?' Mum had last looked like this when Mars, her rabbit, had died of myxomatosis. 'Is it Granny?'

Her grandmother lived alone in a foreign country and was apparently, a little bit mad. Every so often she sent random gifts. The last one had been that Mexican face mask that Lizzie had hung up on the wall in the lounge – much to mum's annoyance.

Her mum, dressed in a high-collared cream blouse and a knee-length black skirt, took one of the plain pine chairs and smoothed the surface of the table with her pearly nails. She shook her head and frowned.

'What then?' Lizzie grabbed a slice of toast and bit into it.

Mum nodded toward the back door. 'Susie has just popped round.'

Susie was mum's best friend. She also happened to be Bee's mum. They lived next door. Of all the neighbours to have.

What had Bee done now?

'It's Mrs Froust.'

Lizzie's throat tightened.

'Lizzie, I'm sorry.' Her mum paused. 'She's dead.'

The toast assumed a lumpy texture, dry, wooden, like sawdust. She swallowed.

'How?'

She had nearly told mum about the black mark the other night. But the words wouldn't come out right and then mum had told her off for mumbling so she'd ended up talking about normal stuff instead. That was all they ever talked about anyway.

'Apparently she got hit by a double decker bus outside the Angel tube. The bus pulled out and hit her.'

'A bus?'

Mum grimaced. 'It was quick, thankfully. I've made a pot of sweet tea. Here, drink some.'

She handed Lizzie her favourite mug, even though they had argued about throwing it away for ages because it was chipped and might carry germs. Lizzie lifted it to her lips and blew across the tan liquid. Through the steam she saw a hazy vision of her teacher splattered on the road in a pool of dark red blood. She blinked and the image disappeared.

'I'm running late for work.' Mum's eyes fell on the stainless-steel clock. 'I've got an important meeting today.'

Mum worked long, erratic hours as regional sales director for a chain of boutique clothes shops in southwest London. Lizzie couldn't remember a time when mum hadn't loved her job. She must do because she brought it home with her every night. Working in fashion also meant she got discounts on all the designer clothes. Lizzie had got used to getting these clothes for her birthday. Clothes that always seemed to look better on other girls than her.

'You'll be ok, Liz?'

She nodded faintly.

Mum linked and unlinked her fingers and then stood up. With a small nod in Lizzie's direction, she gathered her leather purse and car keys off the table and made her way down the hallway to the front door.

It was still too early for school and Lizzie might have sat there indefinitely if not for Joopy. He scratched at the back door and she leapt up, tugged the door open to let him in and pulled the dog into her arms. She sunk her face into his fur.

'Dead?'

The kitchen seemed to shrink, so with Joopy clutched in her

arms, she stepped outside and took a big gulp of air.

The back garden was mum's pride and joy. A neatly mowed lawn surrounded on three sides by flower beds arranged with a carefully coordinated color scheme. She spent hours out here on the weekends making sure everything looked in its place. There was something so quaintly *English* about it all.

The skies started to drizzle.

Lizzie hated drizzle. Why couldn't it just rain properly? She longed for hard rain. Dramatic rain that ripped through the lining of the sky. Rain that stung. Rain that *hurt*. Drizzle wasn't rain, it was just damp air that made her hair frizz even worse than it already did.

She ducked inside the greenhouse. This was her second favourite place in the world. Hidden from view of the Buckingham's house next door, and overhung by the ghostly branches of their silver birch tree, the greenhouse had a hushed, furtive feel about it and she often escaped in here. Sometimes she even slipped inside the glass walls in the middle of the night when everyone else but her was asleep. Those were the best times. There was something so forbidden about it. So secretive.

Inside it was humid, musky smelling, ripe with the scent of plump tomatoes. It was the one place in the garden her mum could not tame. Lizzie felt far more at home in here amongst the wild tangle of untidy vines than she ever did inside the obsessively tidy house.

She picked one of the tomatoes. It even smelt homegrown. She popped it in her mouth and it exploded with a burst of flavour.

Mrs Froust was dead!

The thought sent shudders through her body and for a moment she sat doubled over. It was almost as if the bus had hit *her*, and not Mrs Froust. Joopy licked her hand and the feeling passed. But she still felt coated in something clammy.

She shuddered again as a wave of nausea passed through her.

Even though she hadn't said anything, all week the other girls had been going on and on at her about the black mark. It was worse than the usual comments. She could handle stupid jokes about her hair or her eyes, but this felt different. Like they'd caught onto something real. Something about her that they could *use*.

'Hey, frizzo! Are you hiding?' Candyfloss pink lips framed by a blond mane appeared through the glass.

Just her luck.

'Have you heard about Mrs Froust?'

Lizzie nodded and glanced away, towards grey clouds that threatened rain, sodden in the sky like wet handkerchiefs.

'I heard her head got splattered all over the road and there was bits of brain everywhere.' Bee's eyes glittered as she looked around the greenhouse. She had a perfect heart-shaped face and sexy bee-stung lips. She was beautiful in a way that made Lizzie feel even more plain and ordinary. She looked down and noticed she had some tomato pips splattered on her white blouse.

Bee raised a perfectly plucked eyebrow. 'It's a bit of a coincidence, don't you think?'

'What is?' Lizzie's throat tightened.

'One week you see this mysterious black mark above Mrs Froust's head and the next week she's spread all over Upper Street. Some people might even think the two are connected.' Bee snaked the tip of her tongue across her lips. 'As if you could *see* it happen.'

'See what happen?' Lizzie whispered.

Bee leant forward. 'See that she was going to die. You know, like she was *marked* with death or something.'

Lizzie's heart paused for breath. She let out a long exhalation. 'That's not….true.'

But deep down in a place where all answers sat, she knew it *was* true. The heat rose to her cheeks unwillingly and she looked up and stared straight into Bee's eyes.

She stared because staring was the only weapon she had ever had. It was the one thing she could do that always made Bee back off. That made everyone back off. She had the kind of stare that unnerved people.

Bee's olive skin paled. 'It's true, isn't it?' she whispered. 'You *can* see when people are going to die!'

Every muscle in her body froze.

'You don't just look like a freak,' Bee jabbed a finger towards her chest. 'You really *are* a freak.'

Lizzie looked at Bee's horrified face and gulped hard.

It was true.

She was a freak.

Chapter Four

It was only after Bee had gone that Lizzie unclenched her fists. Why did her mouth always go dry around Bee? It hadn't always been this way. Once upon a time they'd been best of friends, just like their mums, but now they were worlds apart. Their childhood friendship had collapsed in the first week of secondary school. Bee had simply decided Lizzie was not good enough .

And that was that.

'What's wrong with me?' Lizzie cuddled Joopy and pressed her cheek against his fur. She wished someone could tell her.

But not Joopy. He barked, reminding her that he hadn't been fed and that it was time for school. She threw down a bowl of dried biscuits for him, topped up his water bowl, double-locked the front door and set off for the bus. The cul-de-sac she lived on, in this colourless part of north London, so far north it was hardly London at all, appeared dead on this June day. Semi-detached houses with comma shaped driveways, all dozing whilst their owners worked their days away. The sky so low she could practically touch it with her fingertips.

The truth of Bee's words reverberated around her skull.

There *had* to be a connection between the black mark and Mrs Froust's death. No wonder Bee had recoiled in horror. Lizzie had predicted death. She had seen when someone was going to die and maybe she could have done something about it.

The very thought made her stop dead in her tracks. And a cold, pale breeze washed over her.

Already she felt sick.

She pushed the other question back under the surface. Where Mrs Froust was gone was a question she might never know the answer to. Who knew if *anything* existed after death. And how could you ever know anyway? Not unless someone came back and told you all about it.

Biting her lip, she joined the back of the line of people waiting at the bus stop, juggling her school bag from hand to hand, overhearing snippets of conversation. It was all about Mrs Froust. The bus. The blood on the road. Her brains splattered everywhere. The story growing gorier and gorier the longer they waited. Occasionally, a finger would point her way or someone would nod their head over at her. She chewed her lip and kept her eyes pointed straight ahead. She noted Bee's blond hair a few heads up in front bobbing up and down animatedly. Someone ahead of Bee was holding up a tatty black umbrella.

She dropped her bag.

It wasn't an umbrella.

It was a black mark.

Not exactly the same as the one she'd seen above Mrs Froust's head, this had the appearance of two wings joined together. It was more solid looking somehow. She craned her neck to see whom the mark belonged to: it was an old lady wearing a thick black duffle coat and leaning on a walking stick.

The bag still sat on the pavement where Lizzie dropped it. As she leant over to pick it up, vomit filled her mouth.

And the rest of the world carried on. Bee threw her head back in laughter, there was the whine of a distant motorbike, the smell of exhaust as the bus pulled up. One by one the passengers climbed on. Lizzie gritted her teeth and getting on the bus she saw the only seat free was the one beside the old lady.

They locked eyes.

'Hello dear.'

Lizzie ignored her and perched on the edge of the seat. She could still see it though. It was a sooty charcoal colour and every so often it twitched as if it was alive.

The old lady smelt musty and she was grateful when the bus lurched to a stop outside her school. She swung out through the doors the second they opened. She looked back.

Should she say something?

How *could* she say something?

The old lady pressed her face against the glass. For a moment, their eyes connected, and then that moment was gone, leaving behind an imprint of a white face and a blurred black mark. She blinked a few times, as if to wipe her vision clean.

'Freako Fisher!' yelled a red haired boy.

She didn't even know his name. He was just a zitty face she'd seen in the corridor a few times. Her step faltered for a second, then she ducked her head and scurried around the outskirts of the playground, trying to melt into the building itself. The boys from her year stopped their game of football.

'Hey, Lizzie!'

She could recognize Nathan's voice anywhere. Always an octave lower than everyone else's. Cool and sardonic. It was a clever voice laced with sarcasm. She clutched her bag to her chest. What now?

He walked over. Her mouth felt dry. She looked up into his green eyes. So sharp, they could cut her. Somewhere in the background she was aware of a group of people gathering. She willed herself to act normal.

Nathan looked down on her and smiled. He really did have a beautiful smile for someone so heartless. Against her will it made feel special. As if she were the most gorgeous girl in the world and he had eyes only for her. She pulled her bag tighter to her chest.

To her surprise, he ruffled his hand on top of her head and ran his fingers through her hair.

He turned back to his friends. 'No. Nothing there.' He took his hand away and laughed. 'No horns.'

The heat seared her face. 'What?'

He lowered his voice. 'Bee says you can see when people are going to die. Is it true? Is it true . . . you're not human?' He smiled once more, a cool self-satisfied smirk, and then turned on his heel and walked away.

Lizzie stared after him and wished for one sick moment that she could see a black mark above his head.

* * *

The day didn't get much better.

She was now Lizzie Fisher: the girl who could predict death. It wasn't as if she had ever been popular but at least she had never been *unpopular*. Until now.

As soon as the final bell rang, she dashed for the door and ran across the playground to escape via the main gates. She couldn't face getting on the bus with everyone else so she trudged home along slippery gray pavements. The low hanging clouds drizzled non-stop. She even saw one more black mark. It was above the head of an elderly Indian guy who stood in the doorway of an off license store.

She scurried past him.

At the bay window of number thirty-four Joopy's face shone through. His muzzle had started to go gray but his toffee eyes still lit up like a puppy's as soon as he saw Lizzie. Just seeing his face made her burst into tears.

She fumbled with the door key, collapsed into the house and buried her face into his soft fur. He stood patiently whilst she sobbed the day away. It was not often that Lizzie cried, but whenever she did, Joopy was always there for her. *Always*.

The doorbell rang.

Looking through the frosted glass, she spied the familiar short skirt and long legs. Bee. Lizzie unintentionally caught a glimpse of her own face in the hallway mirror and thought she had never looked quite so ugly. For one fleeting second, she wished she could go to the same place as Mrs Froust, and then she wished she had never had that wish. Who knew where Mrs Froust had gone?

'I know you're in there!' Bee's face pressed against the glass.

Even distorted it was prettier than her own. 'C'mon Lizzie, open up.'

Lizzie hid her face in Joopy's fur.

'I won't make fun of you. I promise!'

Bee placed her palm against the glass. It was something they used to do when they were kids, hand to hand, a sign of friendship. Lizzie hesitated and then slowly opened the door. Bee smiled. Honey-colored hair dripped over her shoulders, sky-blue eyes blazed with unfed curiosity and her shirt was opened just a little too indecently for comfort.

Lizzie scowled at her.

'Read this.'

Bee handed her a note. Her nails were freshly French manicured. Lizzie, whose own nails were always uneven and broken, however hard she tried to keep them neat, gingerly took it and unfolded it into an A4 piece of paper. On it was a list of names with the words 'Hate List' at the top.

She crinkled her brow in puzzlement. 'What's this?'

'The list of people who *never* want you to talk to them or touch them again.'

There must have been about fifty names on the list. Lizzie recognized about half of them, kids from her maths class mostly, and others in her year, including Nathan Parks. The rest were just names.

'There's more,' Bee added and pulled out a thick wad of paper from her bag. There were about ten sheets jam-packed with names.

Lizzie tightened her fingers around them.

'Why?'

Bee smiled sweetly. 'Because you're a freak?'

Lizzie's heart quickened.

'What could I do?' Bee said, widening her eyes.

Lizzie scrunched the paper up into a ball and closed the door in Bee's face.

'Not sign the list,' she muttered, and pressed her hand against the glass. But Bee had already gone.

Chapter Five

She took a long hard shower, got changed into her combats and T-shirt and sloped downstairs. Joopy hovered by the front door in expectation of a walk. Miraculously it was sunny outside and boy, did Joopy love the sunshine.

'You can't come,' she snapped and then hated herself for snapping. She cuddled his face and kissed his muzzle. 'I'm sorry,'

Then she stepped out of the door quickly before he had a chance to escape. Without Joopy to slow her down (he was nearly twelve and much slower than he used to be) she made it to Milton Graveyard in under twenty-five minutes. She sweated under her black fleece. It was the first time she'd come here by herself.

The wind suddenly swept up and brushed her hair against her face like cobwebs. She took a sharp intake of breath.

'Don't be silly,' she muttered out loud. Her voice sounded odd and she shoved her hands in her pockets and hurried on through the heart of the graveyard until she found the angel. She started when she saw his face.

'Hi.' She ran to his side and threw her arms around his torso. Her heart throbbed in her chest. Not for the first time, she wished he had arms so he could hug her back. She couldn't remember the last time she had been hugged. Not even by mum. As her breathing settled down she began to relax and as she relaxed she told the angel about her day, down to every last detail: from the lumpy toast, and Bee's glistening eyes, to the old lady on the bus all the way through to Nathan rubbing her hair. She paused.

'How will anyone ever like me now?'

The angel didn't answer. It never did. Not for the first time, Lizzie wished he could speak. She continued to talk until all the hurt had seeped out.

Then she took the list of names, folded it up into a tiny square and buried it in the dirt next to fifteen-year old Elizabeth's grave.

* * *

'Liz? Is that you?'

She'd tried to open the front door as silently as she could but mum appeared like an apparition.

'Where have you been?'

Every single light in the house was on and Lizzie blinked a few times as her eyes adjusted.

'Where have you been?' Mum repeated with that familiar nervous twang. Lizzie kicked off her trainers and then under mum's frown, carefully placed them side-by-side on the mat.

'It's late.'

"It's 8pm. It's not *that* late.' She tried to brush past her but mum grabbed her shoulders.

'You didn't leave a note.'

Lizzie rolled her eyes. 'So?'

Soft brown eyes, the colour of milk chocolate, bored into her own. She shifted on her feet.

'So I was worried.'

'I can look after myself. I'm fifteen, not five!'

Mum tightened her grip on her shoulder. 'I don't care how old you are, young lady, this is my house and you follow my rules.'

And with that, she released her grip and marched off into the kitchen. Lizzie cursed under her breath. Living here was like living in a tomb. She hated it.

'And remember to wash your hands before dinner!' Mum's voice floated out.

Lizzie stomped into the downstairs toilet and turned the tap on full blast. Water sprayed over the edge of the sink onto her top. Ignoring the perfumed soap, she shoved her hands under the water for all of two seconds and then rubbed them dry on her combats. She grinned at herself in the mirror.

'Dinner's ready!'

She grimaced. What day was it? Tuesday. That meant lasagne.

The air smelt of garlic and Lizzie hesitated for a moment before going into the kitchen.

Mum glanced up as she took a seat nearest the door then crinkled her brow at the water stains on Lizzie's top. 'How was school?'

She shrugged.

'I suppose they were all talking about Mrs Froust, weren't they? Poor thing.' She splashed in some red wine. 'It's such a terrible thing to happen. She wasn't even that old.'

Mrs Froust must have been mum's age. Not that she looked it. Mrs Froust had looked different from all the other teachers. She had worn long, flowing skirts which sometimes looked unclean and she even went to music festivals. Once upon a time she used to be in a band. Lizzie had always wanted to ask how she ended up just being a teacher in school. But it was too late now.

'Liz, I know it's been a horrid day but please stop staring at me like that.' Mum sighed.

Lizzie bent down and rubbed Joopy's ears. *He* didn't care how hard or long she gazed at him.

'Lay the table will you, please?'

Lizzie took the familiar crockery from the drawer and as she did she noticed a white envelope on the tiled surface. The handwriting was big and loopy, childlike, and the stamp was foreign.

She didn't recognize it at first. It had been years since the last one. Just like this. Sitting on the kitchen surface, unopened, and then days later she'd seen the letter in the bin. It was from her grandmother.

She muttered something under her breath.

'What's that love?'

Mum turned round, having first tested the sauce with a satisfied smack of approval.

'Why don't you answer her?'

Mum's shoulders stiffened. And then she gave the sauce a

vigorous stir.

'Not now, Liz.'

'But I want to know!' Lizzie heard her voice rise and didn't even understand why she wanted to know all of a sudden. It just became very important that she *did* know why her mum behaved the way she did.

'I'll tell you another day when you've calmed down a bit.'

Lizzie chewed her thumb nail and accidentally bit off a bit of skin. Blood spotted. She tore off a bit of kitchen towel, wrapped it around her thumb and laid the rest of the crockery on the table in silence.

She felt all churned up inside and couldn't even understand why.

Mum never wrote back to her grandmother, never sent her a birthday card or a present at Christmas, never called her up. But at the same time, mum hated Lizzie's dad because *he* never sent Lizzie any cards or presents. Why couldn't mum see she was just as bad?

She'd never met her dad but she supposed she must look like him. He hadn't hung around much after she'd been born. Apparently he' d left mum for another woman and had just disappeared from their lives from that point on. It was hard to miss someone you didn't know.

She looked so little like her mum though that sometimes late at night when she was still awake, Lizzie thought that they couldn't possibly be related. Mum was tall and angular with dead-straight glossy black hair. She was chic. Glamorous. Like she belonged in a magazine. In fact, the *only* similarity was their ivory white skin. But that was it. Half the time mum acted as though she wished Lizzie were different. How many times had she compared her with Bee? Bee was so pretty. Bee had so many friends and was out all the time. Bee had a boyfriend. Those clothes looked fabulous on Bee.

Mum turned round as if she'd read her mind. 'How did Bee

cope with the news?'

Lizzie pulled a face. 'Who cares about Bee?'

'I wish sometimes I knew what went on in that head of yours.' She sighed. 'I thought you two were friends.'

Lizzie laughed.

'You used to be so close.'

'When we were six years old! And it was only because you were best friends with her mum.'

She couldn't stomach another lecture about friendship. Not today. She flicked a fork off the table and it clattered to the floor.

'Don't just put it back on the table! Wash it first.'

She stood up.

'I'm not hungry.' She pulled Joopy up by his collar. 'C'mon you.'

'What about your dinner?'

'Who cares about dinner?' She felt the emotions flare up like a firework. 'I don't care about dinner. I don't want to eat dinner. I'm not hungry. My maths teacher died today and all you can talk about is dinner. You might not care about people dying but *I* do.'

As mum's mouth dropped open in shock, Lizzie grabbed Joopy by the collar and ran out the room.

'Goodnight.'

Chapter Six

She dreamt of something murky. Something dragging her down. Of darkness and cold. The weight of the dream pressed down on her and she woke with a start. Struggling to breathe.

It was Joopy.

Marmalade fur, soft fluffy ears, one ear always half cocked, the gentlest most loving eyes (even if they were a bit squinty) and a face that seemed to grin at everyone. Especially Lizzie.

Light sifted through her narrow bedroom and landed on the dog's head. Just like a comforter, he always slept at the foot of her bed. This morning he had a black mark hovering above his head. *A black mark.*

Lizzie screamed.

And screamed.

And screamed.

She grabbed Joopy and pulled him close to her chest, her heart pumping at about a million beats a minute. It was hard to draw air. The dog lay squashed in her embrace and she rested her face against his neck. She could hear his pulse.

The door burst open.

'Lizzie?' Mum was still pulling her pink silk cotton dressing gown around her waist. She felt a sharp sting of guilt for the way she had talked to her last night. Suddenly she wanted her mum to tell her everything was going to be ok. She wanted her mum to put her arms around her and hold her.

Mum didn't though. She walked to the foot of the bed and knelt in front of it. 'What's up?'

Lizzie's eyes felt too huge for her head. She knew she was staring wildly. Looking blindly around the room. She groaned and didn't even realize the sound had come from that part wedged deep within herself.

Mum struggled to find her voice. 'Did you have a bad dream?'

Oh God, *please* make this a dream.

She pressed the dog tighter against her and he whimpered. Lizzie looked at mum and then back to Joopy.

The words tumbled out in short, sharp breaths. 'He's got a black mark!'

Mum rubbed her eyes. 'A what?'

'A black mark! Above his head!'

She clutched him even tighter and heard her heart hammering hard.

'What's the matter, love?' Mum said. 'What do you mean by black mark?'

'There!' Lizzie stabbed the air above Joopy's head with her forefinger.

Mum looked blankly at her and pursed her lips. She couldn't see what she saw. Nobody could. Mum tucked the duvet cover in. This was not the first time Lizzie had had bad dreams. When she was younger, she'd had them all the time and mum would come in and sit with her until she fell back asleep.

'Lizzie, there's nothing above Joopy's head. Look.' She moved her hand across the space and fluttered her fingers. 'There's nothing here.'

Her long fingers passed through the black mark like ink. Lizzie shrank backward and whimpered.

Mum's eyes narrowed in concern. 'Lizzie, what is it?'

There was a huge silence. A silence as vast as the universe itself. Mum shifted her weight from one knee to the other. Joopy whined.

She clutched him tighter still and he squirmed. She felt her heart burst.

Her hair fell over her eyes. 'I don't want him to die.'

'Everything has to die at some point. Even dogs.' Mum said.

'No!' her eyes were wet. 'I don't want him to die *now*!'

She sank her face into Joopy's fur and rocked back and forth. Please, not Joopy. *Not Joopy.* She couldn't imagine life without him. He was her world. The pain came from a place so deep within her she hadn't known that place existed. Mum stayed by her side for an hour, trying to get her to speak, but how could she understand black marks? Death meant nothing to her.

In the end, mum was late for work.

* * *

There was *no way* she was going to let Joopy out of her sight. As soon as mum had gone, Lizzie shook off the pretence she might actually be going to school. As if. She had Joopy to look after. For the rest of the day she clung onto him as if he were her conjoined twin. She kept him on a lead, watched his every move, and that night, as much as possible, she avoided sleep.

Nothing happened.

She kept up the vigil on Thursday and Friday. In the morning she pretended all was fine to mum and then as soon as she had gone to work, Lizzie locked the doors and kept Joopy by her side. And still he seemed fine even though the black mark started to grow denser. On close inspection, it looked like a swarm of flies. It moved. Lizzie ran her hands through it a few times. It was a strange feeling, as if she were running her hands through water. Except there was no water. But the air above his head had the same resistance as water. As if her hand were passing through something.

It made her shiver.

She vowed to do everything in her power to look after him.

Apart from one scrape with a hedgehog, Joopy had always been healthy. Heading toward the twilight of his life he had slowed down a bit over the past year, but he still had keen, bright eyes. Surely, it wasn't his turn yet?

She kept up the vigil over the weekend but on the fifth day she had a massive argument with mum about going back to school. Who *cared* if it was Monday? They shouted so loudly at each other that the walls shook. In the end, mum stormed out and Lizzie kept Joopy in the house all day.

Nothing happened.

On the sixth day, completely ignoring her mum, she kept him locked in her bedroom. But unlike Lizzie, he could not entertain himself with books and he whined at the door for most of the time.

When he wanted to go outside she carried Joopy under her arm like a toy. The black mark was so heavy now that even Joopy seemed aware of it. His eyes rolled upward every so often and he would bark for no apparent reason.

She knew with a billion percent conviction that as soon as she let Joopy out of her sight, something terrible would happen, imagining his death in a multitude of ways. Each one more painful than the last.

The sixth night she couldn't sleep so she locked Joopy in her room and padded downstairs to get a glass of water. Mum and Susie Buckingham were talking in the kitchen. The low, hushed voices seeped out into the hallway.

Mum said something about 'appearances' but it was too low to catch properly.

'It's not normal,' Susie's strident voice piped out. 'Have you considered getting her some *help*?'

Mum's reply was muffled.

'Psychiatric care is nothing to be ashamed of these days,' Susie said in a voice which implied the exact opposite.

Lizzie went back to bed and curled up tight around Joopy. Her heart thudded.

Tomorrow was the seventh day.

Chapter Seven

'I won't go!'

Mum, dressed in a dark blue trouser suit, rolled her eyes. The black mark bristled above Joopy's head like coal dust. It was heavy and dank and full of foreboding. Nothing had ever felt worse than this moment. Lizzie stood facing her mum in the kitchen. The air smelt of burnt toast.

'It's time to go back to school. No buts.'

'But I have to look after Joopy!'

'I said no buts.'

Lizzie was wearing the same dressing gown and slippers she'd worn for the past week. Joopy was tucked under her arm. He was heavy. She was tired.

Mum took a deep breath. 'Lizzie, you have to stop all this nonsense. Let's get you back to school. Enough is enough.'

She stared back. Her mum's brown eyes softened momentarily.

'If you want we can arrange for you to see a child psychologist. They can help you come to terms with Mrs Froust's death. Will that help?'

Lizzie moved Joopy to her other hip. Susie Buckingham's words rang through her head. *It's not normal.* Lizzie tightened her grip and felt her cheeks flush.

'No!'

'Death affects us all in different ways.' Her mum paused to take a sip of coffee. 'But life goes on, and I know this sounds cruel, but you have to start moving on too.'

Lizzie's insides bridled so she gave her mum one of her stares. After a second or so, her mum looked away and poured the rest of her coffee down the sink.

'I'm afraid there's no room for discussion here. You're going back to school and I'm going to take you there myself.'

Joopy barked twice and Lizzie felt her insides melt.

* * *

Her stomach growled but she wasn't about to admit she was hungry. Instead she sat curled up in the passenger seat of mum's silver sports Ibiza and internally raged. They were nearly at the school gates and mum was still twittering on about some important meeting she had today and how she was going to do some powerpoint presentation. Like she cared. The closer they got to school, the more she ground her teeth. There was no way she was going to stay there.

The car pulled up outside the school gates and Lizzie spotted Nathan Park's thin-lipped sneer immediately. Bee was tucked up under his arm like a bird of paradise. They lolled against a red brick wall stained with graffiti and looked straight at her. She shrank back in her seat.

'What's up?'

Like she was going to tell mum.

'Nothing.' She squared her shoulders and pushed open the door. It wouldn't open.

'Hang on.' Mum unclicked the child safety lock and Lizzie sighed heavily as she opened the door.

'See you later, Liz.'

Lizzie didn't look back. She heard the car roar off. Mum always drove too fast.

She stood awkwardly on the pavement facing Nathan and Bee.

'How's your dog?' He leered.

'What?'

Bee sniggered.

'Your dog. Isn't that why you've been off school?' He took a step forward. 'Because Lizzie's little pet dog is poorly sick.'

Lizzie bristled from head to toe and her anger rose up like a dragon. 'Get a life.' She snapped.

Nathan's eyes flickered in surprise. Next to him Bee shrugged and feigned indifference. In amongst her pain Lizzie allowed herself this small victory before turning on her heel and running off.

She had more important things to take care of.

As soon as she was round the corner she kicked off her school shoes and shoved on her trainers. Swinging the bag on her back, she sprinted off down the street and back toward home.

Today was death-day and she had to do *everything* she could to stop it.

Ragged breath, a stabbing stitch, screaming lungs, None of it mattered. The only thing she cared for was Joopy. She *had* to get there before something dreadful happened.

* * *

She ran past rows of Victorian terraced houses, past corner shops, past slumbering taxis and past pubs with outside benches. She ran until her sides stung with pain. She ran and she ran.

And in the sky the sun shone down as if today were like any other.

Joopy hated nothing more than being cooped up indoors when the sun was shining. A slither of guilt shot through her heart for keeping him indoors all weekend. But she had been doing what was best for him, hadn't she?

She ran until she neared the corner of her cul-de-sac. A familiar silver car whizzed past her.

Too fast.

Way too fast.

She turned the corner just in time to see the impact.

Lizzie blinked and wanted to keep her eyes shut forever.

When she did finally open them again her mum cradled the dog in her arms. It was as if lightening had struck Lizzie. She felt the blood drain from her face and her legs buckle and as she stumbled over, she realized that hearts could scream too.

Joopy lay on the road with his head in her mum's lap. His hind legs were splayed at an awkward angle and a small pool of blood had gathered. Lizzie shoved her mum aside and knelt down. She ignored the intense throb of the black mark and focussed on his face. Joopy's soft toffee eyes brightened as soon as he saw her. She rested a gentle palm on his muzzle and felt something inside of her rip.

A single tear hovered in one of Joopy's eyes and she wiped it away. He gazed lovingly at her for what could have been eternity, but was actually seconds.

Then he died.

As the final breath left his body, the black mark curled up like smoke and a long, aching sob burst from Lizzie's lips.

She pressed her fingers to her eyes and felt the chokes burst up, like bubbles, from her chest. She never wanted to open her eyes again. A gulp beside her reminded Lizzie that her mum was still there. She looked over.

She had never seen her mum cry before.

It was then that Bee rounded the corner, she was talking loudly on her mobile and her laugh stung the air. She took one look at the scene and ran over. She looked from Joopy to Lizzie and then to Lizzie's mum.

'I'm so sorry,' she whispered.

Chapter Eight

When Lizzie was twelve, one of the first assignments she'd been given in her new English class was to write a story entitled 'Pain.'

Lizzie laughed at what she had written. Some dumb story about coming last in a sports day race and how embarrassed she'd felt because everyone had laughed at her and called her names. It was nothing. *Nothing!* Compared to how she felt now.

It was like a tangled knot bunched up in her chest. In her grief, she learnt just how much pain could hurt.

She hadn't spoken to mum. She hadn't been able to *look* at her, let alone speak to her. Mum had tried to tell her what had happened. But who cared about mum's dumb meeting? It was *all* her fault Joopy had escaped. If she hadn't have come back to the house after dropping Lizzie off, then he'd still be alive. She'd needed some memory stick or something for her stupid presentation but in her rush she'd left the front door open and Joopy had sniffed fresh air and run outside.

Sure, she *said* she'd looked for him. But how hard? How long? In the end, she had given up and driven off, but even that wasn't enough was it? No, mum had to come back again to the house because of something else she'd forgotten and this time she was late for the meeting, so she was driving way too fast and she had killed Joopy.

Slammed into Joopy.

Murdered Joopy.

Things could *never* be the same again.

It didn't matter that she'd taken a day off work and spent the whole afternoon in the garden making a small wooden cross with her bare hands. How did that help now? Three times she had come up to her bedroom to say how sorry she was, but each time Lizzie had refused all eye contact and buried her head under the duvet.

What did anything matter now?

She lost track of time. Day came, night fell, Lizzie stayed in bed. Mum went back to work and the house took on an eerie silence. It was quieter than a graveyard but less peaceful. The air felt stifled and close. The way it felt before a thunderstorm. Bee came up on a brief visit after school. Lizzie guessed mum must have talked her into it. She hovered in the room, fingering the telescope with mild curiosity.

'Oh Lizzie!' She said softly and for a moment, Lizzie saw a flash of their childhood friendship sizzle in the air. Once upon a time they had lain out on the lawn searching for stars together.

Lizzie hesitated. For some reason making friends had come easy to Bee and not so easy for Lizzie. Whereas Bee surrounded herself with people, Lizzie was often alone. To be honest, she preferred it that way. She liked to keep her secrets hidden. But once in a while, she ached for someone to confide in. Momentarily a glimpse of the angel in Milton Graveyard flashed through her mind. She blinked.

Bee stepped forward. 'What's up?'

Lizzie pulled the covers higher and clamped her lips shut.

'You haven't left the house, you know, since *it* happened.' Bee picked up a framed photograph of Joopy. 'You didn't leave the house before it happened either.'

Lizzie reached out to grab the photo but Bee held it out of reach.

'Mum said apparently you were acting all weird around Joopy. You know, not letting him out of your sight or anything. Then he died, so it made me think if you'd seen another one of those *things*. Above his head.' Bee handed the photo to Lizzie. It was a shot of Joopy when he was a puppy. Looking at it made Lizzie's heart feel tight in her chest.

Bee lowered her voice and sat on the edge of the bed. She handed Lizzie a tissue. 'Did you see one, Lizzie?'

Lizzie stared at Joopy's face. Where was he now? Was he still out there somewhere? She ran her fingertips over the glass.

Suddenly she remembered the way the black mark had coiled up like smoke. What was that?

'Did you?'

She shook herself back to the present. Bee's whining voice. Who cared any more? Lizzie reached into herself and found nothing but pain.

'Yes.'

The bedroom seemed to pulsate with silence. Then Bee sprang off the bed.

'Really Lizzie,' she said. 'First Mrs Froust, then Joopy. Anyone would think you're the kiss of death!'

She told her that her parents thought Lizzie needed psychiatric care.

Lizzie barely listened.

'Can I borrow these?'

Bee had sifted through Lizzie's wardrobe and made a fairly sizeable pile of clothes, the ones that mum had bought her. Lizzie shrugged. She never wore them.

'He's called Byron.'

'Who?'

'The guy I met on the internet.'

'What guy?'

Bee frowned. 'The one I've just been telling you about? Really, Lizzie, you must snap out of it.'

Had Bee been prattling on? Lizzie rolled over onto her back.

'What about Nathan?' She asked dully.

Bee dismissed him with a laugh. 'Do you want to know something?' She leant over the bed and Lizzie could smell her perfume, like sunshine on a rain-sodden day. 'I showed Byron this on camera.'

Bee pointed to her left breast, small but pointed under her clinging red sleeveless top.

'At least I've got some eh?' Bee tossed her honey hair and

winked. 'Bye then.' She paused at the doorway. 'By the way Lizzie, you can trust me, I won't tell anyone about the *latest* black mark.'

* * *

One week passed and July reared its head.

Lizzie had spent the week shut in her room, refusing to go to school. It didn't matter how much mum yelled at her, or pressed at her, or even bribed her. She would *not* go.

Mum was worried. Lizzie knew that because she'd taken two days off work and mum taking days off was a rarity. Even when Lizzie was little and got sick, mum called in Susie to look after her. Susie didn't have to work. Susie had Mr Buckingham to do that for her. Over breakfast, mum asked her again to go back to school.

'Why?' Lizzie said sullenly. 'Because *you* want to go back to work?"

Mum frowned. 'No. You'll get better, that's why.'

'Well, I don't want to.'

Mum's hand tightened on her mug. 'You can't keep missing school, Lizzie. It's been nearly two weeks now. Enough is enough.'

'Enough of what? Grieving over my dog who *you* killed?'

She took a sharp intake of breath. 'It was an accident.'

'I'm not going. I don't care what you say, I'm not going back.'

Her mum put the mug on the kitchen table with a thump. 'You have to go back.'

Lizzie glared at her and walked to the door. 'And how exactly are you going to make me?'

She pondered this in the greenhouse later that day. The air had that meek summer glow to it, the sun pale and watery, the English skies streaked with pastel. Mum was cutting the hedge in quick angry thrusts and putting the leaves into small, piles, each one evenly sized except for one unruly pile which the wind kept sifting out of shape. Watching mum's impatient progress, Lizzie wondered if anything would ever be normal again, or if life was destined to mark her out as the odd one out, as the misshapen pile of leaves.

The skies had darkened, and she hadn't even noticed that mum had disappeared. She left the greenhouse, side-stepping Joopy's grave (the freshly dug turf still gave her a lump in the throat) and opened the back- door. It was Thursday so her mum was making chicken and mushroom casserole. Lizzie walked straight through into the living room ignoring her. She turned on the television and nestled down into the terracotta sofa.

Lately Lizzie had begun to understand why people watched so much television.

It was brain numbing.

The channel was automatically tuned to BBC news and before Lizzie could find the remote to start surfing, she caught sight of the screen.

It was squirming with black marks.

She gaped at the news report for a few seconds, something about a famine in Africa, and the sight of so many black marks, wriggling like maggots, made her cry out loud. A short sharp yelp, almost unhuman, she hardly recognised it, came from within her. She found herself shaking.

Mum raced in, bringing in a smell of onions.

'What is it?'

Lizzie clenched her eyes shut and pointed at the screen.

Mum fumbled with the remote. A second passed and the TV was switched off. Lizzie peered through her fingers. She saw her mum's face loom large, like a full moon, staring at her with an emotion she couldn't place.

'For Christ's sake Lizzie, tell me what's going on!'

Mum ran her fingers through her hair, something she did when she was nervous.

'I can't,' Lizzie whispered. 'I . . . can't.'

There was a pointed, heavy silence, the kind which seemed to be falling between them more and more these days, until Lizzie's eye was caught by something over her shoulder.

A hideous thing mum hadn't wanted to display at all. It was a gift from her own mum, sent years and years ago when Lizzie was about seven. She'd been entranced by the bright colours. Her grandmother had bought it from some Mayan tribe in Mexico, meant to ward off evil, and for some reason Lizzie had managed to talk mum into putting it up in the lounge. Normally the face mask was turned inwards so it looked fairly inconspicuous. Tonight, somehow, it had managed to swivel round so the garish purple and reds blazed outward in a riot of colour.

With a sharp tug, Lizzie pulled the mask off the shelf.

'My grandmother,' she said with a flash of insight that seemed to surf right out of the sky. 'Why can't I go and stay with her?'

Mum's face paled immediately. 'Are you joking?

Lizzie hugged the mask to her chest and felt it burn into her skin. 'It'll get me away from here.'

From you.

'Absolutely not!'

'But why not? There's only two more weeks until school holidays…'

'Lizzie, I said no.'

However hard Lizzie begged, cajoled and pleaded, her mum wouldn't shift. It was out of the question. Certainly not up for discussion. Never in a million years.

'Over my dead body!' Her nostrils flared and she stormed out of the living room.

Lizzie sat on the edge of the sofa, the mask still cradled in her hands. It had just been an impulse. Why did mum *always* have over react? She reached out for Joopy and then with an ache she realized he was not there.

'What should I do?' she murmured. It wasn't beyond the

realms of possibility that she could book her own ticket. She had some savings. But neither did she have any idea of where her grandmother lived or how to get hold of her.

'I hate it here.' She heard the choke in her voice and cursed herself for crying again. Why couldn't she get rid of the pain in her chest? Why did it *hurt* so? She closed her eyes and pictured the stone angel and tried to imagine how she would feel if she were around him. Her breath was still ragged but at least some of the pain seemed to seep away. 'Please help me get away. Please help me find some peace.'

She hadn't even realized mum had come back in the room. Her long shiny hair fanned down her shoulders and shone in the light. Lizzie blinked. Mum wore the red slippers she'd got her for her birthday last month.

'Is this what you want, Lizzie?'

Lizzie stared at the slippers and sensed victory.

* * *

The plane ticket was booked for the day after tomorrow.

Mum took her shopping to buy some essentials and she spent the rest of the time packing. There wasn't much time to think about where she was going. She still didn't know much about her grandmother, other than she lived in a hot country, had traveled a lot, was prone to sending bizarre gifts and that last night was the first time in over three years that mum had spoken to her.

'She hasn't changed a bit,' mum muttered as she hung up the phone. She glanced anxiously toward Lizzie. 'Are you sure you want to go?'

'Yes,' Lizzie nodded.

But by the time mum was loading the suitcases into the back of the car, her palms felt clammy.

'Going anywhere nice?' Bee appeared on the driveway, unable to resist nosing. It was still early so she had not had time to do her hair or put make-up on. In the grey dawn light, she looked pale and ordinary.

'Yes,' Lizzie replied as she stepped into the car. 'Somewhere where I can get a tan and somewhere where I don't have to see you.'

And then she slammed the door, put her hand up against the window and smiled.

Mum drove her to the airport and it wasn't until they neared the check-in desk, that Lizzie remembered the angel. She hadn't been to Milton Graveyard since Joopy died and as the chaos of the airport swirled around her, she wished she had gone. Just to say goodbye. Too late now. But then perhaps all she had to do was picture him and he'd be with her anyway.

She shifted on her feet and mum touched her shoulder tentatively. For a second Lizzie thought her mum was going to hug her and then that second passed. Don't be stupid. They never hugged. And besides, she could still not bring herself to forgive her, even now and as her mum's chocolate eyes melted, she stared at the scuffed floor.

Mum sighed.

Lizzie pulled her cap lower over her brow. She had worn the baseball cap for two reasons. Firstly to avoid seeing black marks at the airport, and secondly, it flattened her hair. Of all the things to pack, the hair straighteners had gone in first. Then her make-up. She didn't know what Spanish girls looked like but at least she could *try* and fit in. Be like them. Act normal.

It was a new start, wasn't it? She could reinvent herself. She'd packed a lot of her mum's clothes. Probably too many. But they would help her blend in over there, make her seem like any other regular English girl on her summer holidays.

When the time came to say goodbye, it was quick and neat. A light kiss on Lizzie's cheek, a twenty-euro note in her hand and a reminder to drink plenty of water.

This was her first time on an airplane alone. She sat by the window and the two seats next to her were empty. The plane hurtled down the runway and nudged its way through thick, bubbly cloud.

England disappeared.

About half an hour after take-off, in the midst of a dream about an ocean with no floor, she woke up with a start. Someone had sat in the aisle row. Still wearing her cap, she peeked across at him. Probably in his thirties, he was strong and attractive, in a rugged, larger than life way. He had silver grey eyes almost as pale as hers and burnt toffee coloured hair.

He seemed familiar.

'Hello Lizzie.'

She jumped in surprise. How did he know her name?

'It's not a curse.' A shaft of sunlight slid in through the window, illuminating his face. For a moment, it looked like he had a halo. 'It's a gift.' He leant closer. 'Do you want to know what that gift is?'

He leant closer still and Lizzie could smell him. He smelt of earth and leaves. He whispered and his whisper was like a breath on the breeze.

And then she woke up. There was no man, only a beam of sunshine which played happily on the aisle seat like a toddler, and the whisper Lizzie had heard coiled above her hair until it evaporated.

Seconds later the plane dropped suddenly. Her stomach heaved but she also felt something else. Not fear. What was it? She scrambled to place the emotion as it raced through her veins. It wasn't something she'd felt for weeks. Not since the first time when she had found the hole in fence and crept into Milton Graveyard and knew she was doing something forbidden. Not since the last time she'd been out in a thunder storm and turned her face up to the rain. *Excitement*. A guilty thrill raced through her as the plane rocked from side to side with the turbulence.

Someone at the front of the plane screamed.

'It's ok,' she whispered to herself as she clenched the armrests. Her knuckles turning white. 'We're going to be ok.'

She looked out the window and saw her reflection. 'No black mark,' she murmured. And as if it heard her, the plane levelled out.

Above the clouds the sky was blue.

* * *

Malaga arrivals lounge was messy.

Lizzie felt conspicuous. Of all the trolleys to choose, she had to choose the one with wayward wheels, didn't she? It moved awkwardly, just like her. She trailed behind a British family of four. Their trolleys were laden with suitcases and sunglasses perched on top of their heads.

A sea of faces swam in front of her.

She had no idea what to expect.

And even if she *could* have expected something, she never would have come up with what actually manifested in front of her.

She actually gasped out loud.

The woman striding toward her wore a jewelled purple kaftan and a long sunshine yellow dress which sparkled in the dusty air. Her wrists jangled with bracelets and a pair of grubby gardening gloves were tucked under her arm.

With a confidence that Lizzie envied, she parted the crowd and stood before her.

'Hello Lizzie. I'm your grandmother.'

Lizzie smiled and bit her lip.

'None of this granny nonsense though. You must call me Ariadne.'

She then clasped Lizzie in a long, tight hug which left her breathless. Close up, her grandmother smelt of lavender, not the fake air freshener kind, but real fresh sprigs of lavender. In contrast, her skin felt rough.

Ariadne released her, but still holding her shoulders with a firm grip, she scrutinized her grand-daughter.

'Take off that cap so I can see your face.'

Ariadne's voice was so commanding, Lizzie obeyed without even thinking about it.

As Ariadne studied her, Lizzie shyly looked back. Her grand-mother's face was covered in fine lines and whilst it did not look youthful, there was something about Ariadne that was ageless, as if time itself could not mark her.

'So Lizzie,' she said. 'Are we going to get along do you think? I rather think so, don't you?'

Eyes, the colour of peacocks, glinted with mischief. 'Welcome to Andalucia.'

She wrapped an arm around Lizzie.

'Welcome to my life.'

Chapter Nine

As soon as they stepped outside the terminal, the heat wrapped around her like cling-film. It was the heart of high summer and Lizzie cooked in her skinny jeans. Why hadn't mum warned her it would be *this* hot?

Ariadne strode on ahead, dragging the suitcase behind her. Lizzie trotted to keep up.

The air was so bright she wished she had brought sunglasses. Ariadne, as if reading her thoughts, peeled off her own pair and handed them to her.

'Walk the light,' Ariadne said as they entered the car-park. 'Do you know what Andalucia means? Walk the light.'

Not exactly sure what she was meant to do with this piece of information, she said nothing.

Ariadne stopped by a dusty 4 x 4. She unlocked the passenger door, wiped the seat clear of junk, let Lizzie clamber in, then jumped in herself and started the engine. It took two attempts. Having settled her feet on a sea of empty water bottles, she wondered how Ariadne could even see out the windscreen, it was that dusty.

'You don't say much do you?'

Lizzie shook her head.

'Your face doesn't give much away either, does it? I've never seen a face so – how should I say? So enigmatic! That's it. You have an enigmatic face, I don't suppose anyone's ever told you that before have they?' She chuckled without waiting for an answer. 'How will I ever know what you're thinking if I can't read your expression?' She opened the glove compartment, rummaged in the chaos and retrieved another pair of sunglasses. 'How fortunate that I should love mysteries.'

She smiled to herself and as they pulled out of the car-park and followed the road signs out of Malaga. Lizzie stared out the window. A new country. A new start. A new grandmother.

And a new word to describe her face.

It sure beat being called freaky. Lizzie smiled. She knew she was right to come here even though it was so cloyingly hot.

They followed the motorway and even with the windows down Lizzie's clothes were wet with sweat. She shifted uncomfortably in her seat every few minutes, hating the way her thighs were glued together. After an hour in which Lizzie kept checking her watch they turned off the motorway and headed inland, toward jagged topped mountains that pierced the deep blue of the sky. They slowly climbed a nauseous mountain road, winding round and round. The terrain was brown and bare, panting for water.

Along the way they passed through two tiny white villages with not a soul in sight. Villages full of unevenly sized white houses that slotted together like lego pieces. All the houses touched each other and seemed squeezed into a tight space. Ariadne explained that Spaniards loved to live close to one another.

'Except for me, that is. But then, I've always been the odd one out.'

After thirty minutes and with no obvious sign-posting, Ariadne swung the car off-road and headed down rutted earth tracks that seemed to lead nowhere.

Nowhere led to home. And home did indeed have a lot of space. There was *no* other house in sight.

Ariadne lived in the bottom of a deep valley in a landscape much wilder and fiercer compared to the gentle contours of England. Splashes of color stood out, the candyfloss pink of an oleander that followed the stream, the matted green of the olive trees, a deep purple bourgainvillea that crept up and over the house.

Ariadne turned off the engine and jumped out next to a faded wooden sign which said *Casa del Sol.*

'Leave your bag. We'll grab it later.'

She headed toward the house and Lizzie followed.

There was no form or shape to the house; it was a ramshackle mess, a collection of rooms piled together in one place. Misshapen and odd. From every angle it looked different. Peeling white exteriors and a collection of different heights. Not huge by any means, but unique.

Ariadne strode across a terracotta tiled outer courtyard overhung by long wooden beams dripping with vines.

'Coming?' she called back.

An open-air barbeque sat on bricks and bourgainvillea leaves scattered the ground like confetti. In the middle, a set of rainbow colored metal patio furniture. A lone cockerel scuttled away as Ariadne opened the door without even unlocking it.

Lizzie, who was used to traffic, people and jumbo jets scouring the sky, felt the silence of the countryside descend. There was no internet connection, they lived off solar power electricity, they had to go to the top of the nearest hill to get a mobile signal *and* the nearest neighbour was a seventy-year-old goat herder called Gabriel who lived alone with his grandson.

Doubts started to creep in about her decision to come here.

There was no moisture left in her mouth to swallow but she swallowed anyway and walked across the courtyard. The cockerel spluttered into noise and she jumped a mile.

Ariadne poked her head out of the doorway and grinned. 'Everything ok?'

'Sure.'

Lizzie stepped into the kitchen and immediately noticed the drop in temperature. Thick walls and tiny windows meant the room was kept cool. She took a deep gulp of air.

'Here.'Ariadne handed her a glass of iced water. She drank it in one.

Looking around her, she tried not to gasp for the second time that day. Whereas her mum's kitchen was the epitome of hygiene and disinfectant, Ariadne's was the complete opposite. Strings of dried chilli hung from the ceiling, cardboard trays of eggs scattered the surface of a rickety wooden table, the cupboards had thin wispy curtains instead of doors and the sink was full of crusted washing up.

Worse than all this was a sticky, gluey band of orange material which hung down from the centre of the room which had dozens of dead flies clinging to it.

'Disgusting, I know. I hated it at first. But this is Spain in summer and the flies do get everywhere.'

A few of the stuck flies buzzed angrily.

'But they're still alive!' Lizzie said, hating having to watch the flies suffer and hating herself even more for even caring about a silly fly.

'It's them or me,' Ariadne said, wiping a black and white cat off the work surface.

It was the most grotesque things she had ever seen but Lizzie walked over to it. One of the flies was only attached by a wing tip and so she gently prised it away. It plopped down into the palm of her hand and sat forlornly. One of its wings had been torn off. Lizzie held her hand closer to her eyes. Suddenly curious to know if she could see black marks on flies.

It was impossible to tell.

Ariadne appeared at her shoulder and she jumped.

'Sensitive little thing, aren't you? Your mother was the same at your age too. I can take it down if you want.'

'No... it's ok.'

'Rule number one if you're going to stay here for the summer with me.' Ariadne clambored up onto a chair and pulled it clean off the ceiling. 'Never say things you don't mean.' She threw it across the kitchen floor and it landed in the bin. 'Done.'

Lizzie sat down on a spare chair and caught her breath. *This* was her mum's mum?

Another black and white cat wandered in.

'Meet North and South. North's the one with the chunk missing from his ear.'

North pushed his face into her hand and purred.

'Why do you call them North and South?'

Ariadne rolled up her sleeves. 'The stars.'

The stars! She wanted to ask her grandmother about the constellations and how bright the sky must be here without any light pollution, but Ariadne had already turned her back and was filling the sink with water. The words stuck in her throat.

'I must do this washing up.' She pointed toward an interior door. 'You get on with exploring the house. Find yourself a bedroom, there's three spare rooms to choose from. And let me know when you're hungry.' She winked. 'Whatever you do, have fun.'

She smiled suddenly and Lizzie had the impression that whenever Ariadne did smile, it was as if the sun itself were shining. It made her glow. She had never met anyone so warm before. This was probably how most people felt when they first encountered Ariadne.

For some people making friends was easy.

'See you in a bit,' Lizzie said and Ariadne nodded.

Beyond the kitchen lay an L-shaped hallway with rooms spiralling off either side. There was also a short staircase which led up to Ariadne's bedroom (the door was ajar, Lizzie didn't go inside but she knew it was Ariadne's room because of the fresh smell of lavender drifting through the doorway). It also led to a large, airy room filled with bookshelves stuffed with books of all shapes and sizes. The Library. A chaise longue sat coyly in the sun and a variety of books lay scattered on the floor. She turned one over with her toes. It was in Spanish.

She closed the door behind her and going back down the short flight of stairs, she tried a few other doors, finding a bathroom, a spacious but empty dining room, a lounge that was dominated by a huge open fireplace, and a room which had no window at all.

It wasn't until she'd looked in all of the rooms that it hit her.

There were no mirrors.

Not even in the bathroom. Not that Lizzie relied on mirrors as much as Bee did (she had no less than five in her bedroom alone!) but it did feel bare without them. How on earth did Ariadne do her hair or make-up? On second thoughts – an image of Ariadne's straw-like hair and naked face sprang into her mind – maybe she didn't bother.

It was the same with the three spare bedrooms. No mirrors. But that didn't detract from the prettiness of the rooms. Her favourite was the one that overlooked the rear of the house, gazing down on the oleander. She could just about hear the faint gurgle of the stream. The bedroom was not huge and it smelt funny, but it did have a four-poster bed which was covered in a mosquito net. The kind of bed a Princess slept in. How Bee would envy her now!

She walked over the window and put her hand up against the wire mosquito mesh. Outside the sky was a vivid blue and everything seemed so still, even the trees were too hot to sway.

Out of the corner of her eye, she caught a flash of red as someone emerged from the oleander.

Ariadne?

No.

This was someone closer to her own age. Someone male. Spanish by the dark, gypsy look of him. He had wavy black hair tied into a loose pony-tail and wore a red towel round his waist and little else.

He looked up toward the window. She started.

So intense was his gaze it sent goose bumps up her arms. He had hooded eyes and the fiercest gaze. There was something unnerving about the way he looked at her. They locked eyes for a moment.

She didn't wave and neither did he.

He turned abruptly and disappeared back into the oleander.

As he walked away the towel fell. Not just fell, but dropped. As if he'd done it on purpose. Had he *really* done that? She caught her breath as she stared at his naked body from the back. All of him tanned like almonds.

It was suddenly clammy in the room. She felt her breath come in hot bursts. She wiped the sweat off her brow and sat on the edge of the bed. Her mind fluttered.

She'd never seen a boy naked before. In fact she'd only ever been kissed once and that only lasted ten seconds. And even when their lips had touched and his tongue darted into her mouth like a lizard, she'd thought of the angel's cool lips rather than the boring computer geek called Daniel from the year below.

She'd felt nothing. No fireworks or heat. No flush or spark.

She rubbed her eyes. The sunlight coming through the window was so bright it was like Aslan's breath, warming her up and bringing her back to life, as if she really had been a statue all these years and now she was awakening.

Less than four hours ago she'd been on a plane climbing through the gray clouds of England and she had been the *only* person on that plane who knew they wouldn't crash and die.

But no-one here needed to know about that did they? She shifted her gaze to the window and the burning ball of sun. The *last* thing she wanted was Ariadne or anyone else knowing that she was different.

She lay back on the bed and took a long time to fall asleep.

Chapter Ten

She woke covered in sweat and couldn't work out where she was. Her head thudded with a mild headache and she was relieved to see a glass of water by the bed. Her suitcase was carefully placed by the chest of drawers. Outside the light was pink. Her first sunset in Andalucia.

She'd had a strange dream about the angel from the graveyard. He'd been trying to talk to her but his lips wouldn't move and so she couldn't hear him. She'd pressed her ear against his chest and actually heard his heart beat. She woke up not knowing the answer to something. It bothered her.

Too tired to get up properly, she gulped the water and then fell back asleep.

This time she dreamt of a Latin skinned Andalucian boy with dark gypsy looks. And this time they were both naked.

* * *

'Sleep well?'

Lizzie blushed as the dream came back in full force.

Ariadne smiled, it was as if she could read her mind.

It was breakfast and the table was laid with uneven slices of wholemeal bread, a jar of marmalade, some Spanish ham which Ariadne called *jamon,* a bowl of oranges, and a black and white cat. Her grandmother was reading a book, some crime mystery novel, and every so often she'd raise her eyebrows, purse her lips or even curse out loud. Lizzie had never met someone so animated in the art of reading before.

Lizzie cleared her throat. 'Why aren't there any mirrors in the house?'

The question seemed to catch her off guard. Ariadne's face changed expression a few times before settling into a smile.

'Illusions, that's why.'

'What illusions?'

'The illusion of what we look like. Quite frankly it's the least important part about ourselves.' Ariadne waved her book in the air. 'As you can see I gave up caring years ago.'

There was something about Ariadne's answer that seemed incomplete. Never mind. She was too hot to work out what it was. She pushed a hand through her own hair. She'd spent nearly an hour straightening it this morning.

'Who's that boy?'

Ariadne put the book down on the table and smiled slowly. 'Boy? What boy?'

She felt the heat rise to her cheeks again. 'The one I saw yesterday. Outside by the stream.'

'Ah, *that* boy.'

Lizzie's eyes widened and in that moment of widening she felt Ariadne dive straight into her pupils. She froze as her grandmother's eyes bore into her own, digging deeper and deeper into her depths. And then the moment passed. Ariadne chewed her bottom lip thoughtfully and nodded her head, as if conducting an internal conversation.

Lizzie concentrated on the reflection of herself in the knife she was using.

'Oh, I wasn't looking at *that* Lizzie!' Ariadne chuckled. 'As I said, I rarely look at the surface of people. No, what I'm looking for is gold.'

'Gold?' Lizzie repeated.

'Gold dust to be precise. I think it exists in everyone don't you?'

It wasn't a thought she'd ever had before. And to be honest, she had no idea what Ariadne was talking about.

'You have it in abundance.' She smiled and licked the knife clean. 'Good marmalade, huh?'

She had only tasted marmalade once before, it had been bitter and she hadn't liked it much. But this tasted so fresh that it almost felt alive in her mouth.

'Home made.' Ariadne winked. 'He's my neighbour and my gardener.'

'Who?'

'The boy you saw yesterday. He comes by most days. He was probably cooling off in the dip pool.'

Ah. So *that* was why he was half naked. For a gardener, he certainly felt at home.

'Fancy a walk in the garden?'

Not bothering to wait for an answer Ariadne stood up from the table and threw Lizzie a well-worn straw hat. 'Wear this.'

Lizzie held it by her finger-tips. It was hideous. Foul. The kind of garment Bee would *never* wear.

'Don't worry!' Ariadne's voice softened. 'No-one will see you.'

She put it on her head tentatively. 'What's his name?'

Ariadne opened the kitchen door and a burst of sunlight fell in. 'Rafa.'

Trying not to feel too silly, she followed her into the bright outside. She was immediately glad for the hat. The light smacked her in the face and the force of it made her stumble. Ariadne chuckled, not unkindly, and held Lizzie's arm for support.

'It's quite all right,' she said. "I've lived here over twenty years and I still haven't got used to the light.'

Lizzie squinted her eyes against the glare. It came from the great big ball of sun that hung in the sky like a basketball hoop. How searing the heat was. She wished she had put some suntan lotion on this morning, but she hadn't because it was the kind of thing mum would have told her to do, and Lizzie had felt a small stab of pleasure at disobeying her.

She soon regretted it.

Ariadne took Lizzie on a grand tour of her 'garden'. All three thousand square feet of it. She showed her the citrus orchard first and its display of orange, lemon, grapefruit, lime and tangerine trees. There were *so* many. All roughly the same round shape, about twice the height of herself, with rich green leaves. In the middle of the orchard was a small, circular clearing. Its peaceful aura reminded her of the graveyard.

All that was missing was the angel.

'How do you water them all?'

'I don't.' Ariadne pointed out an irrigation system on the earth. 'Rafa does. With a little help from his grandfather, Gabriel.'

She pointed out almond and walnut trees and whole hillsides of olive trees. They passed the chicken pen.

'Twenty-five chickens, seven ducks and one pair of geese.'

She pointed out two bee hives on the far side of the hill. 'My one great vice.' She sighed deeply. 'All things sweet.'

They crossed the stream, which was really only a trickle in the summer months, although in winter it 'roared like a tiger', and Ariadne showed her the secret tunnel through the oleander that led to the dip pool. The place where Rafa had been yesterday. Naked.

The dip pool was manmade, where a boulder had been placed in the flow of the water to create a dam effect. It had created a small pool of transparent water, the size of a Jacuzzi, shaded by the tall ferns. You could sink up to your neck apparently.

'You'll probably end up coming here everyday.' Ariadne dipped her toe in. 'It's the closest we get to heaven round here.'

Lizzie trickled her fingers in the water. It was surprisingly cool and refreshing. She had a sudden urge to jump in now. Dressed as she was. No wonder Rafa came here.

'One more thing. You ready for a climb?'

Her limbs felt weary but Ariadne's face was so excited she didn't want to say no.

'Sure.'

'I want to show you my tree of life.'

They ducked out of the oleander and came face to face with the house again. Lizzie could see the blue shutters of her bedroom and realized she was standing in the same place as Rafa had yesterday. Except *she* was not naked. Ariadne had already started striding towards a steep bank. Without pausing for breath, she started to climb the bank, setting off little clouds of dust with every footfall. Lizzie followed.

'Here, take my arm. This bit's tricky.'

They passed scented bushes of flowering jasmine and clumps of spiked cactus with funny prickly pear shaped fruit. At the top of the bank, when she was sure she was about a billion degrees hot in temperature, she collapsed by the roots of an old olive tree.

'There's something very special about this tree.' Ariadne ran her fingers along the gnarled trunk. It was the kind of tree, if hobgoblins and fairies existed, where they would be hiding in the branches. The trunk had immense character, thick and knotted, as if it teamed with magic and hidden stories.

'Touch it.'

Lizzie, whose mouth felt as dry as the earth, walked over and pressed her palm against the tree. The bark felt warm and alive under her touch.

'Look. There's where Rafa and Gabriel live.'

Ariadne pointed toward a small, one level house on the top of a neighbouring hill. There was a huge red-roofed outbuilding right next door to it. 'The goat shed.'

So not only was Rafa a gardener, he also tended goats. She wondered if he went to school or college. Or even if he had any education at all. He looked a couple of years older than her.

'And now look this way.'

She directed her gaze down the V of the valley toward a horizon so hazy it was too difficult to make out. But she knew what it was anyway.

'The sea!'

'Beautiful, isn't it? Especially in winter when it's clear.' She smiled and pointed toward the olive tree roots which had formed themselves into a natural seating arrangement. 'I sit there sometimes in winter and I watch Africa.'

'You can see Africa from here?'

Ariadne nodded and pointed toward the horizon. 'Just a few bumps on the horizon. And voilà, a brand new continent.' She turned to Lizzie and put her arm around her shoulder. 'Doesn't get much more special than that, does it?'

Lizzie felt the warmth of her grandmother and for the first time in weeks, she felt a surge of happiness. It had been the right decision to come here. She could put all of the past behind her and look forward to a beautiful summer. A *normal* summer.

'So why are you really here, Lizzie?'

The words were like rain.

Lizzie pulled away. Of course, there would be questions. That's what grown-ups did. They nosed into things, not giving up until they'd trampled over all the parts that were meant to be kept private. She felt a headache begin at her temples. How could she think just coming to a different country would change things?

And then she felt it. The soft, tender touch of her grandmother's fingers brushing against her chin. So lightly it could have been the breeze. She looked up and Ariadne was gazing at her with such warmth that she felt something stir in her chest. It was the same kind of feeling she'd had when she'd first got Joopy as a puppy.

'It doesn't matter what's happened in the past, Lizzie.' She felt her breath on her face, sweet like honey. 'What matters now is that you're here. And here is for living, don't you agree?'

Her face was so close she could almost count all the fine lines around Ariadne's mouth. They were like little smiles. And for the first time she noticed the necklace her grandmother wore, a simple gold chain with half a sun dangling just beneath her throat. She wondered where the other half was.

Ariadne squeezed her shoulder once more. 'I'll leave you in peace.' She walked back down the hill. 'Don't get sunburnt,' she called out halfway.

Lizzie stared down the valley, toward the sea she couldn't see and an African continent just out of sight.

* * *

It might have been hours, in reality it was only minutes. But her skin soon felt the force of the sun. In England, her pale, almost translucent skin stood out and made her look like a ghost. Over here, she might well have been anaemic.

She moved her wristwatch and recoiled at how pink her arm had got already.

Too pink.

She hurried down the steep bank, slipping and sliding on the clods of earth, scratching her arms on the cactus and even grazing her knee on a sharp pebble. And now she'd ended up not in the orchard by the oleander but at the other end of the house completely and her new cut-off shorts were ripped.

This part of the house had an unlived feel about it. Even outside was bare. No lovingly tended herbs or flowering jasmines. Just neglected scrubland.

And she would have turned back because it really was *that* uninteresting had it not been for the door.

An invitation into the unknown.

She hesitated. Rubbed her knee. Licked the blood off her hand. Smoothed down her hair. And walked toward it.

Up close she could see that panels of cheap plywood had been nailed across the door frame. The wood was rotten and the first panel pulled away easily. She peeked through the gap and blinked. Underneath was a dark, wooden door divided into four panels. Compared to the rest of the house she'd seen, run-down, faded, dusty, this door shone. Like gold. The wood was expensive, that much she knew. She ripped off another slat, and then another. How could anyone have covered this door? Three of the panels were bare except for the top right. This one had a crude carving of a sun cut into the wood.

It seemed a shame to mark the wood so callously and yet the sun, although roughly drawn, did had a certain beauty about it. It was simple and uncomplicated. She ran her fingertips over the wood, feeling the cut grooves under her skin. And then curiosity took over.

What was through the door? She knelt down and peered through the keyhole but could see nothing. She tried the handle but it was locked and shut so tightly, it didn't even rattle.

What could she do?

She turned round and came face to face with Rafa.

Chapter Eleven

'What are you doing?'

He had a soft Spanish accent. And eyes that seemed bottomless. Dark, flashing pools which Lizzie couldn't help but stare into. How could anyone have eyes so black?

It took an effort to drag herself out.

Close up he was skinny, not even that tall, with slicked back black hair. Even though it was greasy she noticed how it frizzed at the ends. The closer he came, the more the details fell into place. A longish face, a slightly hooked nose, full lips and one ear pierced with a chunky wooden ring. She tried hard to imagine someone like this fitting into school back home.

And couldn't. Just like her, he'd end up orbiting the popular people. But maybe even worse. He smelt. Not of sweat or smelly feet. It was something she couldn't recognize. Something pungent and clingy. She tried not to crinkle her nose.

'Rafa?'

He wasn't good looking. He was...? She tried to think of a word that fitted him. Dishevelled? Scruffy? Untidy? Strange? Then she realized she was staring at him. Not only that but she'd already seen him naked. She remembered the dream she'd had last night and accidentally dropped the piece of plywood on her feet. She yelped.

She caught his half-smile and frowned.

'Who are you?' He asked.

'Lizzie,' she muttered, determined not to rub her toe even though it stung.

'Why are you here?' He cocked his head to one side. He wasn't good looking at all and not only that, he smelt so bad she wanted to cover her mouth.

'So?' he repeated. 'Why are you here?'

'In Spain or here?' She pointed to the door.

'In Spain?'

Except he didn't say Spain like she did. It came out with a Spanish lilt. Which could have sounded romantic had it not been from his lips.

He stared at her waiting for an answer.

She sighed. 'On holiday.'

'For much time?'

'The summer.'

He nodded. 'It is a beautiful place. I think you will have very good summer.'

'I hope so,' she said, trying not to inhale as she spoke. Why couldn't he just leave her alone?

'If you want me to show you around,' he waved his arm in the air and she almost recoiled with the smell. 'I invite you a drink.'

The very thought of spending time with him made her stomach curdle. She didn't want to spend her summer with him! She'd come to reinvent herself. She'd come to be normal. Or at least try.

She offered a thin smile. The kind of smile Bee used when she dismissed someone. 'Thanks. But, no thanks.'

'No?'

She couldn't read the expression that ran over his face. Surprise? 'I'm here to spend time with my grandmother.' She cleared her throat and waited for him to answer. When he didn't she rushed on. 'I've never met her before.'

A tiny cloud passed over his face. 'No problem.'

'I'm sorry.' And for some reason she did feel a bit sorry, as if he were one of the flies caught on that thing, buzzing to be set free. She almost took the words back but another wave of his smell hit her nose. There was no way she could spend even ten minutes in his company.

He shrugged. 'No problem.'

She waited for him to go. But he didn't. It was rude but she turned her back anyway and faced the door again. If she offered him her back, he might get the hint.

'You cannot go through that door.'

'Why not?'

'Because it is locked.'

It was *because* it was locked she wanted more than ever to see what was on the other side.

Did he want her to say she wouldn't go through? She turned round and stared at him. He stared back. And in the end it was she who felt uncomfortable, as if he were seeing past the straightened hair, past the thin layer of foundation she'd put on, past her very skin. For the first time in ages it was Lizzie who looked away first, but not before she'd seen the small smile on the edges of his lips.

Before she could say anything, he'd walked away.

'Enjoy your swim!' she yelled out. Not even sure where the words came from or why she suddenly felt so bold.

He paused but didn't turn round.

* * *

She woke up from her siesta with a jump.

Tentacles of hair clung to her neck like an octopus and her back felt sheathed in sweat. She shifted on the bed. Disorientated. The dream coiled in the air. She'd dreamt about the wooden door. It had opened easily under her touch and when she stepped inside she'd come face to face with the stone angel from the cemetery. Except the statue had started to move, to transform, as if the angel were coming alive. Not stone any more, but human.

It left her with a hungry desire to see what was on the other side. Not that she expected to come face to face with the stone angel in real life, but the dream felt like an invitation. No, not an invitation, more like a command.

An icy feeling passed through her body.

It was insistent in a way she didn't like. She picked up the cut-off shorts she'd been wearing earlier and examined the rip. Mum had bought them from the boutique at the end of last summer in the sale. Lizzie had laughed at the price tag. Over a hundred quid for a pair of shorts! And now look at them. She smiled but put them on anyway and rummaged through her suitcase (she hadn't bothered to unpack yet) for a fresh top.

The door opened. Ariadne popped her head round and beamed. 'Dinner time!'

Her hand hovered over her make-up bag. If only she could get Rafa's sneer out of her mind. The way he'd looked *through* her. Acting on impulse she threw the entire make-up bag in a drawer and slammed it shut. And with it came a wave of relief. The foundation just sweated off in this heat anyway. She pulled a hand through her hair. Was it her imagination or did it seem less frizzy here? Of course, there was far less humidity in the air. An unexpected bonus. She grinned.

Ariadne had prepared a light salad. 'Home grown,' she smiled proudly. 'We'll eat in the kitchen tonight, though normally we eat outside in summer. It's still a bit hot out. Hotter than usual. They're talking of a heat wave.'

She was glad to be inside. Her skin felt tight from the sun and already it felt warm to the touch. She'd got a bit sunburnt today and she was sure she had a bright pink nose.

A flash of Rafa's brooding eyes popped into her mind. She shoved it to one side. Though not before feeling hotter still. Maybe she could have been more polite to him. It wasn't in her nature to be rude and she wasn't even sure why she had spoken the way she did. Something about him had got under her skin.

Probably his smell.

As she smiled there was a tap at the back door followed by a guttural cry that she failed to understand. Ariadne stood up, her serviette still tucked into her blouse like a bib.

'Must be Gabriel,' she said. 'He often pops by in the evening.'

The smell entered first. The exact same smell that Rafa had carried. But even more pungent. It *stank.*

What is that?' she crinkled her nose.

Ariadne laughed. 'It's the goats. Sssshhh.'

In walked Gabriel stooped low like a crab, wearing baggy blue workman's trousers and an ill-fitting green check shirt. He carried a plastic container full of a honey colored liquid and in the other hand was a bag full of ice.

On his head was a flat cap.

His face was so lined it looked exactly like a walnut.

Ariadne spoke quickly in Spanish to him and did the introductions. He grinned toothlessly, shuffled over to Lizzie and leant over. She shrank back.

'He wants to kiss you?'

'Kiss me?'

'It's the custom. Don't be alarmed.'

Garbriel brushed his lips against her cheeks, one side and then the other, and Lizzie held her breath. He kept smiling, touching her cheek and talking in Spanish. Ariadne tried to translate.

'He says you're *"guapa"*, you'll hear that expression a lot. It means pretty.'

Ariadne was still translating. 'You have lovely eyes – which you do by the way – very unusual I noticed them straight away. What colour are they exactly? Gray? Silver? They're very distinctive, aren't they?'

Her eyes were *lovely*? Lizzie almost laughed out loud at the very thought. No-one had ever said that before.

'He's enchanted to meet you and he hopes you'll be very happy here.' She stopped suddenly and frowned.

'What?'

'He says you must get used to my eccentric ways.' She patted his arm affectionately. 'He thinks I'm mad. An old English woman living out here by myself in the middle of the countryside .' She lowered her voice even though he couldn't understand her. 'He likes to look after me. He calls himself my guardian angel.'

Gabriel's eyes twinkled and he handed Ariadne the bag of ice with a wink. 'Ooh, fresh *rosada*!' She pulled out three white fillets, and with her hands still fishy, she hugged him.

He didn't seem to care.

Then she lifted the container, sniffed the contents, and poured the wine into three glasses. 'Here you go, Lizzie. Just a splash.'

She poured Lizzie a smaller glassful. Ariadne and Gabriel raised their glasses.

'He's making a toast to you. He says welcome to the most beautiful and most magical place on this planet, Andalucia.'

'To Andalucia!'

They all clinked glasses and then Gabriel and Ariadne took large gulps, whilst Lizzie sipped hers. It wasn't the first time she had tasted alcohol. But this was too sweet and she didn't like it much. As Gabriel kept staring at her for some kind of response, she nodded her head enthusiastically but when he went to pour some more into her glass, Ariadne covered it with her hand. She wagged her finger at him.

Ariadne cooked the fish on the barbeque and after eating they left the dishes inside and drifted out to the courtyard. By now it was nearly ten o'clock. The light began to fade and the atmosphere was still clingy. There was a balmy feel to the night, as if the air was velvet and stroked the skin. The night flowers started to waken and slowly filled the air with their musky scent.

Gabriel snapped off a flower from a bush and handed it to her.

'It's called a dame of the night,' Ariadne translated. 'Certain flowers prefer the night to the day, just like people. Are you a day or a night person, Lizzie?'

'Night,' answered Lizzie without thinking.

Gabriel said something and Ariadne nodded, grinning at Lizzie.

'What?'

Ariadne laughed again at something Gabriel said.

'Tell me!'

'He wants me to translate a story.'

Lizzie glanced over at Gabriel. He smiled.

'There is an old Spanish belief that when two people belong together they are like day and night.'

Gabriel babbled a bit more. Ariadne nodded.

'He says a day without night will never shine and a night without day will never sleep. Even though they each have a beautiful gift to share with the world, they are destined never to find happiness by themselves. One will always be searching for the other to make them feel complete.'

Gabriel jabbed Ariadne in the arm and then pointed at Lizzie.

Ariadne paused. 'Gabriel thinks you are the moon to Rafa's sun.'

Lizzie just about managed to stop herself from bursting into laughter. Thank *God* it was dark. She remembered the heat of Rafa's skin as he'd stood in front of her. Yes, he certainly had made her feel hot and bothered. Not in a good way though. How could *he* be her day?

No way.

The conversation moved on and Ariadne and Gabriel talked late into the night, deep in a dialog Lizzie couldn't understand. No matter, she sat back in her seat and gazed at the sky. One by one the stars popped into view. Nothing like the light polluted sky in London. She could identify almost every constellation she'd ever seen in a book *and* see the Milky Way. Why hadn't she brought her telescope instead of all those clothes?

'Beautiful, isn't it?' Ariadne leant closer, the pale pink of her dress rustling in the air. 'I could stare at the sky all night. Do you want to know a secret?'

Ariadne's face shone.

'Sometimes I sleep out here in summer and before I fall asleep

I look for shooting stars. And each time I see one I make a wish.' She smiled and reached forward to take Lizzie's hand. 'I've made a lot of wishes over the years. And many of them were to meet you.'

'Then why haven't we met before?' The words were out before she could stop them.

Ariadne sighed. 'A long story, Lizzie. Has your mother told you anything about me?'

Lizzie shook her head and then realized Ariadne couldn't see her. 'No. Nothing.'

'Then we have many things to catch up on.'

'Tell me,' Lizzie said, turning round in her seat. 'I want to know. Why don't you get on? What happened in the past? *Why* have you fallen out?'

Ariadne shifted in her seat but said nothing.

'It's horrible that you don't speak,' Lizzie confessed. 'I wouldn't like that. I don't really get on with mum but not to talk to her for years? That's so....'

'Cold?' Ariadne answered for her. 'I don't much like it either.'

'Then why couldn't you try to make up?' Lizzie leant forward. 'Why not both make an effort? Why do you *both* have to be so stubborn?'

Ariadne laughed. 'You're so much like your grandfather. He wanted to make everything perfect too.'

'My grandfather?' Mum never talked about him. All she knew was that he'd died when her mum was about her age. She felt Ariadne tense and bristle. A subtle shift in the air that made it crackle. 'What happened to him?'

An owl hooted.

'Why do you want to know?'

At which point Gabriel coughed. Typical. Just when Ariadne might open up and tell her what she was burning to know, the goat-man had to spoil it. Lizzie drew her knees to her chest and wrapped her arms around them.

'I'm curious, that's all,' she muttered, not really intending Ariadne to hear, but her grandmother must have ears like a cat's because she leant in and whispered.

'Of course you want to know. Just like I want to know *your* secret.'

It wasn't cold but Lizzie shivered anyway.

'We can never run away from our past, Lizzie,' Ariadne continued softly. 'However hard we try.'

Chapter Twelve

Nothing else was said.

Ariadne leant away, poured another glass of wine and resumed her conversation with Gabriel. In fact, Lizzie could have almost imagined it. But she knew she hadn't. Ariadne wasn't stupid. She knew something must have happened in England for Lizzie to be here. She told her grandmother she was going for a walk.

Ariadne didn't ask any of the normal questions mum might have asked, like how long she'd be gone, or where was she going. She didn't even tell her to be careful. She just nodded and continued talking to Gabriel.

Lizzie didn't really know where she was headed. If she were back home, she'd go to the greenhouse, but she wasn't home. She could do anything she wanted. Such freedom almost felt disabling. What *did* she want to do? Her tummy gurgled so she went to the orchard and picked the plumpest peach from the tree. There was simple joy in not having to wash it first. She sank her teeth into its ripe flesh and smiled as the juice ran down her chin and dripped onto her T-shirt. When she had sucked the stone dry, she picked another and then wiped her hands down her shorts.

And now what?

She lay on her back on the dirt and gazed up at the sky. It was black like coal and studded with stars. The moon shimmered and she looked up at it through hooded eyes. This was the same moon she'd seen in England, wasn't it? Except that the stars seemed brighter and the moon was fuller and riper.

She lay on the dirt for hours watching the sky shift and change. Was this what it would be like to sleep with someone for the first time? Not to have sex, but to actually *sleep* alongside them? Watching them as they passed through all the subtleties of sleep, mapping the dreams that passed across their face and the whispers on their breath. Spying on all their night-time secrets.

It was as the moon set (who knew a moon could set?!) and sank to a low tangerine colour that she finally stumbled to her feet.

'Thank you,' she whispered upwards and blearily made her way back toward the house.

Something dark flapped against her face and she stopped. It was probably just a bat but it reminded her of her dream.

And the angel.

As the sky started to turn pale gray, she walked round to the other side of the house, right up to the door and turned the handle.

The door was unlocked.

It opened easily and as soon she entered, a yellow light flickered on, then off, then on again. She stood in a narrow hallway full of a bizarre assortment of objects, obviously from Ariadne's travels. African masks, Peruvian panpipes, even a didgeridoo. Crates and crates of artefacts and objects stacked on top of each other. Framed pieces of art rested against the wall, tussling for space against lamps, vases and wooden statues.

And at the far end, there was a stone angel.

She gasped.

It wasn't her angel, of course, it was more of a cherubic angel with cherry red lips and fat cheeks. But even with the angel there was something strange about this room. It was much colder than the rest of the house. And more than that. It *felt* different.

This room carried something. Something dark and heavy. Even the air felt thick. Amid the stale dust and the sour smell, there was something else in this room. Something which made Lizzie shiver.

Should she leave? She hesitated but the dream nudged its way back into her mind, urging her to move forward.

'You better not let me down, angel,' she murmured and stepped forward.

The deeper she entered the room, the colder it got. There was a part of her that wanted to turn back. But the stronger, braver part of her urged her on.

'It's just stuff,' she muttered out loud. 'It can't hurt me.'

Crates and crates of stuff. Cobwebs dripping off them. The scuttling of spiders. Other noises too. She scurried forward.

Because at the end of the room next to the angel cherub was a door handle.

She had to yank three crates out the way before the door was clear. The dust rose and she coughed. Just a moment's hesitation before she grasped the door handle and yanked it open.

What was on the other side?

She widened her eyes in surprise. 'Oh my God.' She stepped forward one pace. 'Here they all are.'

Mirrors.

A square shaped room and every single surface of the walls lined with mirrors. They were all identical in shape and size and they each looked like a sun. The effect was dazzling. A thousand suns. All staring at her.

But why all here? And why all in one place?

Normally she hated looking at her reflection, especially in the hairdressers, but now she couldn't avoid herself. She could see her head from all angles. Before she knew it, she was standing in the centre of the room and turning her head this way and that way. It was like a mirage, a split TV screen, the effect of seeing her reflection from so many angles. And really, from the back, her hair was not *that* bad. Could she, in certain mirrors, even be considered pretty? If she bit the inside of her cheeks and plumped her lips out? OK, so she was a bit pink right now, but what if she arched her eyebrows and pulled her hair back? She tried a variety of different facial expressions but she couldn't help but think she looked strange. Her skin was too pale, her eyes were that weird gray colour and the less said about her hair the better. Even though Ariadne was ancient, and wasn't conventionally beautiful, she still had one of those faces that would *never* be called ordinary.

Lizzie stopped posing because it struck her how ridiculous it was to be standing in front of hundreds of mirrors and pulling silly faces.

Apart from the mirrors there was just one other object in the room. A box.

It was made of a wood that matched the main door. Was it mahogany?

She thought of Joopy. A memory of curly wood chippings caught in his fur. The memory hurt.

Like a treasure box in shape and size. It was not menacing like the black mark. It was solid and real, like a hundred-year-old tree was solid and real. Looking at the box gave Lizzie a calm feeling in her chest. There was some quality about it that oozed tranquillity. Like the angel.

'Just do it!'

She took seven large strides across the room and flipped open the lid.

* * *

'It's come all the way from Africa, you know?'

Lizzie looked up from the rosemary bush, wild and tangled in the roasting summer months, Ariadne had said it didn't need much watering. She held the hose in one hand and sprayed it with a splash of water before moving on to the lavender. Bees hurtled out of the way.

She had slept in. And when she woke up the light was so bright it sluiced its way into her eyes. Ariadne had knocked on her bedroom door mid-morning and announced that Lizzie could start helping her in the garden as of today.

The first day of the holiday was over.

Responsibility began now.

The sand she referred to was everywhere. It had come in the night whilst they slept. It had come on the wind. Ariadne had another hose and washed the terrace tiles clean. The sand was red.

'All the way from the Sahara desert.' Ariadne pointed in a direction, presumably toward the sea, although they couldn't actually see the sea from where they were standing. 'Amazing, isn't it? That a wind picked up in the deserts of Africa can find its way into my backyard. That's nature for you.' She put a hand against her hip as she straightened her back. 'Though not good for the arthritis.'

Lizzie's back ached too. Though not from arthritis. It ached because she'd had the *worst* sleep on living record. When she'd finally got back to her bed, the wind had howled. Battering the blue shutters. Demanding to get in. It was so noisy. Even the trees sounded like they were having a party.

And then there had been the bad dreams. Something about being trapped in that cold room. The big mahogany door slamming shut and leaving her in there. With just reflections of herself for company. And all the time, thinking about what she had found in that box.

'You still with me?' Ariadne touched her shoulder. 'You've been watering the lavender so much its drowning. Time for the jasmine.'

Lizzie hadn't mentioned anything about going into the hallway and didn't intend to. Everything in those two rooms seemed locked to Ariadne's past, especially the mirrors. If *she* didn't pry, then maybe Ariadne wouldn't pry either.

'I got a phone call from your mother. The second one in three years.'

The hose slipped in her hand and she ended up watering her own foot.

'Asked if you were settling in ok. I said perfectly. As if you belonged here. It's true, isn't it?'

Lizzie nodded and to her surprise she felt the sting of tears. She rubbed the back of her hand against her eyes and hoped Ariadne hadn't noticed. No such luck. Ariadne had the kind of eyes which saw everything. And more besides. Stuff that no-one ever usually saw. She had a way of peeling past layers and seeing right into people.

'It's fine to feel homesick.' Ariadne patted her arm.

'I'm not homesick though,' she said and paused. 'I *do* feel at home here.'

How could she not? Living here with Ariadne was a million miles from attending school on a gray English summer's day. This place was so wild and untouched, just like the graveyard. From almost the first moment she'd got here she had felt free, as if she could be anything she wanted, as if she could start again.

Ariadne paused the hose a moment. 'Don't worry, I won't tell your mother. By the way, she said she wanted to organize a set time when she could phone each week. I did tell her that we don't do time here but you know your mother.' She grinned. 'Sundays at 8pm it is.'

Ariadne turned the hose back on and turned it towards the red-headed geraniums. 'It's a good thing, you know. Being wild. Take the sand, for example, some people fuss because it gets everywhere. On the cars, on the patio furniture, even in the house. But I rather like the idea of having Africa in my living room. It's only sand.'

Sand.

Lizzie's mind flipped back to what she'd found earlier this morning.

When she had finally opened the mahogany box all that was inside was a jam-jar half-filled with sand.

A jam-jar in a box. *That's all.* A jam-jar half-full of sand. Sand made up of gold, amber and bronze. It was the prettiest sand she had ever seen though. Each time she'd sifted the jar, the sand had shifted shape and a new colour had emerged.

The lid was so tight it might as well have been super-glued on. It had been a moment's hesitation, that's all, before deciding to take the jam-jar to her bedroom. And even as she'd closed the box, she knew she had shifted things in some way, as if she had shifted time itself.

She'd left the jar on the chest of drawers.

The dreams came and went. Sleep came and went. The wind picked up. She had no idea what time it was when she sat up and reached for the glass of water. In the dark, her hand fumbled. It happened in a flash. The jam jar slid off the edge. She tried to grab it. One slippery palm. Fingers like ice. It slipped.

It fell.

For a split second the wind dipped and all was silent and then the jam jar hit the cold tiled floor and cracked into a thousand pieces. The wind exhaled and the shutters flung open suddenly. They whooshed open back and forth and the African air entered the bedroom.

She felt it brush against her face.

There were stars in the night-sky and she thought momentarily of Joopy, of Mrs Froust, of the grandfather she had never met, of all the people in all the world who had died and gone someplace different. She saw stars. All alive even though some of them were dead.

'Quite wonderful up there sometimes, isn't it?'

'What?' She caterpaulted back to the present.

Ariadne watched her intently. 'I said you can visit the *pueblo* today, if you like. Gabriel has invited us for lunch in the plaza. I can't leave just yet but Rafa has offered ride you in.'

She turned away to water the rest of the herb garden. It was important to water them before the sun got too hot.

'Ride me in?' Lizzie repeated.

'I said you wouldn't mind.' Ariadne turned round. 'A girl like you likes a bit of adventure, don't you?' She smiled impishly. 'You can ride on the motorbike with him.'

As if on cue, a roar of dust and noise exploded round the corner of *Casa del Sol*, and a huge yellow motorbike galloped up to their feet.

Chapter Thirteen

Rafa sat astride the bike wearing biker's boots, black jeans and a black T-shirt. To Lizzie's surprise, Ariadne flung her arms around his neck and pulled him into a tight embrace. And Rafa hugged her back. Their relationship was obviously much closer than Lizzie had thought.

He pulled off a red helmet.

'*Abuela*!' he laughed. When he smiled he looked completely different.They spoke rapidly in Spanish for a few seconds. Was it her imagination or was his voice gentler in Spanish than it was in English? He had a soft Spanish accent compared to his grand-father. His voice almost had a lilt to it, as if it could rise and fall on the breeze, like a melody.

Lizzie realized she was gawping.

'Rafa.' Ariadne switched to English. 'Let me introduce my grand-daughter, Lizzie.'

Rafa leant in. What was he doing? OK, leaning in for the customary two kisses. She leant forward, feeling the heat of the bike rise up like steam, and then the gentle brush of his lips against her cheeks contrasting with the rough stubble that grazed her skin.

It was only after she pulled away that she noticed there was no smell today.

'We've already met,' she said.

'You have? When?' Ariadne turned to them both and raised her eyebrows so high they almost took off.

'Yesterday morning,' Rafa answered. 'In the orchard.'

She turned to meet his gaze and couldn't read the expression in his eyes. For some reason, she had the feeling he was laughing at her. He hadn't mentioned the conversation by the door and she didn't know why. His dark eyes danced and he turned back to Ariadne. 'I had been swimming and was not … expecting to meet anyone.'

Ariadne threw her head back and laughed. Lizzie blushed so brightly she wondered if she could get any redder.

'No wonder you didn't tell me.'

Still chuckling she crossed over to the other side of the terrace and started to water the geraniums on that side. Lizzie felt bare without her.

'So we meet properly then?' Rafa cocked his head to one side and studied her through impenetrable eyes that seemed to rake over her face. She'd put on factor five million this morning and wore the same torn cut-off shorts as yesterday and a clean white T-shirt that had probably cost her mum a thousand pounds. Oh, and Ariadne's tatty straw hat. Not the most *together* look.

'I am enchanted.'

Enchanted?

'It's what we say here.' He coiled a strand of stray hair around his finger. The rest of his hair was scraped back in a greasy bundle. 'Much more romantic than "pleased to meet you", don't you think? *Encantado*.'

She coiled a strand of her own hair around her finger. Then stopped when she realized she was mirroring him. 'Sure,' she nodded, praying that Ariadne would come back and rescue her. For some reason, Rafa made her feel uncomfortable. There was a quality to him that made her feel on edge, as if he had the capability of seeing straight through her. When she was around him it was as though the sun had got brighter and everything around her, even the trees and the plants, had a sharper focus.

'You are Ariadne's grand-daughter, no?' His eyes bored into her but Lizzie refused to look away first this time.

She nodded and held his gaze. He smiled and looked back.

In the end she looked away first. Damn him!

His eyes crinkled. 'I am sorry that you must go with me today.'

'What?'

'Yesterday, you say you are here to spend time with your grandmother. Today you must go to San Juan with me. I am sorry.'

The way the corners of his mouth turned up didn't indicate he was sorry at all. It was like he was laughing at her. She cleared her throat.

'What does abwayla mean?'

'What?'

'A-bway-la?' she tried not to feel stupider than she already did. 'It's what you called her.'

Rafa roared with laughter. '*Abuela*.'

'That's what I said.'

'No. You said Abwayla.' He pronounced it the way she had.

Lizzie gritted her teeth. Who did he think he was? Her *teacher*?

'It means grandmother,' he said softly.

'But she's *my* grandmother!' She said automatically and then felt about five years old.

'I know,' he said. 'And you are getting to know her now. This is why you said no to my invitation and now here we are. She is not my real grandmother but how do I say in English? She is *like* my grandmother to me.'

His eyes raked over her again and she felt like was being stared at in the same way *she* stared at people. Rafa had the same way of looking as she did. Nathan Parks never looked at her this way. Nathan looked *over* people, Rafa seemed to look *through* people. She didn't know which she disliked more: Nathan's cool, sardonic look or Rafa's intense gaze.

She broke eye contact, again, and noticed his hands. How dirty and rough they were. How calloused.

'So, you do some gardening for her then?'

For some reason this made him smile. 'Yes. I garden for her.'

She couldn't see how this was funny. 'What do you do?' she asked politely.

Rafa launched into a detailed description of his work. She

listened as he talked about the land, the climate and the vegetation. It was surprising how good his English was. Not one hundred percent accurate, but good. She mentally readjusted her picture of him and now pictured him in some kind of school. An *educated* gardener. Did he still go to school or did he garden full time? He looked about seventeen.

'So, why are you here?' he asked, breaking her thoughts.

Because I see when people are about to die.

As if. Obviously she wouldn't tell him about the black marks! An image of the list flashed unwittingly through her mind and she winced. Even though he was a greasy gardener who smelt, she still didn't want him being repulsed by her. So what could she talk about?

Really, what could she talk about?

Of course. The bike!

She put a hand on the metal then snatched it back. It was boiling. She fished around for something suitable to say. 'Is it safe?'

His lips twitched into a smile.

'Are you afraid?'

Was he teasing her? She ground her heel into the ground and wished, just for a split second, she could tell him she wasn't afraid at all. That she could see the future and knew that they could ride on this bike as fast as he dared and they'd still be safe. What would he say then?

'Right, you two need to head off.' Ariadne returned, waving the hose around in the air. 'I'll drive in later in the 4 x 4 and meet you in the plaza.'

Lizzie glared down the dirt track. The heat bounced off her head.

'Are you afraid?' Rafa asked again.

His eyes twinkled in the same way that his grandfather's did The same way of looking at her as if he were looking at something funny.

She held out her hand for the spare crash helmet.

'Let's go.'

* * *

He rode hard and fast. Jumping over the ruts in the track. She pressed her knees into his thighs and circled his waist with her arms. Close up he was not as skinny as she'd thought. He had a wiry, taut frame. Hardened muscles.

They rode like this for about two minutes, which actually felt like much longer, whooshing past banks of olive and almond trees, and the air rushed past her face. Granules of dirt clung to her lips and her hair streamed out behind her. So much for straightening it. She felt the same guilty thrill she'd experienced on the plane when they'd hit turbulence.

He slowed and pulled over. She wrenched off the helmet and pulled a face. 'Why have we stopped?'

'Because it is dangerous.' He pulled off his helmet and stared back at her. Was it surprise she read in his expression? 'I don't think *Abwayla* would like it if I kill you so soon. And besides,' he looked up and down her outfit with a raised eyebrow.

She looked down at her not so white top. Mum would have a fit. Actually she would have a double fit. Riding on a motorbike was something she was expressively forbidden *never* to do. Well, lucky mum couldn't see her now! She wiped her brow and spoke without thinking.

'It's not like we're going to die.' She clamped her hand over her mouth. 'It's …unlikely, I mean.'

'And do you know this?'

He stared at her so forcefully she shuddered. It was that dark. Almost hypnotic. She jutted out her jaw and looked back down the track. 'I like going fast, that's all. It feels different.'

He studied her face. 'You are alive, that is why.'

She nodded even though she didn't fully understand what he

meant.

He smiled. 'You surprise me, Lizzie.' Except he didn't say Lizzie, he pronounced it *Leeezie*. 'You are so little and so pink. But also you are brave.' He shook his hair. 'Are all English girls like you?'

What had he called her? Little and pink? She pursed her lips and stared back at him. 'Are all Spanish boys like you?'

He laughed. And then she realized. He had paid her a compliment. He had called her brave.

She turned her head away so he wouldn't catch her smile. She didn't want him thinking she *liked* him.

He started the bike again and they set off, this time more sedately. Lizzie was able to see the trees as they rode past. Not that she knew what they were. So different to the trees back in England. They looked like the almond trees she'd seen on Ariadne's land. Sort of thin and spidery.

What was *that* tree?

She turned her head to look at it. And as she turned she saw a flash of silver. The glint of another vehicle coming toward them.

It happened fast.

One minute she was looking at a tree and the next minute the bike swerved. They skidded. He braked. Dust rose up in clouds. She felt Rafa's stomach muscles clench. The bike leant over to the side. She tightened her hold round his waist. She felt uneven. Like she was sliding in the seat. They were leaning too far. Way too far.

Someone screamed.

And then she was in the air. Not flying.

But falling.

She closed her eyes and blackness came.

Chapter Fourteen

'It's a shame your first visit to San Juan wasn't under different occasions.' Ariadne offered a tentative half-smile. 'But for what it's worth, welcome to my *pueblo*.'

The pair of them sat under the shade of a red parasol in the plaza of San Juan. Next to them loomed a huge white church. Lizzie sipped a coca cola. The woman at the *farmacia* had patched up her up and said she had nothing more serious than a few cuts and grazes.

Though at the time it had felt far worse.

Lying on the track in the heat of the sun, on her back, whilst the sunshine poured down in incessant waves. She felt covered in grime and dirt and sweat. Her knees stung. Her hands stung. Thank God she was wearing the crash helmet.

What had happened?'

She rolled over onto her side and feebly tried to pull the helmet off her.

'Don't move!' Rafa grabbed her shoulder. 'Your neck.'

'My neck's fine,' she snapped. 'It's my knee that hurts.'

'We need to get her to a *medico*.' She didn't recognisze the voice. It wasn't Spanish and nor was it English. The deep American drawl was totally incongruous with her surroundings.

The man spoke again. 'I can drive us to San Juan.'

'You should not be driving,' Rafa said in a low voice. 'I will call Ariadne and *she* will take Lizzie.'

'I'm sorry. I truly am,' the man said. She squinted up at him. Aged about sixty, his head was bald and the same rust colour as his cheeks. He had big teeth, *horse teeth*, Lizzie thought to herself, and he perspired a lot.

She wanted to tell him it wasn't his fault. But she didn't trust herself to talk at all. Otherwise she would cry. Hot salty tears. She felt a long way from home. A long way from anything familiar. It wasn't even her mum she yearned for right now. No, it was the cool, calm touch of the angel she craved and the way he always made her hurts go away. Just thinking of him soothed her. In the background she heard Rafa on the phone. Talking Spanish in a quick, urgent cadence.

She managed to sit upright. The helmet felt like a furnace on her head and with a burst of energy, she took it off and shook her hair free.

'Are you all right?' The American man with the horse teeth looked concerned. She smelt something pungent on his breath and the jigsaw pieces clicked into place. Was it even midday yet? 'We need to get you to a doctor.'

Rafa strode over. 'Ariadne is coming now.' He pushed the American man out of the way; no mean feat because he must have been well over six foot tall and he was a *big* guy. But the man was unsteady on his feet and fell aside like a skittle. Rafa cursed when he saw she had removed the helmet.

'It was hot,' she complained.

'And that was very stupid of you,' he muttered. 'We need to get you out of the sun.' Rafa grabbed her arm and tried to drag her toward the car.

'Careful!' she yelped. 'I'm not a goat.'

He said something in Spanish and in one swift movement, before she could even protest, he'd lifted her up by the armpits, heaved her against his chest and carried her over to the car. Her face pressed into the side of his neck and he tasted of salt. She almost gagged. She flailed her legs but it only made them sting even more.

'Better?' he said before bundling her into the back seat.

She flopped back and glared at him. 'You could have hurt me!'

'I thought you are brave?' He raised an eyebrow.

A snarl of anger. 'I am.'

'Be quiet then. Even the goats make less noise than you.'

Before she could answer, he thrust a bottle of water her way. 'Drink.'

She snatched the bottle and drank until it was nearly all gone. The last little bit she poured over her hands and knees. Rafa leant across the doorway like a shadow and watched every move like a hawk. She threw him back the empty bottle. It hit him in the chest.

'Thanks for the help,' she said.

'*De nada*,' he replied, *it's nothing*.

They glared at each other and this time Lizzie was determined she wouldn't look away first. Ariadne's car rolled up in a cloud of dust and exhaust.

'I think *Abwayla* is here,' he said.

'Really? I hadn't noticed.'

'I see you later, Lizzie *the brave*,' he said and turned his back.

'Not if I can help it,' she muttered and inwardly soared when she saw Ariadne's face appear in the doorway.

One hour later the church bells chimed two o'clock.

'What would your mother say?' Ariadne took a swig from a bottle of water and placed it back on the table.

Mum would have had her in casualty by now demanding x-rays. She always over-reacted with any illness and had a first-aid kit the size of a small house.

She didn't say any of this though.

'She'd probably be angry that I've ruined these clothes,' she said with a resigned shrug. Her white T-shirt was torn and her shorts were ripped even more. She picked at the fraying cotton with a ragged fingernail. 'I wish mum was more like you.'

Ariadne frowned. 'Don't say things like that.'

'It's true though. She's so prim and proper and she always likes to do things the right way. You should see the house, Ariadne. It's like living in a hospital. ' She pulled at a stubborn thread of cotton until it came loose in her hand. 'I've never felt at home there.'

Ariadne stroked a strand of hair away from Lizzie's face. 'You're so much like she was at your age.'

Lizzie pulled a face. 'Hardly.'

'Always fighting against yourself. You do know you're special, don't you?'

Her mouth felt too dry to answer.

'Being at home doesn't come from where you live, Lizzie. It comes from *who* you are.' She tapped her on the chest. 'Be happy here and you can be happy anywhere.'

Her heart fluttered against her chest like the beating of butterfly wings. Dear angel. Ariadne made it all sound so *easy*.

'I see you straighten your hair these past two days and I ask myself why a girl with beautiful hair like yours would want to make it go all straight and boring.' She thinned her lips. 'Really, you don't need to do anything to your hair. You know that, don't you? Why try and make it something it's not?'

Ariadne ran a hand through her own thin wisps of pigeon coloured hair, bound loosely in an orange scarf. 'I would *love* to have your hair.' She leant over and squeezed Lizzie's fingers. 'I'm so glad you're here.'

'I'm glad I'm here too,' Lizzie said. Which felt an odd thing to say considering what had happened today. But it was true. She had ridden on a motorbike for the first time in her life and she had *loved* it. She hadn't been killed, had she? Just the opposite, the whole experience had made her feel alive (she reluctantly used Rafa's word now she knew what he'd meant) in a way that made life taste crisp and sharp, like an apple bursting with flavour.

She didn't care what Ariadne said about being happy in yourself, being here helped. Life in Spain felt more on the edge, not neutered and tame like her life in England, but fiercer, full of experiences, full of adventure. It had started on the plane with the turbulence and had continued with the bike ride today. She could feel the blood pumping through her veins in a way she'd never noticed before, like she was waking up from a long sleep.

She felt more at home here than she ever had in England.

'I just wish mum let me *live* a bit more, that's all.'

Ariadne sighed. 'I don't want you to think badly of her. We all have our idiosyncrasies that carry us through life.'

Lizzie snorted. 'Well whatever they are, I'm glad I'm here with you and not with her. I wish I could stay forever.'

Ariadne reached over and patted her hand. 'There's a lot to why people do and don't get along, little Lizzie and most of it is to do with blame and forgiveness – or lack of it.'

She took another sip of water and Lizzie couldn't help but wonder what exactly had gone on between Ariadne and her mum. There seemed to be more to it than met the eye. But wasn't that the same of *her* life too? She turned to look at her grandmother quizzically and an unspoken look passed between them.

'I think *we* can bond. You and I.' Ariadne smiled and it were as if the sun had come out and washed its warm breath all over her.

A lump of emotion rose unexpectedly in her chest.

'Ariadne?'

'Yes?'

She paused. Licked her lips. 'I opened that door. I went in and then I went into that other room with all the mirrors and I opened the box.'

Ariadne downed the rest of her water. 'Well, I did leave it unlocked for you,' she chuckled. 'I wondered how long it would take you to find it.'

'So you *know*?'

'If I saw a boarded up door, do you think I'd leave it alone? Of course not. It's a mystery begging to be unravelled.'

'I'm sorry.'

'Don't be. I've kept it locked away all this time.'

'The jar?'

'That too.' She squeezed her hand tighter. 'But I meant the

past. It's time for it to come out.'

Maybe it was the way she said it. With that fleeting expression of pain that slid in and out of her eyes. It made Lizzie think of the mound of earth in the back garden back home. A small wooden cross.

'Why do you have all those mirrors?'

Ariadne held up her hand to attract the waiter. 'Someone made them for me.'

'Made them for you? Why?'

A slow smile crept over Ariadne's face.

'Love.'

At first she didn't get it. What did love have to do with a room full of mirrors? But the answer came like a shooting star. It shone in her grandmother's eyes, like flecks of sparkling gold. Ariadne had one of those faces that never stood still, it constantly changed expression and mirrored something new. Someone had loved her *so* much he'd made her a mirror to capture every single reflection that life had etched on her face.

Lizzie bit her lip. Would anyone love *her* in the same way?

Ariadne with that knack of reading thoughts, raised an eyebrow.

'Although your face is much more difficult to read than mine. He'll spend a lifetime just trying to dig beneath the surface with you.' She leant closer. 'Men *love* enigmatic women.'

Lizzie found that hard to believe. All her experience to date had proved the opposite. Nevertheless, the idea was a comforting one.

Ariadne leant back and the sun flashed off her necklace.

'Was he your moon?' she asked shyly, pointing to the sun around her neck.

'Yes, he was my moon,' she smiled gently. '*And* he was your grandfather.'

'What would you like to drink?' The waiter's voice broke into the moment. He was tall with a lot of white teeth. Good looking in the cool way Nathan Parks was attractive.

'Two cokes for the *senoritas*.'

'My *grandfather* made all those mirrors?'

Ariadne chinked her glass. '*Salud*. Of course he did. Your grandfather was a very talented man and extremely good with his hands.' She smiled cheekily. 'He had a gift.'

'A gift?' Lizzie sat up straight. 'For what?'

'For making mirrors. What did you think I meant?' Ariadne said. 'He was an extraordinarily skilled craftsman in his day, known throughout the whole of Spain for his beautiful hand-made mirrors. They called him *El Angel de los espejos*. The angel of the mirrors.'

Lizzie gasped. 'The angel?'

'Believe me he was no angel,' Ariadne chuckled. 'But the way he made those mirrors, they said it was as if he had God's hand on his shoulder. God's messengers – that's what they call angels. The giver of gifts.'

Lizzie thought back to the angel in Milton Cemetery. Was it him who had given her this gift?

'Do you believe in angels?'

Ariadne looked at her coyly. 'When you get to my age you have very little choice.' She laughed abruptly and then stopped. A serious expression passed across her face as she looked back into her past. 'I certainly believed that when Seth worked he found an inspiration from somewhere other than himself. He was *touched* by something. Maybe he even heard them speaking to him, who knows?'

'Then why do you keep them all locked away?'

'Is everything ok?' The waiter suddenly materialized beside Lizzie's chair.

Lizzie blushed as his dark eyes raked up and down her. She nodded and he backed off with a wink.

'You've got an admirer.'

Lizzie looked at him then back at Ariadne. 'Don't be silly.'

'Why is that silly? Why wouldn't he like you?'

Because he's too good looking! Lizzie wanted to answer. But how would Ariadne understand that? She was still beautiful, even for someone in her late sixties. She had the charisma and charm that Lizzie could only yearn for.

'You were going to tell me why you keep all those mirrors locked away…?'

Ariadne opened her mouth to answer but the words caught in her mouth because Gabriel chose that exact moment to sit down. They exchanged kisses and Gabriel patted Lizzie's arm affectionately as Ariadne explained what had happened. Lizzie idly wondered where Rafa had gone. Not that she cared. He was rude, unfeeling and he smelt. She cringed just thinking about how he'd picked her up and thrown her in the car. Like she was one of his goats!

Over the other side of the bar someone started to clap. A cheer went up. The owner of the bar, a short fat guy, brought out a hard-backed chair and placed it under the shade of the building. Another person started to clap. She saw someone with long, dark hair stride confidently out of the bar and take the chair. He had a tall, straight back and hair that fell in soft curls onto his red shirt.

He carried a guitar.

'What's going on?' she turned to Ariadne.

'The entertainment,' Ariadne winked.

Gabriel leant forward on his chair. Lizzie turned to watch, peering through the shoulders to get a better view.

Gently at first, plucking the strings of his flamenco guitar idly as if in a random sequence. He cradled the guitar close to his chest, his head tilted to one side, his eyes closed, his legs crossed, with one foot dangling and the other tapping on the ground. Next to her, she could feel Gabriel nodding his head and across the bar someone began to clap in flamenco rhythm. Gabriel joined in and Lizzie watched his hands beat the time.

He played music as though his fingers were gripped around her heart, squeezing and pressing it from all sides. It evoked a feeling inside of her she didn't even know existed. A feeling of pain mixed with intense longing. A blend of emotions that ran as deep as her soul. The music ached within every cell of her body, every fibre, every muscle. It filled her up in a way that music had never done before, in a way that she could focus on nothing else but the sound of it echoing deep inside.

'Who is it?' Lizzie asked, unable to see him properly, not from this angle.

Ariadne smiled. 'Listen.'

Lizzie leant forward. Around her now, everyone had started to clap the same rhythm. She had no idea how it was done and for a moment she felt left out, and so she looked to Gabriel's hands and he showed her the beat. Even though she felt self-conscious at first, after a moment or two she was soon clapping just like them.

The English woman in front of her left her seat and suddenly Lizzie could see the guitarist more clearly. He looked up and brushed a strand of hair away from his face. He smiled. And then she got it.

'Rafa?' she whispered. 'Is that Rafa?' She turned to Ariadne.

Ariadne nodded. 'Who else did you think it was?'

'But he's so….' She ran of words.

'Beautiful,' Ariadne finished. 'He's another one who's touched by angels.'

It was true.

As he started the next song, she was unable to tear her eyes away. The more she looked at him, the more she saw him for the first time. *Why* hadn't she seen this before? All she had noticed was how different he was with his hair and his clothes and the way he spoke so directly. How he'd been rude and brusque after the accident. How he'd smelt. But now look at him! The music transformed him. He lit up from inside and actually shone.

Somehow the music made him beautiful. He was so lost in it, so totally absorbed by playing, that he was no longer Rafa, but someone else. He made all the boys back home look so normal. So uninteresting and boring.

So bland.

Which of *them* could create music like this?

He looked across at her across the cafe. Their eyes connected and as they did, she rocked back on her heels and stopped clapping.

She wanted him.

Chapter Fifteen

'Why didn't you tell me?'

'You did not ask.' Rafa said, in that peculiar way of his that accentuated each word. He collapsed into his seat, the guitar resting by his feet. Having finished the set about ten minutes ago he'd been surrounded by locals and tourists ever since. All clamouring for his attention, like he was some kind of star.

Now he had come and sat with them. He raised a glass of red wine and chinked it against Lizzie's glass. '*Salud*. To your health.'

'But I thought you were the gardener.'

'I *am* the gardener,' Rafa replied. 'I am *also* a musician.'

'That'll teach you to make assumptions,' Ariadne chuckled. 'Rafa's saving all the money he can to go to a special flamenco college in Cordoba next year.'

'You pay him.'

Ariadne nodded. 'Every little bit helps. That's why he does these lunchtime sets. Not only here but in all the local villages. The tourists love him.' She waved an arm around the crowded plaza. 'We're hoping he gets a scholarship to a specialist music school in Cordoba where only the best students go. When do you find out about that, Rafa?' she asked him.

He took a sip of the wine. 'This week.'

Ariadne rubbed her hands together. 'I pray to God you get in.'

'Me too.'

Lizzie looked from one to the other. She knew nothing about flamenco music other than what she had just heard. She cleared her throat. 'Are you any good?'

Rafa threw his head back and laughed. 'What do you think?'

'I don't know.'

'How does it make you feel?' He leant forward and jabbed a finger toward her chest. 'There. In your heart. What do you feel?'

Like her heart was soaring? As if she had a firework in her

chest? As if she were burning up? As if he'd climbed inside of her and breathed on her soul?

She was glad her face was hard to read and she prayed he couldn't see through the veneer. She looked at him and shrugged.

He looked back at her with what amounted to little more than disgust and then muttered something in Spanish to Gabriel.

Ariadne jumped in. 'Rafa is one of the most talented flamenco guitarists in the region. He gets it from his mother.'

'She played the guitar?'

'She sang,' Ariadne said. 'She was one of the most famous singers in Spain.'

'Doesn't she sing any more?'

'She's dead.'

Ariadne glanced across at Rafa and lowered her voice. 'She died when he was very young and his father left shortly after. That's why we're so close. Gabriel was a widower and had the land and the goats to look after and so I helped bring Rafa up.'

'*Abuela*,' Lizzie muttered.

'Yes, he calls me that.' Ariadne smiled.

'That's why his English is so good.' Lizzie exclaimed, and then she bit her lip. How hard that must have been. It'd been bad enough growing up with just one parent. Imagine having none. No wonder he felt Ariadne was like his grandmother. No wonder he felt so possessive of her.

She wanted to say sorry for being rude the first time she'd met him. She'd tried to dismiss him when all he'd done was offer to show her around. Why had she judged him? Because he looked *different*?

The graze on her knee stung. She'd treated him just as she had been treated in the past. She'd been no better than Bee. She looked up and caught him staring over at her.

'Thanks for looking after me earlier,' she said.

Rafa raised an eyebrow. 'Even though I treat you like a goat?'

'You should be so lucky,' Ariadne said. 'These boys treat their goats better than people.'

'We are farmers,' Rafa smiled. 'And sometimes we smell.' He looked over to Lizzie and actually winked.

The sun suddenly felt incredibly hot.

Her heart thrust itself against her chest like it was a living animal. All her nerve endings tingled. Every cell in her body was jumping up and down.

So, this is what it felt like to want someone. She thought she'd had a crush on the angel. But that was crazy wasn't it? Because the angel wasn't even real. No, what she felt for Rafa surged through her veins and rubbed against the very marrow of her being. Had she ever felt so *alive* as she did right now? Like she had a firework in her chest wanting to rocket outwards?

She felt everyone looking at her. Why?

Was she expected to say something?

Ariadne laughed. 'I told you she got lost in her head. Just like I did when I was her age. Always daydreaming of something else,' she laughed a low laugh. 'Rafa asked if you had been in the dip pool yet.'

The first time she'd seen him rushed into her head, so fierce it scorched through her like a flare. She didn't dare look at him because she wasn't sure that her face could actually hold all this emotion in, not when it flickered against the inside of her skin like flames.

She was rescued by the bells, not chiming the hour, but peeling in a heavy, sombre tone. Gabriel said something and Ariadne nodded.

'What is it?' Lizzie asked.

'The death bell. It means that someone has died.'

It was as if a bucket of cold water had been thrown over her head. A shade fell over the plaza as the bells tolled. As they were too loud to talk over their little group sat in an uneasy silence. Lizzie kept her eyes lowered. The sound of death brought up an image of Joopy on the road. The way his legs had twitched in those final moments. The black mark coiling upwards. The bitter urgency of her voice as she saw his life ebb away.

'There she is!' She recognized the American accent immediately and felt a surge of relief because it put a full stop to the memories.

'I wanted to say sorry.' He shouted over the bells with a slurred voice. She smelt the brandy before she saw him. The stench of it on his breath. She winced.

'It's ok,' Ariadne mouthed. 'I'll handle this. Hooper!' She called out brightly. 'I heard you had a little bit of an accident earlier.'

Hooper stumbled up against the table and saluted Ariadne with a hand that wobbled against his forehead. 'Yes, Ma'am. It was very clumsy of me.' He tried to smile but all that happened was that his lips stuck to his horse teeth and the smile seemed strained. 'Small accident. So sorry. Won't do it again.'

'Too right you won't,' Rafa snarled.

Lizzie frowned at him. What was the point in being angry at someone like Hooper? He was just a drunk. One of those characters that lolled around on the edge of society. She'd seen them in London outside pubs at midday. The only difference with Hooper was that he couldn't hide his fate in a city, he was stuck in San Juan for everyone to see his condition.

He did look terrible though.

Creased off-white trousers that were an inch too short, a garish Hawaiian shirt and faded pink espadrilles. The guy was obese, he must have weighed about twenty stone and he stank like a pig with the amount of sweat pouring off him. He had puffy red cheeks, those ugly horse teeth and a black mark.

And a black mark.

Lizzie looked again.

A black mark.

What?

It hadn't been there earlier, had it? Not even a second ago. Just like the mark above Mrs Froust's head, it had appeared from thin air. From nowhere. She stared at it, fixated on it, gawped at it. Unable to tear her eyes away. Except this time she had an accompaniment to death. In the background the church bells continued to toll. On and on. Like an army marching to its last battlefield.

An odd assortment of details went through her head: The black mark above the old woman's head in the bus, puddles in the school playground, Nathan's fingers ruffling through her hair, Bee's smirk as she handed her the list, mum's tears as Joopy had died, the Mexican mask on the wall back home.

She felt tears prick her eyes. She wouldn't cry. She couldn't.

And the bells kept tolling.

Why did she have to see black marks now? *Why?* She thought she'd left them behind in England. She thought she could fit in. Be normal.

No. Shapeless and yet tangible, there it was .

She knew she was staring. Not only was she staring but everyone else seemed to be staring at her. Ariadne, Gabriel, Rafa and Hooper. There were no words. Nothing she could say. Nothing she *would* say. She wouldn't make the same mistake she'd made at school. She wouldn't blurt it out this time and then have to face all the jeers from everyone else. All the funny looks.

Not now.

The bells finally stopped and she forced herself to look away from the black mark which fluttered gently like a flag. She lifted her glass to take a sip of her coke. None left. So she sucked at the ice cubes.

'Everything ok?' Ariadne leant across the table. 'You're not scared of Hooper, are you? He's totally harmless. A drunk of course, but at heart he's one of life's interesting people. He used to be a famous artist you know, and some of his paintings were quite exquisite. But then his wife left him and it's all been downhill from there.' Something flashed in her eyes. 'Such a shame he doesn't paint any more.'

Hooper didn't look like a talented artist. He rocked from pink espadrille to pink espadrille and sloshed his brandy over the side of his glass. He had shiny, glazed eyes and a mottled red nose. Sweat dripped off his forehead and stained the pits of his shirt.

Ariadne lowered her voice. 'If only he would just give up the drink. He was due for a comeback exhibition this weekend but I doubt very much he'll make it. I think the pressure has got to him because I haven't seen him this out of it in weeks.' She frowned. 'Still, there'll be other chances in future.'

Hardly!

Should she tell him?

Her throat felt raw. It was the same feeling she had felt on the bus with the old lady. She hadn't spoken then and now her heart tugged in the same persistent way. Should she tell him to do the exhibition? But if she spoke to him now, then they would all know something was different about her.

She cleared her throat. 'Hooper?'

He didn't hear her. Not over the chatter.

'Hooper?' She said it louder.

He turned to look at her and swayed. 'You're the girl that fell off the bike.' He pointed. 'Whatd'youwant?' It came out as one word.

She opened her mouth. 'It's...' she stuttered and looked around her.

Ariadne had paled and both Rafa and Gabriel stared right through her, right into the part of her she so desperately wanted to hide. She couldn't do it. She couldn't!

'It's...'

'What?' Hooper said, and the black mark seemed to flutter even more urgently, as if it had wings of its own.

She gulped. 'It's nothing.'

Chapter Sixteen

She waited for the day Ariadne went to the coast for provisions before making her move. It had been planned as an excursion for both of them. Ariadne would drive them down to the coast, she'd take Lizzie to a beach restaurant for lunch and then go shopping afterwards. Come Thursday, Lizzie feigned a stomach-ache and although Ariadne peered at her strangely, she didn't press the matter and off she drove leaving clouds of dust rising listlessly in the air.

Lizzie gazed after the 4x4 and waited until it was out of sight. It had been three days since seeing the black mark and every single second had felt heavy, not helped by a rise in temperature which meant the air was close and cloying.

She wasn't sure how she'd got through it. It had been so hot the heat lay like a shroud. She hadn't slept much. She just laid on the bed, sweating. And these were the times she thought about things. In no particular sequence. No, like the flies buzzing around the room in aimless circles, so did her thoughts. Joopy. The black marks. The jam jar she had broken. Hooper. Mrs Froust. Bee. The man on the plane. The black marks. The deep, cutting shame she felt for letting Hooper walk away. Knowing he was about to die. What should she do next.

And when this produced more questions instead of answers, she would roll over onto her front and think of Rafa.

And just when she thought the room couldn't feel much hotter, the heat raised a few notches, and she would get a funny feeling in her body. A feeling she didn't understand. All she knew was that he made her feel something she'd never felt before.

He had transformed under her eyes and now she didn't really know what to say to him. They had bumped into each other a few times and he'd stared at her and she'd stared back and that was that.

Words came heavy and awkwardly. Now she knew he was somebody it made her feel like a nobody. Which was odd. Because when *he'd* been a nobody, she'd felt like somebody. She didn't know why she should feel differently around him just because he was some hotshot guitarist.

But she did.

He'd come to the dip pool most days but even though it was scorching hot weather she felt funny using it. Like she was trespassing or something. So she'd kept clear. It was *his* spot after all.

The sound of the cicadas jarred her back to the present. The constant whining noise indicated how hot it was. She wasn't sure how much time she had so she dropped the hose and took a deep breath.

'Let's go look.'

If the black marks had appeared then she could at least discover why. Surely she could not be the *only* person in the world with such a gift?

She stopped short as she realized she had just referred to her ability as a gift. Was it a gift? If so, what was the point of it?

She headed into the house, brushing past a mewing North and South, and aimed straight for the library. In lieu of the internet, books were the next best thing. Books were the source of all knowledge according to Ariadne. They were the answer to all mysteries. Perhaps even this one.

The library was silent, slumbering gently in the heat. Yet all these books gleamed with love and attention. What was the probability that Ariadne would have a book about life after death or psychic ability? Slim. But worth a shot, *surely*? Lizzie ran her eye over the shelves – they were full of American detective novels interspersed with the odd Agatha Christie.

No book on death.

She ran a hand through her hair in frustration. What was it Ariadne had said last night? That she looked more Andalucian by the day apparently. Gabriel had even claimed that she had the same hair as his daughter, Rafa's mother.

She stopped twirling her hair and frowned. There were no books here that could help her make sense of what was happening to her.

A hot silence sank down. The thermometer had hit forty degrees and the air felt motionless. The last place she wanted to visit was the museum room but she thirsted for knowledge. She needed information. And where else could a book on life after death or paranormal activity be but amongst all that strange, unworldly junk? She trudged round to the rear of the house where the sun had scorched the ground a burnt omelette colour.

She listened for any sounds. Nothing. Not a soul stirring except for her. Not even the leaves in the trees moved. Everything stagnant.

The door creaked. When she fumbled for the light switch her fingers ran through a cobweb. The light flickered but didn't turn on. Lizzie hesitated. The dark didn't frighten her. She could go get a torch after all. But there was something else about this room. Something more than the dark.

It unnerved her.

In a way that the cemetery had never ununnerved her.

Something about the *feel* of it.

The hallway was full of assorted objects. Such a book could be anywhere. She took a deep breath and focussed. This wasn't a time to rely on logic; it was a time to trust her intuition.

'Where are you?' she murmured and looked around the room. 'Of course!'

Stacked in the far corner, behind the figure of the cherub angel, were a pile of crates. She loosely remembered them from the first time because of the Mexican face masks. They'd reminded her of home. She took a step forward. She was barefoot and her footsteps made only a faint slapping sound. Flesh against tile. Another step and then another. The light flickered on and then off. Nearly there now. The next two steps she took quickly. The crate at the top was heavy and she lifted it down. She couldn't really see but she could feel the contours of the masks under her fingertips. It was cold to the touch. She tried to push her hand through but there were too many masks so she had to take some out first.

She piled them on the floor beside her.

It wasn't so much a movement, more a blur.

Like a television which had accidentally been put on fast forward. Out of the corner of her eye. The exact same time she touched a book. Felt the newspaper print under her fingertips. Something blurred at the far end of the hallway. Something silver.

She didn't even know she could scream that loud.

But she did.

She grabbed the book, left all the masks where they were and sprinted out of the hallway and was through the door in seconds.

What was that?

In all her visits to Milton Graveyard, she had never seen anything like that. Never! And by rights, that place ought to be crawling with ghosts. She bent over trying to catch her breath and as she did, something flashed in through the doorway.

North.

He squeezed through the gap in the door, covered in cobwebs, and sat down to clean himself. She stared at him a long time before walking over to the door and closing it.

Outside the dirt rose gently in the air like a cloud and she couldn't shake the feeling that someone was watching her. As if someone had been there the entire time. She clutched the book to her chest and looked around her. Nothing to see.

Nevertheless she scampered quickly to the sunny side of the house.

The book was coated in a yellowing sheaf of newspaper. A headline about a drowning man. She held it in her hands, suddenly nervous about what was underneath so with one brisk rip she tore the paper off and threw it to one side.

Oh.

It had a bright red cover with a picture of a couple kissing on the front. It was called *Flamenco*.

Not quite a book on death. It seemed the hunt was over. Lizzie felt worn out and strangely relieved she hadn't found anything. What did she want to find out anyway? How much of a freak she really was?

She idly flipped the book over and read the back cover. It was a love story set in Spain. But not just any old love story. It was about a flamenco dancer who fell in love with a foreigner and it reeked of passion and excitement and danger.

A trickle of sweat dripped between her breasts. She idly traced it with her fingertip and then stopped. The feeling that someone was watching her passed over her again. Even though she glanced around she saw nothing apart from the newspaper she had shoved aside earlier. She picked it up and smoothed it into a folded square and slipped it inside the pages as a bookmark.

She shook her hair and wished with a pang she had gone with Ariadne to the coast. Today's search had been fruitless and the silence of the house sank around her shoulders uncomfortably. This was the first time she had been here alone.

How many times had she been to Milton Graveyard by herself? But this was different. She was in a totally different country and a long way from home. And it wasn't as if Rafa was going to pop round either. Ariadne had told her over breakfast that he'd gone to Cordoba, something to do with the music school.

The deep blood red cover of *Flamenco* caught her eye. So much for trusting her intuition and finding a book on angels. Mum always said gut instinct wasn't to be trusted.

Mum.

For the first time since being out here she thought of her in a way that didn't pierce.

The first time she rang it went to voicemail so she punched the numbers again.

'Mum? Is that you?'

'Lizzie!' She sounded surprised. 'I'm with a client at the moment. Is everything ok?'

'Yes.' Lizzie looked around her. 'It's fine.' She sat with her back against the olive tree at the top of the hill. Ariadne's tree of life. The only place to get a phone signal. The horizon was bright enough for her to see the blue smudge of the Med.

The line went muffled. 'Excuse me a minute.' She heard mum's heels click, a door open and shut and then the line became clear again. 'Lizzie, it's the middle of the day. What's happened?'

Lizzie went to check her watch and then remembered her watch had broken. She hadn't thought about the time. Only the sudden fierce urge to call her mum and to listen to her voice. She'd missed it. But somehow all that stuck in her throat. Mum's voice sounded exactly the same. Slightly hurried and breathless.

'Nothing.'

'Is everything all right out there? Granny?' Mum hesitated. 'She hasn't said anything to upset you, has she? I knew it was a mistake you going there.'

'No! Ariadne's fine.' Lizzie knew she couldn't tell her that Ariadne had left her alone. She'd explode. 'I like her.'

Mum's silence was longer this time. Long enough for Lizzie to shift position. Sweat dribbled down her back.

'This call must be costing you a fortune.'

'Ariadne says the phone charges have come down.'

Mum still said nothing.

The mobile felt hot in her hand. Clammy. She didn't know what else to say so she went for the obvious

'How's work?'

'Work's good. Busy as usual. We had a new sales promotion start last week so I've been tied up in that. Though I did manage to do a spot of gardening at the weekend.'

An image of their back garden popped into Lizzie's mind. The garden bench, the apple tree, the greenhouse. 'Are there still tomatoes?'

'Plenty. I'm eating so many I'm going to turn into one.'

Over the other end of the line she could feel mum smiling. Lizzie smiled too. Suddenly Joopy's death seemed a long way away. What was it that Ariadne had said about forgiveness?

'Mum I'm….'

'Look Lizzie I really have to get back to this meeting. We're planning the new winter range. It's all reds and blacks this year.' Mum's voice overlapped. 'We'll speak on Sunday, ok?'

Lizzie nodded and then realized mum couldn't see that. 'OK. But mum….'

'Just one minute!' Mum called out and then lowered her voice. Her tone softened. 'What were you going to say?'

Lizzie swallowed. The words stuck in her throat. 'Nothing. Just … that it's hot.'

Mum paused for what seemed like eternity. 'Yes, yes. Spain is very hot in summer.' Her voice tailed off. 'Goodbye then, Lizzie.'

Her eyes stung. Either sweat or tears. She rubbed them. 'Goodbye.'

* * *

How much hotter could it get?

The temperature inched higher and she was wearing a pair of old denim cut-off which clung to her thighs like sticking tape. Her T-shirt wasn't that much better.

She kicked open the flap of her suitcase with her toe.

It felt unnatural putting it on but the cotton blue dress, the colour of the sea, was cool and slippery. Mum had got it for her last birthday and she'd never even worn it. It lapped around her thighs like water.

Like water.

She stopped in her tracks.

Rafa wasn't here today! She grabbed a bottle of cold water from the fridge and her suntan lotion and at the last minute, the book she'd rescued from the museum room. She'd started reading it earlier on and for some reason it held some kind of pull over her. The words were like hot compresses and she wanted them pressed against her. She had to peek through the oleander first to make sure there really was no-one was around. The dip-pool sat silently, beckoning her with a velvety surface.

She jumped straight in, not even bothering to take off her dress. The water rose to her thighs. It was cool and sharp at the same time. She sunk down so it enveloped her and the dress billowed up. The sun gently filtered through and nuzzled her face, softened by the shade and the silky lick of the water.

After a bit, she picked up the book.

Lizzie read hungrily for the next hour. Greedily. Passionately. Thrusting the pages over in rapid succession. Before she knew it she was nearly three-quarters of the way through and her stomach was rumbling. It was the most erotic book she had ever read. Especially chapter twenty seven.

The thing was it was just so hot! Even sitting here in the pool.

After a few more minutes, she crawled out and because there really was no one else around, because the thermometer had hit forty degrees, and most of all because she wanted to experience the feel of the sun on her skin, she shyly stripped off her dress and after a moment's hesitation, her underwear.

If Rafa could do it, so could she.

At first, the rock felt grainy under her thighs and even though there was no-one around, she felt self-conscious. As if the oleander had eyes. But who was there to see? Ariadne kept telling her to enjoy the freedom whilst she was here, didn't she? And just the weight of the sun against her skin gave her a sensation she'd never had before. A sensation so delicious she wanted to squirm in pleasure. Stretching out on the rock on her back, the sun warmed up her body, as if she were a chameleon, soaking in the rays, turning a different shade. When it got too hot, she dropped back into the water, and when her skin got crinkly she crawled back out again.

It was like she was seven years old again and was free to do what she wanted. She splashed the surface of the water and giggled, dipping her head under.

'Hola?'

She sat up, realised she was naked and sunk back again. It didn't help that the sun had shifted in the sky so now it fell directly onto her face.

'Enjoying yourself?'

She blushed from head to toe as Rafa squatted by the dip pool.

'I thought you were in Cordoba!' she squeaked.

'I leave tonight.'

He wore surfer swimmer shorts and nothing else. It was the first time she had seen his chest close up. He didn't have an ounce of spare flesh on him – the contours of his muscles rippling gently with a faint smattering of hair coiling up from his shorts. She dragged her eyes upward. She found him watching her with a bemused expression.

'You are naked?' He sucked in his cheeks. 'You surprise me.'

'Then you don't know much about me then, do you?' she retorted. Of all the people to catch her it had to be him. She'd have preferred even Gabriel to Rafa! She wished the water wasn't quite so clear.

'Don't worry, I can't see anything.' He threw her the suntan lotion. 'Be careful you do not burn.'

She frowned. Actually she did feel a bit red. She squirted some in her hands and rubbed it over her face.

At which point he noticed the book. Or they noticed it at the same time and reached for it at the same time. He got there first.

He opened the book and with one eyebrow raised started to

read.

'No, don't!' Lizzie spluttered and tried to snatch it back.

He pulled the book out of reach. 'Juan Jose ran his fingertips lightly over Carmen's bare back and she arched in pleasure.' Rafa raised an eyebrow.

If her cheeks went any redder she would explode. She reached out to grab the book. He snatched it out of her reach again.

'The feel of his touch burnt her skin and never had she wanted anyone so much as she did right now.'

'Stop it!'

Rafa snapped the book shut. He smiled in such a way that made Lizzie blush to her toes. 'You are not so English after all.' He held up her blue dress. 'Is this yours?'

She nodded.

He handed it to her as if Lizzie sitting naked in the pool was the most normal thing in the world. Thinking back to the first time she had seen him, it probably was. She clutched the dress in the hand. He stared at her.

And she stared back. Why did he have to be so rude? So direct? The way he stared at her. She couldn't feel any more uncomfortable than she did right now. And yet at the same time, she felt a bit dizzy, as if her head had been sprinkled with fairydust.

He kept staring.

'You missed a bit.'

'What?'

'The cream.'

'Oh.' She rubbed her face. 'Has it gone?'

He shook his head and leant over. Rubbed her cheek with the tips of his fingers and as he did, they locked eyes. And something, she didn't know what, passed between them. So briefly she didn't even have a chance to question it. A light. A moment. A connection. A flame.

She pulled away and yanked the dress over her head.

'Perhaps you should get out first before you get dressed?'

'Look away then!'

He shrugged but turned to face the other way.

She stood and climbed out of the pool, feeling it cling to her. He kept his back turned and she stood, torn between wanting to stay and be close to him and another desperate urge to run away.

She stepped past him and headed toward the oleander.

'Your book?'

She froze. And then slowly turned round. He held out the novel.

And winked. God, she *hated* him sometimes.

Two steps later and he called her back. 'Lizzie?'

'Yes?' she looked over her shoulder.

He was smiling from ear to ear. 'I got the scholarship.'

Lizzie squealed and jumped toward him. She wanted to hug him but stopped herself at the last minute. Instead she faced him and grinned.

He grinned back. 'The party's on Saturday.'

Chapter Seventeen

'What time does it start?'

The stereo in the kitchen was on full blast, playing Rafa's music, and Ariadne trailed from room to room like a comet.

'Elevenish until dawn.'

'Dawn?'

'Best time for a party!' Ariadne said as she rampaged through items of clothing from her bedroom. Lizzie stood on the threshold. The room was a mess. Small piles of clothing dotted around the room like multi coloured anthills.

'Should I wear this or this?' In one arm Ariadne held an emerald green silk dress and in the other a magenta cocktail dress. Lizzie pointed to the green.

'These or these?' Huge hoop ear-rings or a small diamond studs. Lizzie pointed to the hoops.

'What are you going to wear?'

Lizzie crinkled her brow. 'I'm going to look now.'

After sifting through the contents of her suitcase three times, she still sat empty handed. What to wear? She hummed and hawed. Apart from the blue dress she'd worn to the dip pool *that* day, the rest of the clothes were either too scruffy or too formal.

Ariadne entered the room. The emerald green silk dress shimmered off her like a mirage. She had wrapped a matching silk scarf around her hair and the two giant gold loops hung from her ears. Her eyes were smudged with charcoal black eye liner and her lips were daubed a deep dark red. And she'd managed all this without a mirror?

'You look beautiful,' Lizzie said.

'And so do you.'

'I haven't even got changed yet!'

'Not what you're wearing, Lizzie. *You* look beautiful. There's a difference.'

She had no idea how she looked and she wasn't exactly going to go into the museum room to check, was she? Her arms and shoulders were now the colour of runny honey. No strap marks either. And the only make-up she'd put on had been a tiny lick of mascara and a smear of cherry pink lip-gloss. After four days of being outdoors, the idea of slapping on a face of make-up felt wrong somehow. For the first time ever she was about to go to a party and *not* straighten her hair.

What to wear though?

She hadn't noticed that Ariadne had disappeared until she reappeared with a long, silver dress draped over her arm.

'Thought you might like to try this on? The colour matches your eyes.'

The fabric was much shinier than anything she had worn before. It had thin shoulder straps and clung to her waist and hips. It was sexy, with a slit that rode up to her thigh.

'Try it on.'

Lizzie stepped into the dress. It did look good, actually. It also made her look completely different. Grown up. It accentuated her body. She didn't have that many curves yet, not as many as Bee, but those she did, came out to play. The dress matched her eyes. Or her eyes matched her dress. She looked sophisticated. Sexy. Hot. Grown up.

She smiled.

Perhaps, even, she could be pretty.

* * *

The party was in a beachside bar which Rafa's cousin's father had hired out for the evening. Bar Oasis sat at the far end of the beach on soft golden sand and was fringed by palm trees. It was past eleven when they arrived and the car park was jammed full. Having taken half an hour to get down the mountain it took another twenty minutes for Ariadne to find a parking space and in the end she parked it illegally.

'We'll be ok,' she said. 'Gabriel's nephew is in the local *policia*.'

They heard the music from over a hundred yards away, a mix between flamenco and chill. It was unlike anything she'd heard before. She liked it. The fact it was laid-back suited the bar. As they got closer, Lizzie's eyes were on stalks as they drank in every detail.

'I've never seen a bar like this before!'

The bar was huge. Massive. Like a warehouse. It had a teak coloured thatched roof and a long pathway up to the thick wooden door. Ariadne told the burly looking bouncer her name and he stepped aside to let them enter. The bar was on three levels and the top tier, the tier they were on, was glass floored and separated into a variety of seating arrangements. There were tiny nooks and crannies purposely created for couples framed by exquisite Moorish archways. Scented candles dotted around the place with their soft glow reflecting off people's faces. Silky cushions of amber, bronze, crimson and rose scattered the soft-seated benches that hugged the walls. Low level mahogany tables carved in intricate detail brimmed with drinks.

The centrepiece of all this was a waterfall.

A waterfall!

It started in the top tier and cascaded down through the lower tier and ended in a dolphin shaped swimming pool. Around the pool was another bar and plenty of soft cushions laid out on a wooden deck. Bar Oasis didn't stop here. A few short steps below this was the golden sand of beach and on the beach were beds.

Beds!

On the beach!

Four poster beds with tousled red sheets. The chiffon netting fluttered in the sea breeze like sails. And listening very carefully, above the music and the shouts and laughter of the guests, there was the soft crashing of the waves.

'It's like a palace!'

Ariadne laughed. 'The Spanish do know how to party.' She pointed out a handful of people on the beach who were dancing around open fires. 'It's what I love best about them.'

The place was packed on all three tiers: the bar, the pool and the middle tier which was the restaurant. Though all ages were present, from Ariadne's age to as young as seven, it was mostly Lizzie's age group that filled the place. Apart from Ariadne and Rafa, she didn't know a single person.

'How many people are here?'

'About two to three hundred, I imagine.'

She snuck a look at some of the Spanish girls. They had much darker skin than her, were all brown eyed and had lustrous black hair. They seemed so grown-up. Or was that just because they were different? She'd caught a glimpse of herself on the way in and had hardly recognized the girl who stared back. Soft brown hair fell to her shoulders in waves and glinted with streaks of gold. Her face had thinned so her silver-grey eyes looked enormous in her face. She stared at herself wondering what other people saw.

Ariadne introduced her to a hook-nosed Spanish girl called Ana who kissed Lizzie on her cheeks and kept calling her *guapa*.

'What does that mean again?' She whispered to Ariadne.

'Pretty,' Ariadne whispered back. 'And don't you forget it. You look gorgeous.'

Lizzie blushed. Compliments didn't feel normal.

'Shall we find Rafa?' Ariadne suggested.

They spent a good half hour searching and eventually found him on the top tier. Lizzie's stomach dropped as soon as she saw him. He wore a dark blue suit, no tie, and the top button of his red shirt had been left undone. She never would have imagined that someone's neck could look so enticing.

'*Abuela*!' He hugged Ariadne tightly and then turned to Lizzie. Their eyes did that funny sparky thing and after a moment's hesitation he hugged her too.

He smelt earthy and yet sweet. Like autumnal leaves mixed with candyfloss. It reminded her of Bonfire Night. And then he released her and introduced her to his friends who were actually cousins, all around seventeen.

He had to shout because the music was so loud. There were four of them. Jesus, pronounced *Hay-sus.* Antonio, Oscar and Felipe. All similar looking, with short black hair, dark brown eyes and tanned skin. They wore smart shirts and they lined up to kiss her.

'Encantada,' she repeated in turn.

Whereas Antonio and Felipe were openly admiring her, Rafa barely glanced at her. It was the first time she'd seen him since the dip-pool and she shuffled on her feet and tried to resist the urge to pull the dress down. If possible she felt more naked than she had that day. He gabbled in Spanish to Ariadne, not that she could understand a word, but she liked the way his whole face was alight, as if there was a lantern inside his head shining a light outwards. It didn't exactly make him better looking but there was something contagious in his smile.

Amazing that she hadn't noticed this the first time they'd met. Had she been *blind*?

Or blinded by the smell?

She smiled to herself. *Stop ogling.* Her eyes would fall out of their sockets in a minute.

'Where's Gabriel?'

'Out front holding court no doubt,' Ariadne replied. 'I'll go find him after I've got the social niceties out the way first.' She said goodbye then glided into the middle of the bar, engaging in conversation with the first person she met and immediately making them guffaw with laughter. She made it look so easy.

Rafa turned his attention to her and as was his custom, raked his eyes up and down her. He said nothing.

'What are you looking at?'

'You,' he replied.

'Why?'

'You look different.' He smiled. 'With clothes on.'

She had been about to take a sip of her coke but froze. He raised an eyebrow.

'Are all Spanish boys like you?'

'Like what?'

She narrowed her eyes. 'Rude.'

'And you are not?'

Then he turned his back! Turned his back and started talking in Spanish to one of his cousins and proceeded to completely ignore her.

'Rafa?' She cleared her throat. 'Rafa?'

Was he ignoring her on purpose? Was this some immature kind of pay back for the first time she'd met him? She seethed. She more than seethed. She wanted to throw her drink over his shirt. But that would make a scene. So she inwardly fumed instead. Bee would know exactly what to do in this moment. How to re-enter the conversation, how to smile at them, how to talk. But Lizzie had no idea what to say. One of them, Jesus maybe, tried to make conversation.

'Where are you from?'

'England.'

'Are you on holidays?'

She nodded.

'You are here for long?

'Until the end of summer.'

'You speak Spanish?'

'Not really.'

The conversation ended. By this point some other boys had joined the group and then Felipe started asking questions and all this time Rafa was *still* ignoring her. Then Jesus said something which made the others laugh and then they *all* started laughing. Was she being paranoid or had they just looked at her? She stood more motionless than before and felt the separation in every cell of her body.

'You ok?' The hand on her shoulder made her jump. It was Ariadne

'I can't speak Spanish to them!' she blurted out. 'I don't even talk English that well.'

The corners of Ariadne's mouth twitched into a smile. 'Don't worry. Why don't you come outside with me and get a breath of air?'

Rafa didn't even notice that she left and with each footstep she walked away, she seethed some more. How dare he ignore her like that? It wasn't as if she deserved it. Just because she had been rude to him the first time they met didn't mean he had to be rude back to her now. He wasn't any different from the boys back home.

She *hated* him.

They passed through the lower bar and stepped out onto the beach. Lizzie yanked off her sandals and stomped out over the sand, passing the small group of people sat around the bonfire.

A hot breeze blew and the scent of the sea rolled off the waves and onto her face. On her lips she could taste salt.

'Rafa's not like other boys. He's very intense. Have you noticed?' Ariadne came over and joined her. 'He doesn't go out much, he rarely drinks, he doesn't show off and I hardly ever see with him with girlfriends.'

'And?' Lizzie muttered, trying really hard to ignore the pinched feeling in her heart.

'*And* music is his life. Completely. He's different from those cousins of his. They'd rather be out partying, chasing girls, drinking and dancing to dawn. But not Rafa. He practises for eight hours every day. Imagine that. Eight hours a day.'

Ariadne picked up a pebble and skimmed it over the surface of the sea. It bounced three times. The water rippled.

Lizzie watched it and bit her lip. The heavy feeling in her stomach sat like an undigested meal and she gazed out unseeingly to the black blanket of sea.

'He's passionate,' Ariadne continued. 'Passionate about music. It's his life. It's the only thing he knows. It's the thing he wakes up for and the only thing he breathes for. He doesn't really know how to do anything else. Let alone talk to a beautiful, exotic girl who has come from overseas and landed in his home and taken his *abuela* away from him.'

It took a moment to register Ariadne was talking about her.

'Have you considered that he might find it quite difficult to talk to *you*?'

Lizzie shrugged. 'You don't have to make excuses for him. He's *rude*.'

'He's Spanish!'

'Are you saying all Spanish people are rude?'

'No, I'm saying they're a different culture to us completely. He's not from here,' Ariadne tapped Lizzie's head. 'He's from here.' She tapped her heart. 'He's Mediterranean. He knows how to feel things but that doesn't mean he knows how to articulate them.'

'Like me,' Lizzie said softly as a wave lapped over her foot.

'Just like you,' Ariadne touched her shoulder. 'You want to know a secret?'

'What?'

'You must learn how to express yourself, how to express what's in here.' She tapped her heart. 'Otherwise we live in our heads and that's not really living, Lizzie. That's not *experiencing* life, that's just *seeing* life, like watching a travel show on television rather than actually visiting the country itself and breathing in its air. Learn to express what is in your heart. Because if you don't express this feeling, how is anyone ever going to know the real you?'

* * *

The party played on. They ate. They moved from lower tier to the top tier and back again. At some point, she thought she saw a Hawaiian shirt but when she looked harder, she couldn't see anything. She'd lost Ariadne and met up with Ana who wanted to practice her English and so for the best part of the last two hours she had been lounging on one of the sofa's next to the dolphin pool.

It was now about two in the morning.

'Now you speak Spanish.' Ana urged.

'I can't!'

'But you can to try with me.' Ana smiled. She had dark red lipstick and hooded eyes.

'It's embarrassing,' Lizzie said. 'I'm *shy*.'

Ana threw her head back and laughed. 'You cannot be shy in this country.'

So Lizzie tentatively tried out a few words and with Ana's encouragement she grew a tiny bit in confidence. It wasn't so bad once the first words were out of her mouth and she realized Ana wasn't going to burst out laughing at her.

'You have good accent,' Ana encouraged her, and Lizzie glowed with the compliment.

The sea breeze caressed her face and she leant back on the cushions and smiled. Someone started to play the guitar.

Her head snapped round.

Rafa.

He stood at the other end of the pool, by the dolphin's tail, leaning against the wall, his head bent over the guitar. Softly at first, he soon began to play louder, and within seconds the music on the sound system had been turned down and a hush fell over everyone.

Lizzie's heart skipped. He was just so beautiful she could forget how rude he'd been earlier. This was the real Rafa. The way he lit up, the way he radiated his music, the way he shone. It wasn't as if the music came *from* him, it was as if it came *through* him.

'You want to dance?'

'I hate dancing!'

Ana shrugged and stood up anyway. She unpinned her hair so it tumbled down her back. Someone wolf-whistled as she swished her skirt and moved with the music, oozing passion. She looked wild and free and incredibly sexy.

If only Lizzie could dance that way! Ana had natural rhythm, she didn't just listen to the music, she *became* the music. Her plain face transformed into something haughty, regal, something hynoptic.

'She is sexy, no?'

Lizzie looked round to see who had spoken. She couldn't place his face at first. Lots of teeth, high cheekbones, sparkly brown eyes.

'Carlos. I am the waiter from the plaza.' He smiled.

'Carlos! Hi.'

'You want to dance?'

By now most people were dancing. She looked across at Rafa but he barely glanced at the dancers. She nearly said no but then she remembered what Ariadne had said about learning to express herself.

'Sure.'

'We dance on the beach,' Carlos touched her elbow. 'It is better.'

It was hard to tell where the bar ended and the beach began. There were people dancing everywhere in a flurry of colour and movement. A couple more fires had been lit and their soft flickering flames licked into the sky. Some people were even in the sea shrieking and laughing. Carlos led her to a space near one of the fires.

'Here,' he linked one hand with hers and placed the other hand on her shoulder.

'I can't dance like Ana,' Lizzie said, desperately wishing her legs weren't quite so leaden. It was as though her feet were in quick-sand.

'I teach you,' Carlos murmured, pulling her close to his chest. Over his shoulder she saw a splash of colour. Carlos's hand slid down her back. The touch of his fingers on her bare skin made her jump. 'You like that?'

Not really. His fingers were warm but his breath smelt of garlic and she felt none of the charge she felt around Rafa. None of the heat. She tried to pull herself away but Carlos clamped onto her arm.

'You don't like that? What is wrong with you?'

'There's nothing wrong with me,' she tried to pull away again. Carlos gripped her tighter. 'Then why are you so cold?'

'I'm not cold,' she snapped. 'Now get off me.'

'Is everything ok here?'

Rafa had appeared from nowhere and she'd never been so pleased to see him. 'Rafa!'

Carlos dropped her arms and smiled thinly. 'I see you later.'

Rafa waited until he had gone. His face flickered with shadows from the fire. 'Be careful.'

A pulse throbbed in his temple and she watched it, wondering if her own heart was beating as furiously.

'Ariadne told me you are upset,' he said at last. 'I came to find you.'

Lizzie ground her toe into the sand. 'She told you?'

'Do not be angry.' He leant closer. 'I came to say sorry.'

'You? Saying sorry?' She laughed out loud and then stopped herself. Forgiveness came in many forms. 'Then I'm sorry too. I was rude the first time we met.'

'And I am rude back and now we are equal.'

'That doesn't make it right.'

'I know.'

He shrugged and turned to move away. 'Rafa?'

'Yes, Lizzie.'

She took a deep breath. 'I heard you play,' she said at last. 'It touched me here.'

'Now you speak my language,' he said softly. 'Where?'

'Here.' She touched her heart and even though it was dark and she couldn't see him properly, she knew he was smiling.

There was another long pause between them where neither of them seemed to breathe. Someone splashed in the sea. The music changed and the air between them thickened. He took a tiny step closer.

'Would you like to dance?'

Before she'd even said yes, she felt the hot graze of his hands on her shoulders. He held her in the same position as Carlos had held her and yet this was utterly different. Where his hands touched her skin, it felt like hot stones had been pressed against her.

Someone, somewhere let off a rocket on the beach and it exploded into the sky with a searing flash. Her heart beat wildly as she rested her cheek against his chest.

'You have to feel the music,' he murmured into her ear. 'In every part of you. You have to *become* the music. Can you do that, Lizzie?'

'I'll try,' she whispered.

'Don't *try*. Be.'

His breath was warm on her face and she let herself relax in his arms, so she became a reed, a sail in the wind, who listened only to the music. Who became the music.

'Good,' he whispered. His fingers fluttered lightly on her back and she arched her spine and shivered. He pulled her tighter and her own breath quickened as she listened to the rapid pulse of his heart. She itched to trace the dark hollow of his throat with her fingertips.

Please, God make this moment last forever.

There was another loud splash in the water and she frowned.

'What is that?'

'It is no one.' His voice was a gentle murmur in her ear and she groaned as his hot breath grazed her skin.

There was another splash and a shout. She wasn't sure what it was that grabbed her attention. Had she even seen the flash of the garish colours at this point or did that come later? Who knew? Right now, all she felt was the cold steely calm that ran over her skin. From nowhere, the angel's face flashed through her mind.

Rafa's embrace turned to stone.

'Oh my God.' She pulled away. 'It's been seven days!'

'Seven days? What?' Rafa held onto her arm. 'I do not understand.'

'Hooper!'

Chapter Eighteen

She pulled away from Rafa and stared at the blanket of sea. Thick blackness. No light. Only nothingness. An icy finger crawled up her spine.

'Hooper is out there?' Rafa asked following her gaze. 'How do you know?'

'I just do,' she murmured. 'Oh God. We've got to get to him.' She started to run toward the shore.

'How do you know?' Rafa repeated. 'I can't see anyone.'

'I've got to help,' she shouted. No time to think. Only act. Her feet kicked up sand and her dressed ripped.

There it was. A flash of bright colours. And then it went.

She was the only one running. Toward the blackness. Nothing to see. Just a vast empty stretch of water. The water slapped against her shins. Someone shouted.

'Lizzie!'

Rafa was behind her. They dove into the water at the same time. Two dolphins. The saltwater streamed down her face and stung her eyes. Keep going.

Behind her people started running toward the sea. She could hear their shouts. A girl screaming and someone yelling at her to shut up. There were other noises too: The pounding of feet on the sand. The splash of the sea. The dull thud of music. The roar in her ears.

She had never been the strongest swimmer but tonight she found strength. Her heart screamed as she pushed herself. Her breath was already ragged. Every stroke in slow motion. Rafa's silhouette pulling ahead. God, it was so dark. The further out they swam, the darker it got.

'Where?' Rafa stopped and her arm clashed into his chest. She dunked underwater. It was colder out here. He bobbed up and down. His hair wet to his head. She looked around. Nothing. No

Hawaiian shirts.

'There's no-one,' Rafa gasped. 'Are you *sure* you saw him?'

Behind them the other swimmers crawled closer.

She took a mouthful of sea water by mistake. Something bobbed up and down behind him. She pointed. Swim again. Just a few yards more. Every stroke hurting now.

Rafa got there first.

'There's a man,' he yelled. 'Over here!'

She was treading water. Her legs were screaming. What could she see?

Rafa's arms. A man's head. A Hawaiian shirt. A white body floating face down.

She swallowed more sea water and gagged. The other swimmers arrived. Dark heads like seals. Shouts in Spanish. They flipped him over.

The water was choppy now and a wave sloshed over her head. Rafa and another swimmer grabbed Hooper by the neck and pulled him toward the shore. The others lifted the rest of his body.

'Follow us!' Rafa shouted back. 'Follow!'

Her throat was raw. Her legs were like weights.

They hauled Hooper toward shore, a hulk of bloated white flesh. A crowd of people waited. Bonfires crackled. People screamed and shouted.

She threw up and a pool of orange vomit floated in front of her. Her legs felt so tired. Alone out in the water.

Alone.

'Lizzie!' Ariadne's voice shouted out from the shore. 'Lizzie!'

It didn't matter that she was crying because the sea washed it away. She willed herself to swim toward the shore, one more stroke, and then another.

Ariadne ran out to meet her, the water swishing around the hem of her dress. 'Lizzie!'

Nearly there. Ariadne came closer so the sea rose to her waist.

At last. Her feet touched the bottom. She collapsed into Ariadne's arms. 'It's ok. You're safe now. You're safe.'

Her stomach heaved and she wanted to be sick again. Her legs felt like dead weights. 'Hooper? Where's Hooper?'

'You've done enough, Lizzie. Don't go there.'

'I have to,' Lizzie said. 'You don't understand. I *have* to.'

She broke free and with the last bit of strength she could muster, she headed for the horde of people on the sea edge. Why did death always draw an audience? She ducked under their elbows and squirmed her way through the people. An elbow knocked her in the cheekbone and she winced, but she had to get through. Before it was too late.

Just one more person to push past. She squeezed past him and took a big gulp of air. Her dress clung to her skin. The first person she saw was Rafa. His hair lay in bedraggled curls around his face and his wooden earring was almost falling off. He looked at her strangely.

'You were right.'

The next thing she saw was a pair of pink espadrilles sat neatly on the shore's edge where someone had left them.

'Hooper,' she murmured.

'What are you doing?' Rafa stood up and blocked the view. 'Don't come any closer, Lizzie. You've....done enough.'

Lizzie pushed past him.

Hooper lay on his back, naked except for his Hawaiian shirt which had been draped over him. His bloated white body was wet with sand and a spool of vomit drooled out of mouth and onto his chest. The skin was puckered and slimy. His legs were coated in something dark where it looked like he had excreted his bowels.

Rafa went to touch her shoulder and stopped. 'It is not good.'

She took a deep breath. 'I don't care. I have to be here.'

Of the many people surrounding Hooper, Lizzie recognized one of Rafa's cousins, Felipe. He squatted by Hooper's side, taking his pulse. He said something to Rafa. His face was pale.

'What did he say?'

'He says he's still alive.'

Lizzie dropped to Hooper's other side. Up close he stank. A mixture of vomit and shit. She wiped a strand of seaweed away from his neck. It was cold and slimy. Revolting. His eyes flickered even though they were shut. Lizzie felt her heart contract, as if someone had squeezed it.

She faintly registered that the black mark above his head had grown darker.

Someone behind her started shouting and then another person shouted louder. Rafa punched numbers into his phone, slapping it against his fist as he misdialled.

She looked around her from the crowd of faces peering in morbidly to those stationed around his body. Someone in the crowd was crying. It didn't matter that she'd run into the water. It was too late.

'He's dying.'

She'd never seen a person die before. Only on television and it was never as raw as this. She didn't know what to do. Sitting here holding a cold, clammy hand and feeling useless. Up close, death was brutal. It smacked her in the gut. So what if she'd managed to pull him out of the water? He wasn't going to make it. As if to prove her point, green slime trickled out of his mouth. She gagged.

His eyes opened briefly, resting on her. The way he looked at her? It reminded her of something. Frightened and vulnerable.

Of course. Joopy.

She was sitting in almost exactly the same position she'd been in when Joopy died. Hadn't he gazed into her eyes until his final breath? And hadn't she willed him with *all* her heart to live and if he couldn't live, hadn't she willed him to go to a better place and be at peace?

She felt something inside her tear. Just a little. Thinking of

Joopy and feeling how much he had hurt back then. Just as Hooper hurt now.

She squeezed his hand more firmly. He wasn't going to die alone in the water where no-one could hold his hand. She was right here by his side. She was here. She had got him out of the water and *she* would make sure he didn't die alone.

He opened his eyes again. Just a slither but Lizzie knew he could see her.

She kept her voice low and soft, how she used to talk to Joopy. Out of the corner of her eye the black mark shifted insistently, and she saw then how much it kept moving. Just like it did with Joopy. Like it was trying to get her attention almost. She ignored it.

The sounds around her faded: the music, the excited chatter of the crowd, Felipe, even Rafa.

'I'm here for you, Hooper.'

Ariadne burst through the crowd. 'Lizzie!'

'Ssshhh.' She waved her hand. 'Take his other hand.'

Ariadne knelt opposite her. 'Oh my God. This is not good.' She said something quickly to Rafa and then took Hooper's hand. 'Not good at all. Has someone called an ambulance?'

As she said it, the sound of siren wailed in the distance. Felipe rocked back on his heels and looked relieved. Rafa passed the phone to him.

'Can I do something?' he looked at Lizzie like she was in control.

'Can you sing?'

Rafa looked surprised. 'Yes. *Claro*. Of course.'

'Then sing to him. Not loudly. Just softly. Sit there,' she pointed to the space next to Hooper's head, adjusting her finger to make sure Rafa wouldn't actually sit *on* the black mark, now so alive it looked like a raven, flapping wildly at the crown of Hooper's skull. 'A lullaby,' she muttered.

She averted her gaze from the black mark and squeezed

Hooper's hand again. His eyes fluttered open in a panic.

'It's ok, Hooper. You'll be ok.'

With her other hand, Lizzie stroked the hair from his face. He moaned and more vomit slid from his mouth. She wanted to pinch her nostrils but instead she called out for a towel and in a few seconds one was passed to her. She wiped his face. He opened his eyes briefly. Their eyes connected and Lizzie smiled at him. He kept his eyes open. She stared into them.

He opened his lips a slither but the words refused to come out.

'What?' She bent her head toward him.

'Can you see it?' he croaked.

At first she thought he meant the black mark. She sucked her breath in.

'See what?' she whispered hoarsely.

Hooper opened his lips a crack but nothing came out. She leant her head closer.

'It's so ....' he murmured indistinctly.

The ambulance siren wailed again. Closer this time. Someone shouted. She looked around her. There was nothing except people hungry for death.

Hooper's face began to soften and as it did the black mark curled in on itself like a vortex and disappeared abruptly with a flash. He opened his eyes fully and widened them in surprise. Lizzie looked to where his gaze fell and blinked. A flash of silver on the shoreline so rapid she almost missed it.

Ariadne touched her gently on the shoulder and she looked away. She heard a faint lullaby. She'd forgotten that she'd asked Rafa to sing. She looked back for the light. But there was nothing. However hard she stared. Just the ripple of the sky as if it had folded in on itself – as one world joined the other. She looked down.

Hooper was dead.

Chapter Nineteen

They drove home in silence.

Ariadne's fingers clenched the wheel, the knuckles of each hand were white. It was pitch black and even though she couldn't see anything because they were on the dirt track and there were no streetlights, Lizzie looked out the window anyway. Outside the world seemed huge. There was no moon.

At last they pulled into *Casa del Sol* and she wrapped the blanket tighter around her and jumped out of the car. She ran her fingers over the rough metal table in the courtyard. Everything felt red and raw. She wasn't ready for sleep. Not yet.

'That was very brave of you,' Ariadne said quietly.

Lizzie sank onto one of the chairs and put her face in her hands. She smelt of death.

Lizzie didn't speak. What was there to say? No doubt Rafa thought she was a freak.

Ariadne switched on the courtyard light and strode back to the car. She returned carrying a battered packet of cigarettes.

'You don't smoke!'

'I do now,' Ariadne grimaced. 'I'm sorry.' She waved the cigarette in the air. 'Only do it when I'm nervous. Or when I see someone die.'

Lizzie shuddered as she remembered Hooper's body. 'It was horrible.'

Ariadne took a puff and slowly exhaled. 'I know.' She stubbed out the cigarette after two quick puffs and ground it under her heel. 'It reminded me of your grandfather.'

'What about my grandfather?'

Ariadne groaned softly. 'It was the same.'

Lizzie recoiled at the pain in Ariadne's voice. 'What happened to him?'

'He drowned.'

Something tried to click in Lizzie's head but the pieces wouldn't quite fit.

Ariadne pulled up a metal chair. It scraped on the tiles. Sucking on her next cigarette, the hollows of her cheeks dug out like caves, she looked old. 'Years ago.' She waved her hand. 'It's in the past.'

The jigsaw pieces slotted into place. Lizzie jumped up and ran inside without a backward glance, into the gloom of the kitchen, and sprinted straight up to her bedroom without turning on any lights. 'Where are you?'

She kicked aside stray garments of clothes and ran her hands over the tousled bed. At last her fingers touched the hard edges of the book. She'd finished it days ago. It had a predictable ending of course. The girl and the boy got together. That's what always happened in books, wasn't it? Real life was much more complicated. But it wasn't the book she was interested in.

It was the newspaper article.

She carefully prized it out and unfolded it and laid it flat on the bed. The shutters rattled and Lizzie flicked on the lamp and read the article:

> Freak Drowning Accident
>
> On Cabo de Gato beach an Australian native, Seth Buchanon, 42, drowned in a freak accident. He leaves behind a wife and one daughter, aged 15.

The article went on to describe that particular stretch of the coast. Lizzie skim-read it. She was more interested in the grainy black and white photo of the three of them on the beach. Although Seth was blurry, Ariadne was unmistakable – full of the kind of vibrant beauty which made men want to make mirrors to capture her face. But it was her mum's face which drew her attention most of all. She had wavy shoulder-length hair and stared straight into the camera in a familiar way.

'I haven't seen that in a long time.'

Lizzie jumped into the air.

Ariadne came in and sat on the edge of her bed.

'May I?'

Lizzie nodded and Ariadne picked up the article and read it silently. Her expression shifted like sand. She ran her fingers over the photos just like Lizzie had done seconds ago.

'She looks just like me,' Lizzie said. Even the way she *stares*.'

Ariadne nodded. 'Your mother was exactly your age when he died.'

She touched her mum's face again. 'She's changed.'

Ariadne stood up and walked to the shutters. 'Yes, people do. Unless they die, that is.'

Outside the sky folded into gray. 'Were they close?' Lizzie whispered.

'Very.' Ariadne turned round. 'She was inconsolable.'

The temperature in the room dropped. 'And?'

'And so was I.' She fingered the half-moon hanging round her neck and with the other hand pointed at the article. 'Where did you find it?'

'In the museum room.' Lizzie paused. 'I was looking for .... something. I found this instead.' She held up the copy of *Flamenco*.

Ariadne laughed. 'Now, that's a book I haven't seen in a long time.'

Lizzie smiled.

Ariadne cleared her throat. 'You remind me of him.'

'My eyes?'

Ariadne nodded. 'That and something else about you both. Something more elusive.' She moved back to the bed and took one of Lizzie's hands in her own. Her skin was papery and she smelt of cigarettes. 'You want to know the real reason we fell out?' Ariadne paused. 'Your mum thought it was my fault that he died that day.'

'Why?'

Ariadne knitted her brow. 'If she hasn't told you after all these years, then it's not for me to say either.'

'She's never going to tell me! She never tells me anything.'

Ariadne turned to her. 'And you? You tell her everything?'

Lizzie clamped her lips shut. What, if anything, did she ever tell her mum? But how *could* she?

Mrs Froust, Joopy and now Hooper all jumped into her mind. The black marks above each of them.

Her throat tightened.

Joopy.

'It's ok,' Ariadne reached out and squeezed Lizzie's hand. Lizzie had forgotten she was there. 'It's ok, Lizzie.'

The roar inside her head was deafening. 'It's not ok!' she cried. 'He had a horrible last few days and it's all my fault!'

'Hooper was unhappy for years. It sounds harsh but he's better off dead.'

'Not Hooper! Joopy!' The tears rushed to her eyes. 'I kept him trapped inside! It was sunny outside and he could have had a happy last few days. But I didn't want him to die. All that time I could have been feeding him his favourite food and taking him out on long walks and doing the things he loved!'

'Lizzie,' Ariadne touched her shoulder. 'You didn't know he was going to die, did you? You couldn't have done anything.'

'But I did know!' she shouted. 'I did know.'

She felt a muscle in her jaw twitch, her insides knot and unknot, her palms sweat. A melody of reactions. All so sudden and violent and then they passed. Nothing but warm air and the sound of silence.

Ariadne watched her. Not judgementally or with scorn, not with fear or loathing, but with a face so full of compassion, so full of love that it reminded Lizzie of something. Something that had faded into the back of her mind, into her unconscious self but with a blink of her eye it was back.

The angel in Milton Graveyard.

'You can trust me,' Ariadne whispered.

Lizzie nodded, wordlessly, as a flotsam of memories floated through her mind. She thought of all the times she'd been to visit the angel, all the hurts and pains she'd thrown at its feet, all the moments when she'd cried, and the only person in the world who'd heard her had been the statue. She thought of the list of names she'd buried next to Elizabeth's grave. She thought of the classmates she'd left behind who had called her names. She thought of Bee. She thought of Joopy. She thought of Hooper.

She thought of what life meant if you knew you were going to die. She thought of what life might be beyond this one.

At which point Lizzie burst into tears.

The crying came from so deep within her, it felt like the pain would never stop. She wasn't sure how long they sat there, long enough for the sky to turn two shades lighter, but in the end she realized she had stopped crying and that she was still sitting there on the edge of her bed.

Ariadne silently passed her a tissue.

She blew her nose.

'You ok?'

Ariadne handed her another tissue. 'You want to tell me about it? From the beginning?'

Any slither of remaining resistance fell away.

Lizzie nodded.

'Why don't you shower first, get yourself clean and then we'll go for a walk.'

'Ok.'

She stripped off the silver dress and dropped it into a pile in the corner of the bedroom. She'd never wear it again. The shower was hot and hard and she washed every single part of her skin and then scrubbed it until it was sore. She dressed in her comfy black combats and her old black T-shirt. *Her* clothes. As she waited for Ariadne she sat in the courtyard, knees hunched up to her chest. When Ariadne emerged the two of them walked.

And as they walked, they talked. At first the words wouldn't come out or they came out all jumbled and out of sequence. A dog on the road. Mrs Froust. Bee. The greenhouse. Joopy. Her parents. The list. The angel. A wooden cross. Maths class. Being sent here. Then after a bit it got easier.

She told Ariadne about the black mark she'd seen fluttering above Hooper head – how it had looked like wings. How it had danced about the moment before death and then disappeared in a whoosh. She told her about the silver light she'd seen when Hooper died.

The only thing she didn't mention was the flash of silver in the hallway.

After she had talked it all out they came to a halt beside Ariadne's tree of life. The sun reared up for another day, the planet they were on was still hurtling through space, and somewhere out there people were still dying.

Ariadne took her in her arms and hugged her. 'You're a brave girl, Lizzie Fisher.' She kissed her forehead as she let her go. 'You have a remarkable ability.'

'You don't think I'm a freak or anything?'

'You silly thing.' Ariadne cupped her cheek. 'I knew you were different from the first moment I met you. When you took off your cap and I looked into your eyes I saw such an old soul and I loved you for it. You're special. You have a gift.'

'Do you really think so?'

'I know so. You have a gift.' Ariadne smiled. 'A gift from the angels.'

Chapter Twenty

She woke up wet with sweat.

There was no sign of Ariadne in the kitchen and when she checked outside, she saw that the 4x4 had gone. Lizzie had no idea of the time – was it even midday? The air was so close she could almost see it. Thick and heavy. It was suffocating. The only thing that could cut through it was death itself.

In the week since Hooper's drowning she had noticed things she'd never even seen before, the tiny, intricate details of life which normally passed her by. Death brought a sharpness. It made the surroundings feel brighter than they were. Every sense heightened, even taste. She was glad to be alive. Pure and simple.

There was no funeral.

He was cremated and flown home to Texas. The post-mortem revealed he'd had a heart attack in the water but it also transpired he'd had cirrhosis of the liver for months and wouldn't have lived much longer anyway. What family he did have, an ex-wife and two daughters, did not fly over. He took the long, final flight home alone to be buried in a cemetery near where he grew up.

He never did make his last exhibition.

Life went on.

But differently from before. This time, Lizzie wasn't alone. As she climbed out of bed, dripping with sweat, she recalled last night's conversation over dinner. It was the first time she'd talked about the black marks with Ariadne since the night Hooper had died.

Ariadne was curious about the gift and had pressed her for detail. What did the black marks look like? How many times had she seen them? Had Lizzie tried to stop it happening? Had she told her mum? Had she experienced anything like this in her childhood?

She also wanted to know what Lizzie was going to do with her gift.

'How are you going to use it when you go home?'

She had gulped. It was only three weeks until the end of summer.

'I don't *ever* want to go home.'

Ariadne reached out and grabbed her hand. 'I suspect your mother might not agree.'

'I doubt it.'

'Don't say that.' Ariadne stood and cleared the plates. 'She's your mother.'

Lizzie watched as Ariadne carried the plates into the kitchen and dropped them into the sink.

'But we're so different!'

'That doesn't mean she doesn't care for you.'

Lizzie sighed as she pulled on the blue dress. The irony of being thankful for her clothes was not lost on her. For the second time since being here she felt a fierce desire to speak to her mum, to try and close the distance between them.

The sky was the color of a bruise and the air enveloped her as soon as she stepped outside. She hardly noticed her surroundings until she stood at the top of the hill, by the olive tree. Her phone beeped and a couple of messages from mum came through. *Mum.* That was weird. The messages asked her to phone but she'd be at work. Even so, she went as far as dialing the number before hanging up.

No. She couldn't stomach another stilted conversation like last week's. And besides she had so many questions associated with her grandfather yet not the words to say them. How did you bring up a dead grandfather that your mum had very rarely talked about?

She stared at the phone in frustration. Bridging the distance between them had never seemed harder.

Her skin felt grimy and the dip-pool flashed into her mind.

Not today. She wanted *more* from today. A longing or an ache for something else. A feeling that she wanted to *live* her life. Not just pass the days. She wasn't exactly sure what she ached for until she stumbled across the boundary to Ariadne's land.

Rafa.

She hadn't seen him since Saturday and in the post-death lull, she hadn't really wanted to see him either. She had revealed too much of herself to him that night and she wasn't sure how he would react.

How much had he guessed about her?

The image of him came crashing back into her mind. The feel of his fingertips against her bare skin. Their dance on the beach. The warmth of his breath on her face.

It took a few paces to realize where she was. In that moment she could have turned back. But she didn't. She kept on walking. Through an orchard very similar to Ariadne's and onto a vegetable patch.

And that's where she found him.

For a split second he stayed in silhouette. A dark, shadowy blur. Then he moved into the sunshine. He wore the same black surfer shorts as before and had wrapped a wet T-shirt round his neck. Drips of sweat slid down his chest.

Neither of them spoke.

He was digging over the ground with a pitch fork and the muscles rippled in his arms. Clods of dirt clung to his hands and a sheen of sweat coated his face. He didn't smile or say a word. He just nodded in her direction and kept on digging. But that was enough. She sat with her back against an almond tree and watched him.

He dug for another twenty minutes. Oblivious to her presence, moving in focussed concentration. The same concentration he had when he played guitar.

When he had finished he took a long swig of water, poured some over his head and walked over .

He offered her the bottle and she drank.

She cleared a space next to her and he sat down, so close they brushed shoulders. She could smell bike oil mingled with perspiration. Not unpleasant. Earthy. Sweet.

'There's going to be a storm,' he said. 'Look at the sky.'

She followed his gaze. 'I love storms.'

'So do I.'

Every cell of her body was acutely aware of how close he was. How near. The air felt charged.

After a while she sensed he was looking sideways at her. He was staring at her so intensely. Eyes like black coals framed by long dark eye-lashes. The kind of eye-lashes Bee would kill for.

'What?' she whispered.

'How did you know?'

'Know what?'

'Know he was in the water. No-one knew. No-one could see him. But you knew. You knew it was *him*.'

She prayed he couldn't read her face. What should she say?

She'd told Ariadne but that was different. She'd *had* to tell Ariadne. She could trust her grandmother. Rafa belonged to a tight-knit community, he was part of a different culture and they didn't even speak the same language. How could she ever tell him the truth? A vision of Nathan ruffling her hair for horns flashed into her mind.

'I guessed.'

'You guessed?' he grimaced. 'When you can see nothing out there?'

'I heard him.'

'I heard nothing.'

She shrugged, willing her face not to say anything.

'You are a good guesser.'

A tiny pulse throbbed in his neck and she watched it, hypnotized.

'You ride with me on the bike and you know you are safe and

then you guess a man is drowning and you know exactly *who* it is even though you don't see him.'

He sat so close she could reach out her tongue if she wanted to and trace the outline of his lips.

'You are *muy intelligente,* Lizzie. Very intelligent.'

He stared at her as if he was trying to read her. And she stared back, willing herself not to look away.

'You are different from other girls.'

She swallowed even though it felt as if she had a mouthful of sand.

'You ran into the sea and you try to save him even though you hear nothing.'

He lifted his hand and she watched it move toward her jaw, as if in slow motion. The tips of his fingers grazed her skin and she wanted to cry out. His touch was hot. Like fire. Rough from the calluses and yet gentle.

'You are brave.'

'Yes,' she whispered.

'Say it louder.'

'*Yes*.'

A fork of lightening splintered from the sky and thunder cracked like a bomb.

'Come with me,' he grabbed her hand and yanked her to her feet. 'We go to my house.'

And at that point, the storm broke and the heavens wept. Within seconds they were drenched in fat splashes of warm rain. The rain was hard. Much harder than the rain in England. Not a pathetic dribble but a powerful, bruising kind of rain. It slapped against her bare legs. It hurt. It stung.

It was also exciting, wild and dangerous.

They ran uphill. Hand in hand. Slipping, sliding. The rain was so hard, she could barely see a thing. Grasping, panting, heaving. She could just about see the red roof of the goat-shed at the top. But apart from that, nothing. No sea on the horizon, no view of

Rafa's house, just thick, blinding rain.

They made it to the top of the hill and now she could see the goat-shed and Rafa's house. She stopped, letting go of his hand, and looked up to the sky. Just as she'd always done as a child.

Not the sky, but the sky *beyond* the sky. The universe. The soul of the universe. Not that she could see anything. She closed her eyes and felt the rain bounce off her skin. Tasted it in her mouth. Sweet rain. Warm rain. Did this come from Africa too? Did it come from a distant shore? Or did it come from even further away than that?

'Lizzie? What are you doing?'

His hair was plastered down his face and water streamed off his nose. 'You're crazy.'

Not that they could talk normally. They had to shout over the roar of the rain.

'I know!' she shouted back.

He looked at her, so dark, so hard, she rocked back on her heels and he stuck out a hand to pull her back. He tugged her toward him and she collided against his chest. She pressed her palms against his bare skin, slippery with rain.

Neither moved.

She kept her eyes open and looked up at him, lifting up her face. He widened his eyes. Her pulse raced. Something else too. Something tingly. Like a firework which licked up inside her, growing brighter and hotter with each passing second. She stared at the fullness of his lips

The thunder came so violently, it shook them apart.

'Come with me.' His hand was wet and warm at the same time. He led her around the side of the house toward an igloo made of stone. 'This is mine,' he yelled and kicked open the door. It was like retreating into a cave.

The rain battered onto the roof but the room was dry and warm. It wasn't a big space. Big enough for a double futon, an old rocking chair, a bookshelf and six guitars lined up against the far wall. The room smelt of him. Earthy. Musty. It was dark and intimate.

'You are trapped,' he said closing the door on the rain. 'For the afternoon.'

Her clothes were soaked through and rain dripped into a puddle on the floor. Rafa grabbed a towel, wiped his face and threw it to her. She rubbed her face, her shoulders and hair. Rafa took a fresh blue T-shirt, turned his back and stripped off his shorts and pulled on a new pair.

It was like that first day. Seeing him naked from her window. Except this time she was close enough to see the smooth tautness of his muscles, the curve of his back, the rich teak colour of his skin.

He had no sense of embarrassment. He tossed her a red T-shirt and a pair of white surfer shorts.

'Get changed.'

'Here?'

'Do you want to get a fever?'

'No.'

He sighed. 'I will face the wall. I won't look, *inglesa*.'

She waited until he had fully turned round before quickly peeling off her clothes, including her underwear, and dropping them onto the floor. Her skin felt puckered and cold and she rubbed it with the towel. All the time she was conscious that she was naked and that any time Rafa could turn round and see her. His T-shirt smelt of him, musty and sweet. Not at all goaty.

'You can turn round now,' she said softly.

He smiled. 'It suits you.'

'Really?'

'Yes. It makes you look Andalucian.'

He sat on the edge of his bed. Picked up one of the guitars, tuning it as he spoke. 'You like my room?'

She looked around. 'It's very private, isn't it?'

He nodded. 'Away from the main house. From the goats.'

'You can't smell them in here.'

'Good.'

'Is that your mum?' She pointed toward a black and white photo on the book shelf. It had to be his mum because she looked exactly like him. Traditionally Andalucian with dark hair and a regal, haughty face.

He nodded.

'She was beautiful.'

'Yes. The men all loved her.'

She sank down into the rocking chair and found herself gazing at him as he idly played the guitar. She admired the curve of his lips, the way his cheekbones left hollows, the dark depths of his eyes, even the mad frizz of his hair as it started to dry. Not that his hair mattered. He was so beautiful when he played. So alive. As if he had a current flowing through him. Where did this current come from? Was it within him or did it come through him? And if it was outside of him, what would happen if this current was switched off?

She looked back at the black and white photo.

'Do you ever think about your mum?'

He missed a chord. 'What a question.'

'But do you?'

He followed her gaze. 'Every day I think of her.'

There was a long silence. She blinked and in the shadows of her eyes she saw a cold gray graveyard, overgrown with ivy and a weathered statue of a stone angel – but with his eyes gauged out.

The image was so sharp and so clear she reached out her hand instinctively to rest her palm on his wing.

'*Que haces?* What's wrong?'

Rafa's deep voice thrust her back to the present. He was staring at her and for a moment she didn't know where she was. Whether she was in a graveyard in London or in Rafa's room in southern Spain. She opened her mouth and nothing came out.

She heard her breath ragged. The knuckles on her hands dead white.

'What is it?'

She shook her head. 'Nothing.'

Rafa's coarse fingers grazed her chin as he tipped her head upward. He studied her face intently. 'What is it with you, *inglesa*,' he muttered. 'You are not like the other girls.'

She pulled away. Picked up the photo of his mum. 'How did she die?'

'My mother had cancer.' He put his hands on her stomach to show Lizzie the area. 'Here. I do not know how to say it in English.'

His hands were hot. They spread warmth into her belly.

'And then it went to her lungs and then her brain and then everywhere.'

He picked up the photo and looked at it. 'In the end I pray that she die so she stop suffering. I go to church and I ask God to please take my mother because she is not my mother any more. She is like an animal suffering. No better than a goat.'

'But she's in a good place now though,' Lizzie whispered.

Rafa snorted. 'There is no *good* place. Because if there is, that means there must be a God. And that God he make my mother die like an *animal*.' He spat out the last word with frightening venom.

'But people do die in different ways, don't they? It doesn't mean there's nothing else, you know, someplace else we go.'

'With angels?' Rafa scoffed. 'You are like *Abuela* who believes in this nonsense. There is nothing out there. *Nothing*. Because my mother she would have come back. She said before she die; if there is another world beyond this one, I will come back and tell you. I *promise*, Rafa, with all my heart I will come back and give you a sign. But she never come back for me.' He rubbed his eyes. 'I wait every day and every night for a sign from her. I pray at my bedtime, 'please give me a sign that you are still out there' but never do I hear anything.'

Lizzie held her breath until she could hold it no longer and then heard it leave her body like a rattle. 'Never? Are you sure?'

He turned round to look at her and she winced under the sharpness of his gaze.

'Yes. I am sure.'

The pain of it hit her in the chest. There was an entire universe out there. How could people just *die*? They went someplace else. Didn't they?

'Yesterday, when Hooper died he said something.'

She chewed her lip wondering if she had said too much but unable to stop herself.

'What did he say?' Rafa pulled a face.

'He said "can you see it?"'

'See what?'

'That's just it. He didn't say. But it could have been *anything*.'

Rafa shook his head. 'He was a dying man, Lizzie. He was, how you say, delusional. He probably have damage on the brain from the water.'

'It's like you don't want to believe!' Lizzie cried. 'Who knows what Hooper saw but I'd rather he saw *something* than *nothing*. I want to believe. It makes death more . . . .comforting.'

'And I do not,' Rafa said, glaring at her. 'I do not believe in any of that.'

'Well, we'll have to agree to disagree then.' She glared back at him.

'You are not normal.' He raised his voice. 'You see things which do not exist. You are ….'

'What?' She shouted back. 'What am I?'

A gigantic crack of thunder made them both jump. The atmosphere shattered.

'I'm sorry.'

'Me too.' He looked at Lizzie curiously. 'Things always happen with you.'

'And?'

He smiled at her under hooded eyes. 'You speak from your heart.' He tapped her chest with his index finger and she took a sharp intake of breath. 'You are *passionate* . . . for an *inglesa*.' He laughed.

She couldn't help but laugh with him. 'Why don't you play a song?'

'For *you* I play.'

He played a song that started slow and then switched in tempo to become loud and voracious. It was like the thudding of her heart. And so time passed. Cocooned away from the rain, sheltered from the outside world, they shared the afternoon. Sweetly. He played the guitar, sometimes to her and sometimes as if he'd forgotten she was there. If he didn't play the guitar he asked her questions about growing up in England and about her family.

She told him as much as she dared and he seemed fascinated by the contrast between Ariadne and her mum. 'Really? I cannot believe that,' he said over and over again as she described the sterile, clean house in London, the neatly tendered back garden and the way she loved routines.

'Lasagne? Always on a Tuesday?'

In return he told her about his mum – how beautiful she'd been and how his dad had left soon after she died and never come back.

'My dad never came back either.'

'But where is he?'

She shrugged.

'Don't you miss him?'

'Don't you miss your dad?'

'No. But I have my grandfather and your grandmother. And

most of all I have this.' He picked up his guitar. 'You do not get on with your mum and you do not play music. What do you have, Lizzie?'

She tried to think of something she owned that was all hers – in the way that Rafa's guitar could only be his. 'I don't know.'

'There must be something. Something you love…'

'I had a dog,' she said after a bit. 'He was called Joopy.'

'Joopy?' Rafa raised an eyebrow.

'It was short for Jupiter.' She paused and waited for the familiar ache that came when saying his name. For once, it didn't come. 'When I was young I named all my pets after planets. The rabbit was called Mars and my goldfish Saturn.'

Rafa's lips twitched. 'Why Saturn?

'Because it used to swim around in rings.'

Rafa threw his head back and laughed. 'You do make me laugh.'

As the rain continued to pour he played her some Spanish music from his laptop. 'You don't know *any* Spanish music?!'

He played her song after song of famous Spanish bands, contemporary tunes and old songs, and after a couple of hours of this, she suddenly noticed that the rain had stopped.

Lizzie sat up reluctantly. 'Ariadne's probably wondering where I am.'

'I walk you back.'

Stepping out of the hut was like stepping out of a tube station back onto the busy streets. She blinked a few times. The air smelt fresh and cleansed. The sky was peppered with stars.

'Let's go.'

They walked in silence down the track past the goat-shed – now full of shuffling, stinking goats – past the *finca* and back through the land to the boundary. The trees dripped with water and the land was muddy. Once or twice Lizzie slipped and Rafa reached out to steady her. As she slipped for the third time, he grabbed her hand and held it tight.

'I hold you close,' he said with a smile in his voice. 'I will be your angel.'

She cuffed him on the shoulder.

'No, I am serious. Angels are not up there,' he pointed toward the stars. 'They are down here taking care of damaged souls like you.'

'I am not a damaged soul!'

'Yes you are. You are like me.'

Lizzie didn't bother arguing a second time. The truth was the truth.

They neared *Casa del Sol* and she saw that the lights were on.

He stopped in the orchard keeping hold of her hand, and turned to face her.

'Bye Lizzie.'

She could barely see him in the dark of the night. Just an outline of his face standing close to hers. The musky scent of him mingled with the fresh smell of the earth. All around them the leaves dripped with water, a pitter patter that matched her heartbeat. She swallowed as her tummy flipped and turned inside her. He moved closer and she held her breath as his fingers gently caressed her cheekbone. Now they were so close all she needed to do was tiptoe up and lift her lips. She could feel his hot breath on her face.

'Rafa,' she murmured.

'Lizzie!'

At first the voice didn't register. All she noticed was the chill between her and Rafa as he'd stepped back. Her lips ached and her heart thudded.

'Lizzie!'

The voice didn't belong. She heard the crackle of twigs as someone walked toward them. The slosh of mud. A narrow beam of torchlight sought them out.

The footsteps came closer.

'Hello Lizzie.'

The torchlight was directed backwards, like a spotlight, onto the honey coloured hair and perfect heart shaped face of Bee Buckingham.

'It's me!'

Chapter Twenty-one

She opened her mouth two, three, even four times. Unable to say anything, unable to hear anything. Nothing but the roar in her chest. A tight band which slapped across it and left her struggling to breathe. Was this some kind of joke? Bee, *Bee* of all people, was here in Spain. Not just Spain but at Ariadne's house?

Bee swept the torch over Lizzie, feeding on her scruffy clothes, her tangled, frizzed up hair, her sun-burnt nose and ending on her mud-caked trainers.

At which point the outside light clicked on and all three of them lit up.

Bee looked as if she'd just stepped out of a fashion magazine for a holiday shoot for Wags. Shorts so short even Lizzie found herself staring at Bee's legs, so shapely, so sculpted, so annoyingly perfect. She wore a see through yellow sleeveless blouse tied at the waist with a white bikini underneath and her blond hair tumbled over her bare shoulders. She'd had her navel pierced – this was new.

She tilted her head to one side and peered up at Rafa. 'And you are?'

'Rafa.'

'Bee,' she murmured, holding out her hand. 'Bee Buckingham.'

'*Encantado,*' Rafa said, ignoring her hand and leaning forward to kiss her cheeks.

Bee nibbled her bottom lip and then smiled. 'Hello Rafa. How *very* nice to meet you.'

And all Lizzie's insecurities came crashing back like a tsumani.

'So, this is where you've been hanging out?' Bee ran her fingertips over the bobbly surface of an orange tree. 'How very *rural* of you, Lizzie.'

The jibe was lost on Rafa.

'What are you doing here?' The words that had been pressing up against her all this time bubbled out.

Bee snapped her head round.'Got expelled. I've been such a *bad* girl.'

She grinned and looked at them both expectantly.

'And?' Rafa asked. 'What happened?'

Bee paused and then turned to Lizzie. 'It was your mum's idea. She thought you might be getting a little lonely out here.' She looked sidelong at Rafa. 'Obviously not *that* lonely.'

Lizzie folded her arms across her chest. 'It's not like that.'

Bee raised an eyebrow. 'Isn't it?'

Lizzie looked to Rafa for a cue and held her breath. He cleared his throat and then said nothing. She turned round abruptly, trying to ignore the stabbing pain of rejection in her chest, and in the process almost toppled him over.

'Where are you going?' he caught her shoulder and she yelped. His fingers were hard.

'To see Ariadne!' Lizzie snapped.

'*Inglesa.*' He said. '*Que pasa*? What's going on here?'

At least he was looking at her now. That was something. But she probably looked so boring and so *normal* next to Bee she avoided his gaze and folded her arms against her chest.

'Bee?' Rafa spoke softly but firmly. 'Tell Lizzie what is happening.'

A frown crossed Bee's forehead. 'I got expelled.'

'What for?' he asked.

'Because I had sex.'

Rafa shrugged. 'And? Goats have sex all the time.'

'What have goats got to do with it?'

Rafa smiled. 'I just say that sex is nothing unusual.'

Lizzie looked sidelong at him through narrowed eyes and tried to ignore the heat that rose in her belly like flames. Sex nothing unusual? Not to someone who had never done it before.

Bee was staring at them both.

'I did it at school.'

Lizzie gasped. Bee looked across at her and smirked. 'Not real sex. *Virtual* sex. Remember that guy from the internet? The seventeen year old from Melbourne?'

'Byron?'

Bee nodded. 'We did it on the library computer.'

Rafa burst into laughter. 'We hear stories all the time about how easy you English girls are – and apparently it *is* true.'

Bee scowled. 'It wasn't like that.'

And Lizzie who had known Bee since she was five, saw a shadow beneath the bravado. Just a glimpse. Nobody else would have noticed it. Not underneath all that make-up. The thought that Bee had weaknesses, was not perfect, was a new thought. She ran it around in her head for a while and watched how Bee arranged her face before speaking next.

'Dad thought I would be safer here.' She looked around her at the nature surrounding her on all sides. 'Away from distraction.'

'There is always distraction,' Rafa said. 'And sometimes we must ignore it. Now I must go to practice. My afternoon was how do I say . . . *angelic,*' he looked sideways at Lizzie giving her a funny look and she didn't know if he was teasing her or not. 'It is nice to meet you Bee, but I must go home.' He turned to Lizzie. 'I see you soon, *valle*?'

There were no lingering looks at her or even a hint of the intimacy they'd had earlier. He simply walked away.

Bee stood staring after him whilst Lizzie tried to get a handle on the explosion of emotions she felt. It was like Bee had been cut out of her London life and pasted onto this scene. It felt so *wrong* having her here. So incongruent. Just her mere presence made her feel small. Instead of feeling like an Andalucian beauty on the verge of a love affair, she now felt like plain old Lizzie Fisher.

The freak.

How could everything have changed? Just at the point where

he'd been about to kiss her! A dull thud pressed against the inside of her chest. Bee snapped out of her reverie. She turned to Lizzie and reached out and touched her over-sized T-shirt.

'Is this the fashion out here?'

Lizzie hated the way just one sentence made her feel insecure. 'Actually, it's Rafa's.'

Bee narrowed her eyes and smiled. 'You're wearing *his* clothes? You're a fast mover aren't you?'

'It's not like that!'

'Isn't it? "*Sex is not so unusua*l",' she leered. 'He is something, is he not?'

Lizzie opened her mouth to protest but Ariadne's voice bellowed into the orchard, bouncing from tree to tree like a pinball.

'Lizzie! Bee! Are you there?'

Bee looked down at the rutted path and pulled a face.

'Girls!'

Bee rolled her eyes. 'What a witch! I couldn't believe it when I saw her at the airport. I nearly *died* of embarrassment.'

'She's not a witch! She's....' Lizzie started but Bee had gingerly stepped ahead, tottering on her heels.

Ariadne appeared at the kitchen door. 'Hello girls.'

Lizzie grunted as she pushed past Bee and her grandmother. She scraped out a chair and sat at the table with her arms folded. Bee carefully took a seat at the other end of the table. They glared at each other.

Ariadne looked from one to the other and sighed. She turned back to the stove and the air thickened as neither girl said a word. 'Bee, which kind of eggs do you prefer, duck or hen?'

Bee wrinkled her nose. 'Neither. I can't eat eggs.'

'Why's that?' Ariadne pulled out a carton of eggs anyway and placed them in front of Lizzie on the kitchen table. 'Lizzie makes a beautiful omelette, don't you?'

'I can't eat eggs.' Bee repeated. 'I'm on a diet.'

'A diet of no eggs?'

'No dairy, no wheat, no sugar and no eggs.'

Ariadne slapped the frying pan down on the stove. 'This is going to be interesting.'

'And no prawns, no coffee, no processed food and definitely no red meat.'

'Right,' Ariadne pulled a lettuce out of the fridge. 'Salad?'

Bee sat with an expression of nausea mingled with disdain. The impact of Ariadne's house had long worn off on Lizzie but she was again reminded of the clutter, the dirt and the smell.

'Can I shower first please?'

'Of course.'

Bee delicately edged herself out of the chair without touching the table and scuttled out of the room, but not without scowling at Lizzie on the way out.

'Everything ok?' Ariadne asked, keeping her eyes on the pan.

Lizzie opened the carton and cracked one of the eggs with such force it spilt all over the work surface. She hardly trusted herself to speak.

'Lizzie?' Ariadne murmured touching her shoulder.

She shrugged it off and took another egg and broke that one too.

'It's ok, it's only you and I having omelette now.'

'Why didn't you tell me she was coming?' She spun round.

Ariadne's eyes softened. 'I didn't know.'

'But you must have known! You went and picked her up from the airport!'

Ariadne sighed. 'I only found out this morning. Your mother phoned and I just happened to be next to the tree so I had signal. It was *very* last minute.'

Lizzie cracked two more eggs into the bowl and beat them with a fork until her breath had calmed down.

'I thought Bee and you were friends? That's what your mother said.'

'Hardly.'

'I can see that now,' she chuckled. 'Actually I saw it as soon as I met her.'

'It's not funny!' Lizzie spun round with the fork still clenched in her hand. 'I *hate* her!'

'You *hate* her?' Ariadne exhaled slowly. 'Hate is such a strong word, Lizzie.'

Lizzie shrugged.

'I don't think *you* hate anyone. Not the Lizzie I've come to know.'

She paused and sought the right words. 'You're so special that you have a gift nobody else has. And you know why you've been given that gift? Because you're the kind of person who *loves*, not hates. You don't show things but you *feel* things.' She pressed her palm against Lizzie's heart. 'And that's a far more beautiful place to come from.'

In the background, the bathroom door slammed shut. Lizzie beat the fork so hard against the bowl it pinged out of her hand and clattered on the floor.

'Where you've been today?' Ariadne picked it up and handed her a new one. 'Anywhere interesting?'

The butter in the pan spat with heat. '*Nowhere.*'

'You must tell me where that is. Is it a good place to visit in a thunderstorm?'

Lizzie poured the egg mixture into the pan and sighed. 'I was at Rafa's.'

'Really?' Ariadne raised her eyebrows sky high. Now that is interesting.'

'Not really.' Lizzie looked toward the hallway where the sound of running water drifted through. 'Not *now*.'

'Oh. So it's like that?' Ariadne murmured.

'It's not like anything,' Lizzie shoved the pan away and tried with all her strength to hold back her tears.

'Oh, Lizzie.' Ariadne pulled her into a tight hug, just like the first day at the airport and she still smelt of lavender. 'Do you honestly think he'll prefer her to you?'

Lizzie snuffled. 'Maybe,' she said in a small voice.

Ariadne didn't answer. She just laughed.

Chapter Twenty-two

Why had she laughed?

Lizzie stood by the open window of her bedroom. Every part of her body felt tired, even her bones, but she couldn't sleep. She leant her face against the blue shutter. It must have been gone midnight.

Even the stars didn't capture her tonight. They flickered and glistened, but all Lizzie could concentrate on was the distant drum of music coming from next door – Bee's bedroom – no doubt either coming from her phone or her laptop. She'd brought four suitcases crammed full of clothes and accessories. Lizzie looked over to her own solitary suitcase which lolled open and had clothes dangling out of it. Perhaps it was time to unpack.

She knelt by it and pulled out each item, shook it and then folded it and placed it on the bed. The routine was soothing. She didn't notice the presence in her room until it was standing directly in front of her.

A tall, silver shadow. Not just a shadow – it sparkled, it glistened, it moved. It was a silver silhouette, standing tall and strong in her bedroom, like a person. Except it was not a person, just a mass of shimmering silver right in front of her nose. Her skin went cold and clammy.

'What's up?'

She screamed and the suitcase lid fell down on her fingers. When she looked up the *thing* had gone.

Bee rolled her eyes. 'Jesus, Lizzie. *Drama.* I only asked what's up.' She sauntered into the room. 'This isn't fair. This room's much bigger than mine. Oh my God! Look at your bed.'

She ran over to the four-poster and dived onto it. 'I want to sleep here!'

Lizzie finished packing the clothes in silence. Would it come back in? What was it? Would it hurt her? Her heart hammered erratically.

Bee sat up and started to fluff her hair. 'Where are the mirrors in this house?'

'They're locked away.'

Bee frowned. '*Who* locks mirrors away?' She flopped back on the bed. 'How have you managed to survive?'

'Without mirrors?' Lizzie kicked the suitcase under the bed and then went over to the window and closed the shutter. As she did she saw something sparkle briefly on top of the hill by the olive tree – Ariadne's tree of life.

'Are you cold?' She asked Bee.

'Are you joking? It's about twenty trillion degrees hotter than England. I'm roasting.'

Lizzie pulled on her fleece top.

Bee looked at her like she was some kind of freak. For once Lizzie didn't care.

'I can't believe dad sent me here. It's lucky you don't have one. Honestly, I thought he was joking at first. But no. He said I had made them "ashamed". Like I care! Mum and dad don't even know what virtual sex is. Or *real* sex for that matter.' Bee stretched out on the bed. 'It was your mum's idea. You won't believe how weird she's been acting since you've been gone.'

Something inside of Lizzie snagged. 'How weird?'

'Like coming over to our house *all* the time and asking my mum if she'd done the right thing by allowing you to come here. Like almost *obsessive*. And she's been dressed funny.'

Lizzie propped herself on the end of the bed, around Bee's ankles. She stared at the cerise pink of her nails. 'How?'

'I don't know. She keeps mis-matching her accessories, things like that. And for your mum that's *major*. Anyway, I bet she loved it when I got expelled. Let's send her to Spain! Probably afraid you'd turn into a witch.' Bee looked around the bare room. 'Isn't there *anything* to do here?'

The image of mum not as groomed, not as neat as usual, stuck in Lizzie's head. It didn't feel right. It was like a missed chord in the middle of one of Rafa's song. But then, everything she'd ever thought about mum seemed to be changing these days.

'How far are we from the beach?'

Lizzie pulled her fleece tighter and tried not to think about that night. But it's impossible not to think of something without thinking of it first. An image of Hooper's bloated corpse floated to the surface. 'You'd need a lift.'

Bee groaned. 'I'm not going in that dirty old land rover again. What about that Spanish guy? Has he got a car? Or does he travel around by goat?'

'He's got a motorbike.'

She turned her nose up. 'No thanks. What was his name?'

'Rafa,' Lizzie said trying to sound nonchalant. As if she didn't say his name under her breath a billion times a day. As if his name wasn't emblazoned on her heart.

'Rafa,' Bee rolled it around her mouth. 'Rafa. Like the tennis player?'

'Like the angel,' Lizzie said, unable to stop herself.

'He doesn't look like an angel,' Bee sneered. 'And he certainly doesn't *think* like one.'

'I didn't say he was angel. I said he had the same *name* as an angel.'

Bee rolled her eyes. 'Your grandmother said he was a musician or something. I can't imagine him being in a band though. He's so dirty.'

'He's not dirty. He's different,' Lizzie said and then instantly regretted it. Bee was looking at her with a glint in her eye.

'You like him, don't you?'

'No!'

'Yes you do. I could tell earlier on by the way you were gazing at him. All starry eyed. And you were wearing his clothes.' Bee leant back on the pillows and yawned. 'So, Lizzie likes Rafa.'

Her cheeks flushed unwilling. 'What if I do? Does it matter?'

Bee raised an eyebrow. 'What's got into you, Frizzo?'

Lizzie took a deep breath. 'Actually, my name isn't Frizzo. It's Lizzie.'

'My my, Andualucia *has* changed you, hasn't it.'

'Yes,' Lizzie said feeling the grains of sand under her feet as she sprang up from the bed and paced back to the window. 'And if you're really lucky, it might change you too.'

'*I* don't need changing.'

Lizzie stared long and hard at her, willing the other girl to look away first. Bee laughed nervously. 'Don't look at me like that.'

Lizzie smiled. 'Don't call me Frizzo then.'

Bee pulled a face but nodded anyway. 'So, you don't want to swap rooms then?'

'No.'

There was a long silence. Then Bee yawned and stood up.'Suit yourself. I'm going to bed.'

After she had gone, Lizzie couldn't sleep for ages. Her mind whirled between Bee and the silver shadow she'd seen in her bedroom. What was it? What did it mean? When she did get to sleep she dreamt she was trapped in the museum room. She screamed and beat her fists against the wooden door until her knuckles bled. Behind her the stone angel laughed.

Then she realized she wasn't dreaming. She was awake. Her heart thudded loud. She wasn't screaming but someone was.

Bee.

Lizzie raced out of her room and into the adjoining bedroom. Bee stood in the centre of the room with her hands bunched up into little fists. She was so white she looked like snow. Something black flapped across the room.

'Get it out of here!' Bee screeched.

It flapped across the room again, narrowly missing Bee's hair. She swiped her hands above her face.

'It's only a bat,' Lizzie said.

'I don't care! Get it out!'

Lizzie switched on the light and the bat flew into the corner by the ceiling where it curled up into a tight ball. Bee stood trembling. She had loosely tied her hair back and her face was fresh and clean. It took Lizzie a second to register the difference. No make-up. She looked younger. Sweeter. She almost said something but then saw how much Bee was shaking.

She grabbed a chair, stood on it and reached into the corner. The bat was soft. It quivered when she tugged it gently from the corner and cupped it in her hands.

'Open the shutter.'

Bee didn't move.

'Bee, open the shutter!'

'Just keep that thing away from me.' She ran to the shutter, flung it open and then ran back to the opposite corner of the room.

Lizzie went to the window and placed the bat on the ledge. She closed the shutters. 'It's gone.'

'For good?'

'Yes.'

'Are there any more?' Bee searched the room.

Lizzie checked the corners whilst Bee hung back. It was a small, rectangular sized room with a single bed. Bee had unpacked her clothes and hung them in a color coordinated sequence on the clothes railing. Underneath them sat a long row of shoes. 'Don't think so.'

Bee ran to the bed and threw herself on it. 'I *hate* this place!' Her shoulders shook. 'I didn't want to come here.'

'But you're here now.'

'Yeah,' she snuffled. 'With the bats.'

'Bats aren't that bad.'

'For you!' Bee sat up and rubbed her eyes. 'You like creepie crawlies. I hate them, don't you remember?'

Their childhood sizzled in front of them. The two of them on the back lawn looking for stars. The day their mums had taken them to pick up puppies from the same litter. The list.

'I remember,' Lizzie said.

Something about the way Lizzie said it made Bee look up and narrow her eyes. She squinted at her. 'You still see them? The *marks*, or whatever you call them. The sign of death.'

After a moment's hesitation, Lizzie shook her head. 'No.' Her nails dug half-moons into her palm as the lie slipped out. She thought about telling her the truth but one look at Bee's curled lip warned her otherwise. 'They've gone. All gone.'

* * *

'I'm so *bored*!'

For the second morning in a row, Bee watched idly as Lizzie watered the herbs and plants.

'Is there nothing to do round here?'

Lizzie handed her the hose and Bee took it reluctantly, as if it were a slug, and then handed it back just as quickly. She held up her hands. They were wet.

'No thank you.' She pulled a face. 'Where's the witch?'

Lizzie's stomach tightened at Bee's words but however many times she'd tried to correct her, Bee still called Ariadne The Witch. But, so what? Ariadne called Bee The Brat.

Neither of them liked the other.

In fact, since Bee's arrival, they'd been circling each other like prize fighters, neither of them making a direct punch, just making little sly jabs here and there.

'Gone to the coast to do some shopping.'

'At last! I gave her a list of foods I could eat. They're not *that* hard to find.' As Bee yawned, the enamel of her teeth shone in the sun. 'If there's really nothing to do I'm going to sunbathe.'

She'd found the dip pool yesterday morning and spent the whole day in a tiny white bikini rotating herself as if on a spit.

Bee sauntered off and left Lizzie alone. Good. If Bee said one more time how bored he was, she would turn the hose on her. Now at least she had some peace. How could anyone fill so much airspace just talking about things? Her haircut, her bikini, her nails, her diet, her new mobile.

No wonder Ariadne had gone straight to her room after dinner last night. *Everything* had changed since Bee's arrival. She'd barely had a chance to talk to Ariadne at all and it was like she'd bundled the past back up into the museum room and boarded up the door again. There was still so much she wanted to ask about her mum and her grandfather but they were not the sort of questions she wanted to ask in front of Bee.

When Ariadne came back from the coast, Bee was still baking in the sun and Lizzie helped unload the 4 x 4. Ariadne was quiet and packed the foods away in silence. Even her clothes were muted.

'Have you seen Rafa today?' she asked as she picked up her detective novel and retreated toward her bedroom.

'No.'

It had been two *whole* days since she'd seen him. Two of the longest days of her life. Every minute was like eternity. Why hadn't he come round? Was he avoiding her? Did he regret getting so close to her the other day? What did he think of her? Would he prefer Bee? Questions, questions and none of them she'd been able to answer. How could she think about someone *so* much?

'He's playing in a concert in the plaza tomorrow night and hopefully this one won't be marred by tragedy.' Ariadne smiled wryly. 'I thought you and Bee might like to go?'

'Yes please!'

Ariadne offered a little smile, a tiny ray of sunshine, before disappearing for the rest of the afternoon.

The day crawled past. And the night too. There was so much on her mind. The end of summer. Bee. The black marks. The thing she'd seen in her bedroom. Hooper. And most of all, Rafa. She tossed and turned, tried to relax but couldn't, recalling every moment of the near kiss in vivid detail, the excitement of the storm, then she tossed and turned again, making a mental image of his face. She replayed the moment over and over in her mind, seeing it from an assortment of different angles and each time wondering passionately what he was thinking of her. If only she could get inside his mind and found out.

In the end she got up to get a glass of water. Passing Bee's doorway, she looked in. Bee slept with the light on and her blond hair was fanned over her pillow. In sleep, she was almost angelic looking. She paused a while. Why couldn't Bee be like this all the time? She'd sure as hell be nicer to be around.

She felt it before she saw it. Goose bumps. Her hairs on end. She didn't want to turn round. Not now. *Not ever*. She stood and waited for what felt like hours. Holding her breath. Still as a statue. Bee stirred in her bed.

The hand landed on her shoulder.

She leapt up into the air and screamed.

'Get off me!'

Bee sat up in bed. Wide-eyed.

'Get it off me! *Please*!'

Lizzie twisted and turned, feeling the hand grip tighter. Then it went.

Bee sat up in bed and stared at her with a horrified expression on her face. 'You *freak*.'

Chapter Twenty-three

'Who is *he*?'

'Rafa,' Carlos answered.

Bee's eyes fell out on stalks. '*That's* Rafa?' She licked her lips. '*Hello.*'

Beams of yellow and red lights scissored through the night. It was Lizzie's first public outing since the party on the beach and the first time she'd been in the plaza since seeing the black mark. Many of the people here were those who had seen her run into the water and then kneel by Hooper's side as he died. She wished Ariadne had stayed rather than just dropping them off.

Lizzie had tried to make an effort in her blue summer dress but it was *nothing* compared to how Bee looked tonight. She had gone full out. With her hair in two pig-tails, her face artfully made up, she'd matched it with a short skirt, knee length leather boots and a slashed cream top that tantalizingly exposed streaks of naked tanned flesh.

'*Que guapa!*' Carlos' eyes had practically fallen out of his head.

Bee drew the boys to her like honey. Carlos, Jesus, Felipe, Oscar, two other Carlos lookalikes with gelled black hair, some chubby blond boy she'd never seen before called Gustavo and even a young Spanish kid of about twelve had all taken seats around her.

But once Rafa had taken the stage, Bee had eyes for no-one but him.

'Rafa is one *hot* goat-herder.' She looked sideways at Lizzie.

Lizzie's heart sank.

He was so beautiful. So achingly beautiful that it hurt to look at him. Her heart tightened into a fist. Of course he would prefer Bee! Who didn't? No-one looked at her if Bee was around. And even if he had started to look at her, to feel things for her, to want her, then once he found out the truth about her, he would soon recoil anyway. It wouldn't be long before Bee told him the truth about her.

He chose that exact moment to look up. He seemed to know precisely where they were sitting and he looked directly at Lizzie with dark, hooded eyes. Her stomach lurched. And then he shifted his expression from Lizzie to Bee, staring at her deep and hard. Lizzie's insides tightened even more.

Bee leant closer and whispered in her ear. 'Did you see that? Did you *see* the way he looked at me?'

She couldn't reply even if she had decided to speak to Bee again. Her mouth was too dry. Her chest too constricted. An ugliness reared up inside of her. Swelled around her body like a gray seething mass. She'd never been so jealous of Bee as she was in this moment.

How could he like her? *Why?* It wasn't fair.

She jumped up to her feet and ran to the toilets.

'*Que pasa*?' Carlos blocked the way to the toilet. She shoved past him. '*Fria*!' He shouted as she slammed the door in his face.

The wood felt cool as she leant her forehead against it and breathed deeply. Her skin dug into something sharp. A small handmade metal angel hanging on the door and it was as if she was back in Milton Graveyard standing in that special clearing in front of her own angel. A calmness washed inside her, lapping against her insides like a tranquil lake. Within minutes she felt a sense of peace settling around the jagged edges of her jealousy.

'Thank you,' she whispered.

She cupped cold water in her palms and splashed it over her face and looked at herself in the mirror. Still and calm. If only she could hide in here all night. But she couldn't.

'I'm brave,' she told her reflection in the mirror. 'I'm brave!'

A few deep breaths later and she emerged. She passed Ana at the bar and the other girl smiled over to her and blew her a kiss.

Lizzie sat down and kept her eyes focussed on the stage, cast in an orange glow, the color of a dying sun. Rafa played song after song. Oblivious to his surroundings, lost in his music, each song more beautiful than the last. After he was finished the entire plaza erupted into a standing ovation including Lizzie. Bee stood on her seat and whistled.

It took half an hour for Rafa to wind his way over. But finally he stood and faced them. He had a bottle of still water in one hand and beads of sweat on his forehead.

'Did you like that?' he asked Bee.

'I loved it!' she exclaimed.

'And you?' he turned to Lizzie. 'What did you think?'

She touched her chest and he smiled.

'So is there a party now or what?' Bee asked.

'No party,' Rafa replied. 'I don't like parties.'

'Why not?' Bee giggled. 'I thought *all* musicians partied.'

The corners of Rafa's mouth twitched and he looked from one to the other. 'I am not *all* musicians.'

Bee's face dropped. 'So what do we do now? It's way too early to go home yet.'

Rafa paused. 'You can come back to my house if you want.'

'I can?!' Bee grinned.

'You both can.' Rafa turned to Lizzie. 'I invite you.'

'Both of us?' Bee turned to Lizzie. 'Can't we bring one of your mates along too to make it an even number?'

'I can ask Felipe, my cousin. He has a car.'

Bee coiled a strand of hair around her finger. 'But you have a bike, don't you?'

Rafa nodded.

'Can't I go on that with you?'

Lizzie gasped. 'I thought you didn't like bikes!'

'Don't be stupid. I *love* bikes.' Bee turned back to Rafa. 'Can I?'

He scratched the side of his face. 'I don't know. After the last time with Lizzie.'

'You've been on his bike?!' Bee's eyes widened. 'Oh please let me have a go. *Please*.'

Rafa looked back at Lizzie. Something passed between them. A tiny spark. Alive in the air like a firefly. If she stared at it, maybe it would last forever.

He looked away first.

'Well?' Bee pawed his arm. 'Can I?'

Rafa slid one last look toward Lizzie. Not the kind of look which was easy to read. It could have said anything. He looked at her whilst his lips opened. 'OK.'

Bee squealed and threw her arms around his neck. 'Thank you!'

Rafa stood still. Over Bee's shoulder he stared at Lizzie. 'I ask my cousin Felipe to take you, if that is ok with you?'

He looked at her again, as if he was trying to say something, and she used everything in her body to will her face to stay calm. She nodded.

'Are we going now?' Bee grabbed his arm.

Lizzie couldn't take her eyes off Bee's fingers curled over the tautness of Rafa's wrist. As each finger of Bee's rubbed against his almond skin, it was as though her own skin was ripping.

'Yes,' Rafa looked again at Lizzie.

'See you at my house?'

She nodded and without a backward glance, Bee tightened her fingers around Rafa's wrist and tugged him away.

* * *

It was just as well that Ariadne hadn't arranged to pick them up. She'd trusted that the two girls would be able to find their way home. Though Lizzie never imagined her night would end quite like this.

Felipe drove his BMWX3 quickly over the rutted tracks. He had sat navigation and she followed their progress on the screen. It was funny seeing Sat Nav out there. He'd grown up here and probably knew the dirt tracks like the back of his hand, why the need for directions? Still, it was something to watch as they drove. No point talking. He played his music so loud the windows rattled. She sneaked little looks at him anyway. He had a nice face. Not striking like Rafa's or good looking like Carlos' but one of those pleasant and yet at the same time, forgettable faces. Short brown hair, bushy eye brows, evenly sized brown eyes and a slightly weak chin. Nothing remarkable about him at all.

Perhaps that's what he thought of her too.

She tugged her dress downwards and shut her eyes. An image of the yellow bike and Bee's arms wrapped around Rafa's stomach popped into her mind so she opened them again. Another wave of envy passed through her. What was the point of going to Rafa's anyway?

They reached *Casa del Sol.*

'Can you drop me here please?'

'You no want party?' Felipe asked.

She shook her head. 'Thanks for the lift.' She fumbled with the door latch and Felipe leant across her. He smelt of spicy after-shave. His hand landed on her hand. Neither moved. He turned sideways so his face was right next to hers. He had soft brown eyes. He leant closer and parted his lips.

'No!' Lizzie yanked open the door and jumped out. Felipe looked at her in surprise. 'I can't.'

He smiled anyway. He wasn't mean or threatening like Carlos had been. Lizzie held onto the door a moment longer. He was a nice person. Why shouldn't she kiss him?

And then she thought of Rafa and her heart blazed. *That's why.* Because she wanted someone to set her on fire, not someone nice and ordinary. She smiled and shut the car door. He sped off back towards town. It was dark and it was quiet. An owl hooted. The lights to the house were off. She was tired. Really she should sleep. But how could she sleep? Every time she closed her eyes she thought of those two.

She stood in the doorway. How long had it been now? An hour? Enough time for them to have got back to his bedroom. For him to play her some music. For them to sit on the futon together. She moaned softly.

She couldn't bear it! How could she sit and wait all night? Nothing could be worse than this. She'd walk over there. Decision made. She shoved her feet into her trainers, grabbed a torch and set out.

Any other time she would have stopped and admired the sky. It was ablaze with stars. The universe showing off in its glory. But not tonight. She wasn't aware of anything other than the thin beam of light ahead of her and the storm of emotions inside her. Like an out of tune band they clashed and banged inside of her.

It didn't take long to get to Rafa's. Not at the speed she was marching. The smell of goat didn't even hit her. She was aware of it but only mildly. Gabriel's *finca* sat in darkness. Rafa's bike was propped up against the wall. So they were back. She swallowed and followed the path around the side of the house toward the stone igloo. She'd not noticed much the previous time she'd been here. Perhaps because there wasn't much to notice. It wasn't alive like Ariadne's – there were no flowers or splashes of colour – this was a man's place. Bare, cold, blank. She marched on.

Rafa's guitar playing spilled out like wine. The thick arched door to his bedroom was slightly ajar, a slice of yellow light penetrating the blackness. Having come so far, she stopped. Her breathing felt ragged. Sharp in her chest.

Bee's laughter rang out and her stomach tightened.

Rafa said something but she couldn't hear it. She crept a little closer.

'She's so plain.'

She froze.

'You should have seen her at school. She's never even had a boyfriend.' Bee laughed. 'We called her Freako Fisher. Everyone *hated* her.'

Her hands went numb and she dropped her torch. It landed on her foot with a soft thud. Tears stung her eyes.

'What's that?' Bee said.

Rafa appeared in the doorway and Lizzie quickly crouched down behind a rock. Her heart thudded. He was bare chested and his hair tumbled onto his shoulders in soft curls. He looked around and stared in her direction for a long time.

'*Nada,*' he said and slammed the door.

She wouldn't cry. She wouldn't!

She trembled as she stood up. Her legs were wobbly. She stumbled back across the land. As she crossed the boundary to Ariadne's land she realized she'd left the torch by the rock. But she couldn't go back. For the first time since arriving in Spain she wanted to be back home in her north London cul-de-sac, sitting on the sofa watching television, in a world where everything was ordinary.

Where everything was safe.

She pressed her palms against the olive tree – Ariadne's tree of life. In the darkness it could almost be her angel. It had the same solid presence as the statue. The same feeling of calm. The same feeling of protection. The angel made her feel as though she had someone to look over her. He was someone to talk to one when no-one else listened. Someone whose voice she had never heard but did that mean he couldn't speak?

Maybe angels spoke all the time and yet no-one could hear them because they spoke in a different language.

The voices of angels.

'It's not fair,' she whispered hoarsely. 'Why me?'

She didn't expect an answer. And nothing came except for the whisper of the breeze on her cheek like a soft caress.

She curled up next to the roots and shut her eyes. With her eyes closed, it didn't hurt quite so much. She just could press it into all the other pains. Press it into the folds of the universe.

As the night passed she dropped off into a light sleep. In her dream she heard the distant barking of a dog which sounded so like Joopy she woke with a start. The sky was ablaze with billions of tiny stars and in her half-awake state she blinked against the glare of glistening lights which didn't seem right for some reason. Although she couldn't say why and so she dropped back into a troubled sleep.

The footsteps woke her and at first she was confused. But then she saw Ariadne's worried face and she threw herself into her grandmother's safe arms and buried herself tight into her embrace. The long night had passed.

'Lizzie, what's up? What's wrong?'

She didn't want to say the words out loud. Saying them would make them real. Would make them hurt even more. But they flew out anyway.

'I've lost him!'

Chapter Twenty-four

They stayed up there to watch the sun rise. And as it rose, the sky dripped with red. And so Lizzie poured out everything about Bee and Rafa. She'd expected Ariadne to get fired up on her behalf, to fight her corner, to snarl her lip and call her The Brat. But Ariadne sighed softly and told her not to worry so much.

'It will all work out, just you see. You must trust the outcome, Lizzie. Two people who are meant to be together will always be together.' She gazed toward the hidden horizon of Africa. 'However long you have to endure without him, you must trust he will be waiting for you.'

It was as if she was distracted. Like she was not talking about Lizzie at all but something completely different. She wasn't really making sense. Why would Rafa be waiting for Lizzie? *Hardly*.

'I love this place, you know.' Ariadne murmured. 'Do you feel it?'

'Feel what?'

But Ariadne didn't reply.

A vision of the sparkling stars and that feeling of something strange crossed Lizzie's mind. She felt unnerved for some reason and so she left Ariadne alone, sitting cross-legged in a yoga position to watch the sun as it looped higher into the sky.

She walked back down the hill and found Bee sat painting her toe-nails at the patio table outside. She wore a clingy baby pink dress and the garden hose sat unused on the ground in front of her. She took one look at Lizzie and smirked.

Lizzie clenched her hands and walked around her.

'What happened to you last night? Looks like things got a bit rough with Felipe?' Bee laughed at her own joke. 'Didn't matter though because *we* had a great time. *And* I'm seeing him later.'

Lizzie paused in the kitchen doorway.

'I know you liked him but I can't help it if he likes me instead.'

The outside tap was directly in front of her. The urge was pure instinct. Without thinking she flicked it on. The tap gurgled into life and a stream of cold water spat out of the hose and straight into Bee's face.

Bee screamed.

'You did that on purpose!' She spluttered.

'Yes,' said Lizzie and grinned.

'Turn it off!'

'Turn it off yourself.'

'No wonder he doesn't like you!'

'And that means you had to go and steal him?' Lizzie turned round and squared up to Bee.

'*So*? I rescued him! You could say I was doing him a favour.'

Lizzie stared at a point over Bee's head. 'And now I'm doing you a favour. There's a black mark above your head.'

Bee paled. 'You're lying.'

'Am I?'

Bee ran her hand nervously above her head. 'There's nothing there.'

Lizzie stepped closer. 'How would you know? Only *I* can see them. *I'm* the one with the gift, not you.'

'You're making it up.'

Lizzie stepped closer still until she was right in front of Bee's face. 'No, I'm not. You've got seven days. Enjoy them.'

Bee went white as a sheet and ran into the house and up to her bedroom.

Lizzie tried to laugh but she couldn't. It came out as a sob. She sat at the patio table with North by her ankles and cradled her head in her arms.

Ariadne appeared as a silhouette. She looked worn and she had on a face Lizzie had never seen before. 'It's time you came with me.'

* * *

Andalucia. Blue skies, a yellow sun, parched brown mountain-sides. It felt like she'd been here a lifetime. In reality it had only been a handful of weeks but so much had changed. Most of all her.

The last time they had been on a long car journey was the day Ariadne had picked her up from the airport. That day her grand-mother had been a stranger to her and now she couldn't imagine life without her.

'Where are we going?' She asked.

'You'll see.'

After the argument, they'd left straight away. Ariadne had made Bee and Lizzie apologize to each other but it didn't clear the atmosphere between them.

'You're a freak,' Bee hissed when Ariadne was out of earshot.

'And?' Lizzie replied with a stare. 'You're a bitch.'

Bee had gone to retaliate but Ariadne had chosen that moment to return and dish out strict instructions to water the plants in their absence. As they were walking out the door, Ariadne popped her tatty old straw hat on Bee's head.

'So you don't go all wrinkly.'

Bee tore the hat off her head in revulsion and glared as the 4x4 drove away.

They drove for about three hours, off the mountain, and along the motorway toward Almeria. They didn't speak. Ariadne's mood faced inward and so Lizzie watched out the window the changing face of southern Spain. The further east they travelled the drier the land became. They were heading into the hottest area of Spain, an area of semi-desert. The mountains were craggy and bare and the sky big and blue. Just after the city of Almeria, Lizzie spotted the road-sign and gasped.

'We're going *there*?'

Ariadne nodded wordlessly and took a right turn toward

Cabo del Gato, a corner of Andalucia full of windswept, sandy beaches. And also the place where Lizzie's grandfather had died.

'Why?'

'Because, my dear Lizzie, the reality of death isn't something to joke about.

* * *

She turned the 4x4 down a series of narrow lanes, each one narrower and dustier than the last and drove it as far as she could before parking.

There was no-one else around.

'We're here.'

Lizzie got out and immediately the wind whipped into her face, throwing sand into her eyes. She shielded them with her hands and followed the billowing tangerine dress of her grandmother. If possible, the sun was even hotter here and the dry wind scorched her face.

Ariadne stopped and faced the frothy sea. Her dress fanned out behind her and the sea gurgled around her ankles. She knelt down and scooped some sand through her fingers. It trickled through in a kaleidoscope of colours.

'It's the same sand.' Lizzie crouched down. 'The sand that was in the jar.'

'Yes.' Ariadne picked up another handful. 'This is the beach where Seth died.'

The sea lapped against Lizzie's toes and she watched Ariadne's face. Her grandmother was lost in a faraway place. It was the same face she'd been wearing for the last couple of days. Wherever she'd gone, it wasn't now.

'You wanted to remember him,' Lizzie murmured intuitively getting why her grandmother had bottled the sand. 'So you took the last place on earth he'd been.'

'I used to believe that if I emptied the sand on the floor it would somehow form the shape of his body all over again.'

'And did it?'

Ariadne shook her head. 'Except I never unlocked the jar. I put him out of sight in a place where it wouldn't hurt. And not only that, I put all of the mirrors in there too. All the mirrors he'd ever made me.'

Lizzie ran her fingers through the sand. It was *her* fault that all these memories were being released back into the wild. She had opened that door and let the past tumble back out.

'And then I broke the jam jar.'

Ariadne stood up and looked out to sea. 'It was meant to break, Lizzie. That way we can move on, you see. And it is time now to move on for both of us.'

'But I've only just got here!' Lizzie said, but the wind picked up and carried her words away.

Ariadne touched her elbow. 'There was another reason to bring you here.' She pointed to a tiny stone house standing all by itself on top of the cliff. 'Look up there.'

Before Lizzie could ask any questions, Ariadne had set off down the beach toward the rocky cliff face. There didn't seem to be a path upward but Ariadne seemed to know exactly the best place to climb. Loose shingle tumbled down as they scrambled up. Once or twice Ariadne stopped to catch her breath and at the top she gulped in large chunks of air.

'It's much harder than it used to be.'

She's getting older, Lizzie thought with a pang, and waited for Ariadne to catch her breath.

'Where are we?'

'You'll see.'

She led Lizzie toward the house. It was even tinier close up. Worn by the weather with peeling white paint hanging off the walls in strips. A broken window. Flapping shutters. A feeling of abandonment. Ariadne stopped and grabbed Lizzie by the shoulder, shouting in the wind.

'This is where we used to stay on holidays, every August, up until the year Seth died.'

Ariadne walked up the broken path. The front door was hanging off its hinges and she pushed it tentatively open. 'I think it's safe.'

'It's ok,' Lizzie said. 'I'll go first if you want.'

'No, no, it's fine.' Ariadne held the door open and stepped inside. 'It hasn't been lived in for years.'

It was cold and dark inside with a smell of damp. The house consisted of one large room. In the far corner was a huge open fireplace. The shell of a kitchen remained near the door but apart from that, the room was empty. Ariadne stood in the centre of it and gazed around her. Her face lit up as if she was seeing it as it was, not how it looked now.

'We had a double mattress here and your mother slept over there – there used to be a partition so she had her own room. Of course she *hated* that the last year.'

'Mum lived here?' Lizzie felt her mouth drop open in astonishment. She couldn't imagine for one second her mum being in this cramped house on the beach. 'She never said anything about this.'

'It was a long time ago and in the last couple of years she spent as much time as she could away from us. She said she had outgrown holidaying with her parents.' Ariadne smiled in memory. 'Over here was the bookshelf and in this corner Seth kept his surfboard.'

Seth *surfed*? Today was certainly full of surprises!

Ariadne beamed. 'He wasn't English, you know. He was originally from the Gold Coast in Australia. He loved surfing.'

Her *granddad* was a surfer? Lizzie smothered a laugh. It was all so insane. Like she had stumbled into a parallel universe. A universe she had known nothing about but nevertheless had still existed.

'And then all round the room,' Ariadne swept her hand

around, 'we had the mirrors. Seth preferred making them in summer when the sun was at its hottest. Don't ask me why. Something about being inspired.'

Lizzie looked around the room and imagined the mirrors lining the walls. If she squinted her eyes she could just about see how all the mirrors would have reflected Ariadne back a million times. How she would have shone in each one. It wouldn't have been one Ariadne in here, but a thousand of her.

Maybe that was the reason her mum never spoke about it.

Lizzie walked further into the room. It was almost impossible to believe her mum had spent her summers here. It was so filthy! Though obviously back then it wouldn't have been like this. She looked out through the gap in the wall where a window had been onto the view of the sea. The wind blew in grains of sand and they grazed her face.

'Do you think you will ever make up?'

Ariadne frowned. 'I didn't bring you here to talk about your mum. I brought you here to talk about your grandfather.' She paused. 'It was time to come back now.'

Lizzie wondered when she would ever get to the truth behind her mum and Ariadne. She pushed the thought away for now.

'You must have met other men since? Someone like you, surely?'

Ariadne laughed. 'True. But none that captured me like Seth did.' She touched her sun necklace. 'He said we had a golden love.'

Lizzie let her breath out slowly. 'What's a golden love?'

'More special than you can imagine,' Ariadne whispered. 'You remember the story that Gabriel told? About the sun and the moon?'

Lizzie nodded.

'When I met Seth my whole life changed. Not just that, my whole existence, changed. I became *alive*.' Ariadne ran her fingers along the dusty window pane. 'We were never apart. Not even for one night.'

'Then how do you live without him?' Lizzie asked.

Ariadne looked at her mysteriously. 'I don't.'

The wind whistled around the room and for an illusionary second it seemed to snake into her body. Lizzie shifted.

'What?'

'Come on, let's go.' Ariadne clapped her hands together and pointed the way toward the door.

They strode away from the house and scrambled down the cliff. When they got to the bottom they paced back along the beach. Lizzie looked at the footsteps they had made in the sand. How long would these last until nature blew them away?

Ariadne shouted over the wind. 'People used to think Seth was a bit eccentric, you know. They said he was obsessed by his mirrors – a mad artist. He would work on them for hours and hours, not sleeping or talking, just in this altered state of *creation*. But when you love someone you don't care what they're like. You love them.'

Lizzie brushed the hair from her face. 'Even if everyone else thinks they're a freak?'

Ariadne took a deep breath. '*Especially* if everyone else thinks they're a freak.' She stared back out to sea. 'You were so brave the other night. I was so very proud of you, Lizzie.'

'But I didn't do anything! All I did was hold his hand. It's not like I can stop it from happening.'

'Nobody can stop death from happening.' Ariadne shrugged. 'You can only make the passing more peaceful.'

Joopy's face sprung into her mind and then Hooper's. She had been there for them both at the end. Where were they now?

'Is there something else out there, do you think?'

'Yes.' Ariadne turned to face the sea. 'Yes. . . I hope so.'

They stood in silence facing the sea feeling the wind buffet their faces. Finally Ariadne shifted. 'Let's go eat some dinner.'

They found an inexpensive but busy fish restaurant in the

centre of Almeria and after dinner, they walked around the city for a while, admiring the faded brilliance of a once powerful port. They stopped on Ariadne's silent instruction, somewhere in the heart of the old city, in the shelter of a Moorish patio and side by side they sat on a wooden bench and watched the sky.

It was so vast, so bottomless, so brilliant with stars.

Somewhere in the near distance a dog barked. And somewhere in the far distance, a sun shone. And up there? Beyond all of this? What happened there?

Was there something after life? Was Joopy still alive in a heaven full of dogs? Did Rafa's mum watch her son playing guitar? Could Seth hear Ariadne cry? Was there another world beyond this world? A time beyond time?

Life was so transient and she felt so tiny. Miniscule. Just a speck compared to the universe.

They sat for a few minutes more. 'Ready to go?'

As they stood, Ariadne looped an arm around her shoulders and they walked like this in silence toward the 4x4. And even though they were silent, Lizzie had never felt so close to her grandmother. Everything was out in the open now. No secrets. No hiding. She'd even told her about the silver shadow in the house over dinner and Ariadne's eyes had flashed with surprise and something else Lizzie couldn't place, but she'd said nothing. Nevertheless it was good to share. And this feeling of complete transparency between them made her feel more connected to her than ever. As if they could share anything. When had she ever sat under the stars with mum? When was the last time she'd gone for a walk with her? Or talked about anything other than school or homework or boring stuff like that?

She stopped in her tracks.

'What's up?'

She couldn't see her that clearly in the dark. Which was just as well because she felt strange and awkward saying the next words. They weren't something that came freely to her.

Articulation of emotion.

'I love you' she said at last.

And even though it was dark and she couldn't see Ariadne's face, she knew she was smiling.

The journey home didn't take long. Lizzie must have dozed off because before she knew it they were driving over the rutted track of *Casa del Sol.*

'What the...?' Ariadne muttered as they turned the corner and saw every light in the *finca* turned on. The back door hung off its hinges. A dozen or so cars cluttered the dirt track. And people. People everywhere. Sprawled all over the terrace. Sat on car bonnets. Scattered in the herb garden. A couple pressed up against the almond tree in front of them. The girl's skirt hitched up.

'A party,' Ariadne groaned. 'The little minx is having a party.'

Chapter Twenty-five

Someone shouted something in Spanish. A glass smashed. The music got cranked up.

And somewhere in the midst of this was Bee.

Centre stage, as always, on the courtyard. Dancing. A bottle of wine hanging out of one hand. Barefoot. Wearing Ariadne's emerald coloured head-scarf. Bee was framed in the yellow light which splashed out from the kitchen. She didn't have much else on. Her white bikini and even then, one of the straps had fallen off her shoulder. She wasn't just doing any old dance either. She was belly-dancing, Lizzie realized. Thrusting her hips one way and then the next. Wiggling. Shaking. Laughing.

She could do it too. That was the thing about Bee. She carried off most things that other girls could only dream of.

Someone cheered. Hard to see who it was. Carlos? A hand reached out and grabbed her thigh. Bee slid away and giggled. Poured some wine into his up-turned mouth. Another hand reached out and grabbed her other thigh. It caught her this time and she stumbled. Fell on the group of boys.

Their hands snuck out like octopuses. Reaching, grabbing, feeling, touching, groping. She shrieked. Tried to stand up. Laughed. Fell back down again. Someone cheered. Her white bikini top was thrown to the ring.

'That's enough.' She wasn't sure where she found her voice but it roared up from somewhere. It had a habit of doing that lately. Lizzie strode forward.

They didn't notice her at first. The kitchen light cut just as Lizzie neared the terrace. She moved as if in slow-motion. Everything had an edge to it. The boys laughing. The sudden sound of Bee's yelp as Lizzie yanked her out.

'Cover yourself up.'

One of the boys shouted again. Lizzie shouted back.

'This is not your house. Go home! Just go home ALL of you.'

They all shut up then. Perhaps they were surprised at someone yelling to them in English. Some of them started to get up. Just shadows. Lizzie couldn't make out who. Seconds later the music was turned off. A limp hush fell over the party. One by one they edged towards their cars.

Lizzie caught sight of the couple by the trees. She strode over. It was one of Carlos' lookalike friends. What was his name? Marcos? And some Spanish girl she didn't recognize. Lizzie saw they left something behind. She looked closer.

'Take that with you!' she spluttered.

Marcos looked down at the base of the tree. He had the decency to look embarrassed and picked up the condom wrapper and put it in his pocket.

He shrugged.

People started to emerge from their hiding places and headed toward their cars. 'Don't step on the rosemary,' Ariadne yelled. 'Will someone please turn the lights back on?'

As the terrace sprung into light, Bee side-stepped toward Carlos' Mazda. She stood sullenly by the bonnet. Each time someone came out of the house, blinking nervously and avoiding looking at Ariadne, Bee made a point of rolling her eyes and apologizing that the party had ended. They climbed four, five each into the cars. Drove off quickly.

Carlos climbed into the car. Bee half-heartedly kissed him goodbye on the lips.

'Where's Lizzie?' she asked. '*Where's* the spoilsport?'

Over here. She wanted to say. But she couldn't. Her mouth was dry. Her head pounded. With one hand she clutched onto the almond tree. She knelt and didn't feel the harsh scrape of the dirt graze her knees.

How long passed?

Dimly, she was aware of the last car leaving.

She hauled herself up, clutching, holding the tree for support.

A splinter of bark sliced into her thumb and a perfect pearl of blood wobbled on her skin. It zoomed into focus, sharp and clear, whilst everything faded to muted colours.

The droplet of blood teetered on the edge of her thumb.

'Lizzie?'

She snapped her head up. Ariadne had called out. She stood on the terrace, looking out to the orchard. She was still bathed in light, illuminated by light, shining with light.

And above her head was a black mark.

Chapter Twenty-six

At first she thought it was a mirage. A trick of the light. An illusion. Anything but the truth. Because the truth hurt too much.

She rubbed her eyes. She looked away, she looked back. She said a silent prayer. Anything to transform this moment into something else.

But the truth remained.

The black mark sat above Ariadne's head like a swarm of locusts. It was the colour of ebony and the shape of a hawk. It flew above her grandmother's head like an omen.

Lizzie ran.

It was the only thing she wanted to do. The only way to quell the pain. To run and keep running. Inside it felt as though a jigsaw set was being dismantled. Piece by jagged piece ripped apart from each other. Disappearing somewhere. Down that dark hole where thoughts of Joopy lay undisturbed. A simple wooden cross. Blood on the road. A pain in her heart.

As she ran her chest burnt. It ached. It was so tight. It hurt.

She ran and kept running until she tripped over a rock and went flying. She thudded to the ground.

She stayed there for about five minutes. Flat on the ground. A headache. Grazed knees. The wind knocked out of her. The rock was grainy. Tufts of weed grew out of it. An insect scuttled.

She cried. She couldn't help it. It was like Joopy dying all over again. That sense of losing something. A sharpness in her chest. Pain. Coming from her heart. So open and raw. Except this time she cried silently. No-one could hear how much she hurt. And this made it harder. She pressed her arms against herself. Holding onto her chest. She opened her mouth but nothing came out. Everything was wedged inside. Deep inside in that place where life was unfair.

'Not Ariadne. Please *not* Ariadne!'

She lay there until the light turned grey, all the time, watching the sky and trying to make sense of it all. But unable to. All she had were questions that she could only hurl uselessly at the dimming stars.

'Why?' she cried out. 'Why now?'

The stars couldn't answer, of course, they merely faded out of sight. She was left with a warm dawn morning and an empty sky.

It was time to go back.

She crept back down the hill, heavy-footed, weighed down by her knowledge. The cockerel crowed dawn as she approached. Empty bottles and cans were still strewn about the driveway and terrace so she grabbed a bin liner and item by item, chucked them in. Activity helped ease her churning mind. When this was complete, she took stock of the damaged herbs and flowers. Some crushed stems, a trampled mint plant, cigarette butts. She cleaned this as much she could. Then she watered. When she was busy the thoughts slipped to the edges.

* * *

'Up early.' Ariadne appeared from the kitchen holding two cups of tea.

She swallowed the lump in her throat and nodded.

'Everything ok?' Ariadne came up to her shoulder. So close she could smell the lavender. See the *thing* out of the corner of her eyes. 'You've been out all night again, haven't you?'

She must look a state.

'Try not to think too much about Rafa and Bee.'

She didn't know whether to laugh or cry! Ariadne thought she was still upset about that, but that was nothing, *nothing*! To how she felt now!

'Some homecoming. Well done you for breaking up the party,' Ariadne commented picking up a couple of cigarette butts Lizzie had missed. 'You needn't have cleared up though. Bee has to take responsibility at some point.'

Oh God! Bee. She'd managed to completely forget about her. But what if Bee found out? Worse! What if Bee told Ariadne?

'I can't believe she had a party,' Lizzie murmured, looking not at Ariadne, but at the jasmine. How she even managed to talk normally, she didn't know. But the words came out evenly and she breathed a sigh of relief.

'I can,' Ariadne chuckled. 'I wouldn't put anything past that girl.'

Out of the corner of her eye, she saw Ariadne's fingers pinch off some dead geranium heads. Old hands. Spotted with age. How had she not seen how old her hands were before?

'That girl has a lot of growing up to do.'

Lizzie had a flash to the bikini. The belly-dancing. The moment when Bee fell and her bikini top was ripped off. She'd forgotten all that. It all seemed so unimportant now. If Bee wanted to behave that way, let her. If she wanted guys to drool over her, let her. Including Rafa. If that's the kind of girl he liked, good riddance. But Rafa hadn't been at the party. Bee had been all over Carlos.

Rafa.

Should she tell him?

She tightened her hand on the hose. Ariadne was talking about something or other. At first she couldn't catch hold of the conversation. A party she was planning to have at the house next Saturday. That was it. Ariadne had arranged a gathering for close friends and family before Rafa left for Cordoba. He was leaving in about ten days time. Ariadne would die in seven. The day of the party.

How could she tell Rafa? Ariadne was like a grandmother to him. It would destroy him. What about Gabriel? Should she tell her mum? Should she tell Ariadne? What was she supposed to do?

'Everything ok, Lizzie?'

Lizzie stopped the hose. Took a deep breath and turned to face her. She *could* do this. She *could* conceal something. Even something as huge as this. Didn't she have the kind of face Ariadne said was hard to read? If she didn't look at the thing even though it screamed at her out of her peripheral vision, she could do it. Not only would she *not* look, she would try to act as normal as possible.

And it worked. They sank into their habitual watering routine and chattered about the meal last night, Bee's party and whether Ariadne would tell the Buckingham's (no) and also about Cordoba.

Then, as soon as the plants were watered and Lizzie was out of sight, she ran to the bathroom and splashed her face with cool water. As she rested her forehead against the porcelain of the sink, the realization sunk in again.

No more Ariadne. She was going to die and she had one only week left to live.

Lizzie's insides screamed in denial. How someone with so much life could die? *How*? She was the most colorful person she had ever met! The woman who had travelled the world, the woman with a million facial expressions, with the life force of a sun, the woman who had been loved so much she'd had mirrors made to capture her face, the woman who lived in freedom, the woman who had taught her freedom.

She would die.

What was she supposed to do? Ariadne wasn't Joopy. She couldn't prop her under her arm and carry her around. She couldn't even follow her around. Sure she could keep a watchful eye on her but Ariadne wasn't a dumb animal. All she could do was make sure that her final few days were enjoyable. She had denied Joopy that but she could give it to her grandmother.

She could give her grandmother a beautiful few days. And what was it that Ariadne had said? A peaceful passing. She splashed her face with more water and went to her bedroom and stood by the window.

How much had changed since that first day here.

'Lizzie?'

'Rafa!'

He stood in the doorway holding the torch she'd dropped the other night.

'This is yours, no?' He frowned when he saw her. '*Que pasa*?'

'Nothing...' she rubbed her eyes and hoped they weren't puffy. Rafa was here in her bedroom? 'Where's Bee?'

'How should I know?' Rafa laughed. 'I came to see you.'

A flame inside her flickered back to life. 'Me?'

He stepped into the room and she got a waft of his sweet, earthy smell. She sat down on the bed and tried to breathe.

'You want to come to the beach?'

A million things ran through her head. But the loudest thought of all was that Rafa was here, stood in her bedroom, looking at her with a playful smile on his lips.

'Come with me. I take you on the bike.'

'I can't go.... Ariadne.' She tailed off.

'She tell me to take you.'

'Really?'

'Yes. She said you have not swum in the sea yet, well not for pleasure, and that I must take you before the end of summer.'

The end of the summer. The words sliced through her.

Rafa stepped closer until he stood in front of her on the bed. He wore a red T-shirt and black surf shorts. The heat rolled off him.

'Don't you want to go to the beach with Bee?' She held onto her breath and felt her cheeks flame as she said it.

'I did not come to see Bee.'

'No?'

'No,' he said softly. 'I came to see you.'

Chapter Twenty-seven

'Me?' she stammered.

'Yes, Ariadne said to me yesterday to come over.'

'Oh.' So he hadn't come to see her at all, he'd come because Ariadne had *asked* him to. She tried to quell the huge wave of disappointment that threatened to engulf her.

'And Bee hate the bike.'

'She hates dirt, that's why,' she said flatly. 'She doesn't like to get her hands mucky.'

'Mucky? What is mucky?'

Lizzie sighed. 'It's not important.'

Rafa stepped forward. 'Felipe is taking the car. He can take her.'

'Felipe is coming too?' She remembered the scent of his after-shave and his hand on hers. *Great*. Another opportunity to play gooseberry.

She sighed and stood up, looking back out the window, watching Ariadne tidy the herb garden. 'No.'

Rafa joined her at the window. 'You say no to my invitation again? I ask you the first day and you say no and now you say no again.'

'And the reason why is exactly the same.' Lizzie exclaimed. 'I'm here to spend time with my grandmother.'

'But Ariadne she *wants* you to go. She ask me to take you.'

Lizzie looked at him. 'Are you sure?'

Rafa nodded and Lizzie tried hard to ignore the fluttering in her chest as he stared at him.

'Lizzie?' Bee hammered at the door.

Both their heads snapped toward the door. On Rafa's face was an expression she couldn't read.

'Lizzie! I know you're in there. Just answer me. Have you seen my white bikini? I need it for the beach.'

Lizzie yanked the door open. Bee stood wrapped in a towel with another towel wrapped around her head like a turban. On her face was a thick clay mask. She looked at Lizzie. 'Well?'

Lizzie stepped aside and Bee's face dropped as she saw Rafa in the room. She opened her mouth two or three times but nothing came out.

'Try looking for it in the undergrowth? I think that's where you left most of your clothes last night.' She turned her back and grabbed her beach towel and some suntan lotion from her suitcase.

'*You're* coming too?' Bee's mask cracked into tiny splinters and flakes of clay fell from her face. 'But we can't *all* fit on the bike.'

'Felipe will come and collect you,' Rafa said with a smile on his lips. 'He will be here in half an hour.'

'Felipe?' Bee spluttered.

'Yes,' Lizzie smiled. 'You're going with Felipe. *I'm* going with Rafa.'

'*Fine*.' Bee spun round. 'I'll see you at the beach.'

* * *

Rafa's yellow bike sat waiting in the full glare of the sun, all shiny, hard and bright. It brought back memories of lying on the road.

'You are not scared?' he asked as they walked toward it. 'The last time you ride on my bike you fall off.'

'Not really.' She touched the hot metal and spoke quickly. 'That was the first day I heard you play.'

'I remember.' The corners of his mouth twitched upwards. 'You were shocked because you thought I was the gardener.'

'Are you surprised!' Lizzie turned to face him. 'You treat me like a goat when I fell off and then you go and play the guitar so … tenderly.'

'It touched you?'

She nodded, trying to quell the rage of emotions inside.

'You know in Spanish we do not "play" the guitar. The verb is *tocar*.' He ran his fingers down her forearm. 'It means to touch.'

Lizzie swallowed. 'You touch the guitar.'

'I touch you.'

She swallowed.

'I see it in your eyes that day. The first time you listen to me. You could not stop staring at me.'

She cringed. How embarrassing. How *novice*. Bee would never gawp at a guy so much he actually noticed her looking. She scuffed her toe against the rubber tyre.

'Shall we go?' he asked.

Lizzie paused. Ariadne had wanted her to go to the beach with Rafa so much she'd organized for it. Why had she done that? Since coming back from Cabo de Gato she'd been in that faraway dreamy mood. She looked around for her but she was nowhere to be seen.

'I think maybe she want to be alone,' Rafa said.

'She said that?'

Rafa nodded. 'Now will you come with me?'

Lizzie felt relieved. She hardly wanted to admit it to herself but she *wanted* to go to the beach with Rafa. A powerful draw in her belly pulled her toward him like a drug. She climbed onto the bike feeling the strength of it between her legs like a horse and wave of excitement rolled through her.

Nevertheless each kilometre they put between them and Ariadne felt disloyal, like an act of betrayal. She was leaving Ariadne when she needed her most. The conflicting array of feelings tore at her.

Half a dozen times she almost squeezed her knees harder into Rafa's thighs as a sign she wanted him to stop. But each time something held her back. Curiosity? Desire? Freedom? Adventure? Whatever it was, she tussled with it. And before she knew it, the landscape of Andalucia had flown by in a blur of avocado trees and a smudge of turquoise sea.

He rode fast but not as dangerous as last time.

She was aware of mountains. As if they were flying through the cleft of a valley. Tall and impenetrable. Rearing up one side of the road and leaning down the other. The coastline here was jagged. Less benign. Harsher.

Rafa took a sudden right turn down a dirt track. The bike skidded and stumbled and Lizzie held him tightly. She felt the contours of his stomach stretch. They nosed their way down a crumbling slope toward a sea which beckoned with sparkling fingers. Rafa stopped about a hundred yards short.

'We walk the rest.'

His eyes were dark and hard and she wished she knew what was going on under the surface. The friendly, playful Rafa had momentarily disappeared. This was the Rafa who always seemed so impenetrable. She hesitated. Unsure of what to do. The desire to touch his face was so powerful she clenched her fists. Oh, to reach out and soften out the hardness. To smooth out the lines. But she didn't. She kept her hands by her side and nodded.

'Come with me.'

He took her hand and led her down the dirt path.

Already her mouth was dry and dusty. She looked at her feet as they made their way down the slope. Chipped blue nail varnish from a different life. She didn't look up until she'd reached the bottom of the track and her toes had sunk into soft sand. The color of cream. Hot sand. Scolding.

She looked around her.

They stood alone in a perfect C-shaped cove. Sheltered on both sides by rocks, hidden from the road, perhaps only about fifty meters wide, if that. Absolute privacy and isolation. No sound other than the gentle lapping of the waves.

She'd never seen a sea so clear and calm before. Her first instinct was to move toward it. To feel it lap against her ankles. It was warm. Inviting. The sun drifted down.

For a moment she could forget the events of the past twelve

hours. Forget ever seeing the black mark. Forget that Ariadne was going to die.

'It's so beautiful,' she said and turned to look at Rafa.

Their eyes connected. Just a flash. But it was enough to rock her from top to bottom. The same way he'd looked at her in the storm. The same feeling that life had ripped her chest open and plucked out her beating heart. It made her feel alive. The heat rose to her cheeks and she felt her eyes widen. He stared at her so hard she thought he might climb into her.

She willed him to move closer. Willed him with every inch of her body.

For a minute she thought he would. Then he blinked.

'Are you hot?'

'What?'

'I say, are you hot?'

'Yeah… I guess so.'

'I go and buy water.' He shook his head and took a step back.

'Now?'

'I did not bring any with me.' He turned around and abruptly strode off back up the hill, as if he had all the energy in the world, and he jumped on his bike and went. Clouds of dust puckered the air.

She turned back to the sea. Had he been about to kiss her? Or was it all just in her imagination. She'd wanted him so badly. Now here she was back at the beach. Alone. She walked down to the water's edge.

What was it about water and death? Why were the two connected? Last time death had brushed her she had showered hard to get rid of the smell. The urge was the same. Something primeval, something powerful that pushed her toward water. As if water could cleanse it all away.

She tore off her top. Threw it in a heap on the sand. The same with her denim shorts. She ripped them off as quickly as she could. Wanting no part of it. Wanting to be free. To be clean. The pull of the sea was magnetic. She kept on her bra and knickers and ran into the water. Knee high. Not stopping. Waist high. Diving in. Feeling the water stream over her. Not caring now. Just diving under and under again. Underwater. Where none of this seemed so real. Feeling the water press against her skin. Wanting to *be* the water. Wanting to forget.

She didn't hear the bike.

Didn't see him on the beach.

She only became aware of him when she saw him underwater. A bronzed body, swimming toward her, his hair floating outward. Like a sea lion she thought to herself. He grabbed her underwater. By the waist. Circled his arms around her and held her tight.

They broke the surface of the water at the same time. Sea streaming off them. His hair had flattened against his head. It made his face look more angular. Older. The sun beat off his skin. Naturally brown. Like he belonged in the water. Not smiling. Staring at her. Dark, hawk eyes. So dark she couldn't read them. She tasted the salt on her lips. Felt her skin tighten from the sea and the sun. The feel of the sun, naked on her shoulders and chest, felt intimate. Like she was doing something she oughtn't do. At the same time, it felt natural, like her body was a fruit and needed the sun to ripen.

And she wished this moment could last forever.

He kissed her hard on the lips.

He kissed her as if there was no other way to kiss. So hard it almost hurt. So intense she felt herself explode into a maelstrom of emotion.

And so, *this* is what it feels to be alive.

They kissed and she tasted salt and it stung. They kissed again and their tongues clashed. They kissed even harder and he pulled her tighter still. She felt something inside of her she had never felt before. The strength of the sun on her head, the taste of salt in her mouth, the sensation of her body against his, all of it wild, instinctual, animal. She'd never been in this position before but somehow she knew exactly what to do. All she had to do was follow her own urges. She squeezed her legs tighter still. And this in itself brought a fresh wave of pleasure. And she pressed tighter still.

He groaned. Kissed her deeper. A wave came and rolled over them. But they didn't stop. His hand massaged her back. Firm. Strong. He grabbed her hair and pulled it back. It was her turn to moan. He kissed her neck. The part which was exposed. Rubbed his lips against her collar bone. Pulled her tighter still. Closer. Harder.

Then he stopped.

He abruptly let go. Dipped his head back in the water. Swore in Spanish. And without looking at her, swam slowly back to shore. She watched as he rose out of the water. His bare back. Brown. Walking across the sand where he flopped by the rocks.

She trod water for a while.

Then turned on her back and floated. Looked up at the sun. Felt her breathing settle. She felt ashamed. What had she been thinking? She wasn't thinking, was she? Just acting on some instinct. Would she have stopped him? She floated as long as she could. Until her toes and fingers crinkled. Until she knew she was burning.

Then she slowly swam to shore. Picked up her clothes and pulled them on even though she was soaking and they clung awkwardly to her.

He lay on his back in the shade of a rock. His back was bronzed and taut. It was all she could do to stop herself reaching out and stroking him. How smooth his skin looked.

She dropped down next to him and hugged her knees awkwardly. Neither of them spoke for what felt like eternity. Even if she could speak, she wouldn't know what to say.

'You are burnt,' he said at last.

'I know. I always burn on my nose.'

He cleared his throat. 'You ok?'

She nodded.

'You are not ok are you?' He sat up. Sand clung to one side of his cheek and his hair stood out in crazy angles. He raised his hands and then dropped them. 'I am sorry.'

She drew her legs closer to her chest.

He went to touch her and stopped. 'It is my fault. I got . . . distracted.'

Saltwater dripped off her hair and stung her eyes. 'We didn't do anything. Not really.'

'No.' He picked up a handful of sand and poured it through his fingers. Neither spoke again. The atmosphere was worse than one of mum's moods. Lizzie swallowed.

'Did you get the water?'

Rafa threw his head back and laughed, so loud it echoed round the cove. 'You are funny, *inglesa*.'

'What?' she said, looking up.

'You still do not get it, do you?'

'Get what?'

He had that same bemused expression in his eyes. The same one he always had. And something darker too. Stronger. She found herself staring into them. Endlessly.

He tipped her chin gently up and then she felt his lips lightly brush against hers. Soft and sweet.

'Get what?' she murmured as her heart beat impossibly fast.

'How much I want you.'

And they kissed for the second time. And the third and the fourth. And this time it was sweet and tender and gentle. As light as his fingers on the guitar. The way his lips touched hers, they way they played on her face.

The way she felt inside.

And as the sun rose like an arch in the sky and as its light grew more golden, the afternoon was the sweetest Lizzie had ever known. She wished it would last forever.

'I had water in my bike all the time,' Rafa murmured. They lay entwined on the beach, arms and legs criss-crossed. Sand clung to them. Both their hair was matted with sand. Neither cared.

'You mean you didn't go to get water?'

'No.'

'Then why did you go?'

'Because I knew if I stay here, *this* would happen.' Rafa leant over and cradled her face softly in his hands. 'I would attack you.'

'And what's wrong with that?!' she giggled.

'*Nada.* It is only that I go to Cordoba and then you go to England. We are like this, how do you say, two forks.' He separated his hands and smiled such a bittersweet smile Lizzie's heart almost broke. 'I battle with myself if it is good idea to start something with you but...'

'But what?' Lizzie leant forward so she was millimetres from his face.

'But I cannot stop myself.'

He closed the gap between them and they kissed so hard and so long Lizzie felt something pressing on her insides like an ache. She pulled away to catch her breath. With his hand, he cradled her face so she couldn't look away.

'It is powerful, no? This feeling.'

She nodded. 'Is it always like this? So *intense*?'

'It is like flamenco. So passionate it comes from the soul.' He ran his thumb along her jawline. 'I never have it like this before. What have you done to me, *inglesa*?'

Lizzie felt inordinately pleased she had released something new in Rafa. She felt more connected to him that way, as if they shared a secret. 'Is it normal though . . . to feel like this?'

Rafa laughed. 'I do not know if it is normal but it is very good, no?'

Lizzie laughed too and leant forward and kissed him. Now

she was in his arms, it was easy. It felt like home. She snuggled closer and trailed her fingers along the curve of his waist. He smiled lazily.

'I want you the first time I see you,' he breathed into her ear. The feeling was hot and sweet and so unnerving she pushed him away. 'What's wrong?'

'You make me feel things,' she stammered.

He pulled her closer. 'I am sorry Lizzie. You are like a drug. When I am around you I feel on fire.' He took her palm and pressed it against his chest. She could feel the thudding of his heart. 'I want you the first time I see you. By that door, you remember?'

'Yes,' she whispered. 'I remember.'

'You don't know that but I stand and watch you a bit from a distance. You are like a wild animal trying to break into that door. There is something about you I want. Something I do not understand myself. Only that it is there in my body and it has not gone since.'

'Me too. When I saw you play for the first time I wanted you so much.'

He smiled. 'You remember on the beach when you are dancing with Carlos? I am so jealous I want to throw him into the sea.'

She giggled. 'I didn't feel *anything* with him though.' She took his hand and placed it around her waist as she edged closer to him. 'I only ever feel things with you. Sometimes they're too much. It's all so new to me.'

'And so we take it slow, *inglesa*. There is no rush.'

'But you're going! You said yourself we are like two forks. We don't have much time left!'

Rafa pulled her gently toward her. 'We always have right now. That is the only time there is.'

She rested her cheek against his chest.

'But why me? I thought you liked Bee.'

Rafa laughed. 'You think I like a girl like that?' He pulled her closer. 'You are crazy.'

'She likes you,' Lizzie muttered and then buried her face into his neck so he couldn't see how red she'd gone. 'I *thought* you liked her. I heard her...'

'I knew it was you,' he sighed. 'Bee, she makes up her own stories no? She tell me things but I do not believe them. She is very false.'

Rafa prised her away from his neck and held her jaw in his hand. 'Look at me, *inglesa*. There are many girls like Bee in this world but there is only one you. It's *you* I like.'

She tried to stop herself from asking, but couldn't resist. 'But why?'

'Because you are not like the other girls. It is like you are not of this world almost.' He arched his back as her fingers trailed across his tummy. 'You are different.'

Her heart missed a beat. He didn't know just how different she was. She toyed with telling him about the black marks. If there was a moment, now was it. But who knew how he would react *especially* considering everything he had previously said about death. No. Not just yet. Surely she was allowed to have this moment with him? Just like any other normal girl.

'You want me to tell you all the beautiful things that you are? You need that?'

Lizzie shook her head. 'I'm not like Bee. I don't need the compliments,' she murmured trying to pretend that she actually meant it.

'I will tell you anyway because most of the girls they like to know how special they are. Because you stand in a storm and you love it and you don't run away because you are scared you get wet. Because you ride on a bike like a boy and you want to go faster. Because you have beautiful eyes which are not afraid to look at people. Because you feel things from the heart. Because under your calm face I know you are like fire inside.' He leant closer and rubbed his finger along her cheekbone. '*Because* I can't keep my hands off you.'

He kissed her with a gentleness that took her breath away. He kissed her like he was playing music. It was tender and it was pure. She wished it would never end and at the same time, at the back of her mind she knew that it must. As if he had read her mind, he looked up at the sky.

'We must go. It will get dark soon.'

She got to her feet reluctantly and as they walked hand in hand toward his bike, she mused on all the things he had said. She had never seen herself in that way.

She was all those things because if he saw them in her then they existed as truth. But there was one other thing she was too which Rafa did not know about.

He handed her the helmet and she pulled it over her head.

She was also a girl who could predict death and she couldn't hide forever.

Chapter Twenty-eight

He dropped her at the end of the track just as the sun whispered its last goodbye.

'You're not coming in?' She clung onto his hand knowing she was being clingy, but unable to let go. If she let go, the magic of today would disappear and worse, she would have to go back inside and sit across from Ariadne and pretend she couldn't see the black mark.

'I must go practice. Today has been full of distractions.'

'When will I see you again?'

Rafa smiled softly. 'I see you tomorrow, *inglesa.*' He leant forward and kissed her. 'And the day after that and the day after that. Every day until the party on Saturday.'

'And then what happens?'

He touched her hair. 'Remember what I say on the beach. We must keep living in the moment. It's what the Spanish do best. We do not think of tomorrow.'

But little did he know she could predict the future. The end was coming. Not just the end of summer, but the end of Ariadne. Selfishly, she wondered what would happen to them then. If Ariadne wasn't here, then how could she come back and visit? It was the end of everything.

She gripped his hand tighter.

'You ok?'

She switched herself back to the present. She couldn't let Rafa find out about the black marks. Not yet. Not in this precise moment in time anyway. Why spoil their day?

So she leant forward and kissed him hard on the lips. 'Goodnight!' she whispered and then before he could answer she ran off toward the house.

She flung open the kitchen door and the bright yellow light stung her eyes.

'Well, well, well. Look what the cat dragged in.' Bee stood with her hands on her hips in the centre of the kitchen and a sour expression on her face.

Lizzie shielded her eyes with her hand and ignored her. 'Where's Ariadne?'

'Probably concocting a witches brew for all I care! It's not *her* I care about. It's Rafa.' Bee stepped across the kitchen floor. Her face was pinched with two spots of colour on each cheek. She looked like she'd been crying. 'Why didn't he come back and get me?'

In all the fireworks of emotions on the beach, she had completely forgotten about Bee. Under her pink dress she was still wearing her white bikini and the strap marks had left red weals in the back of her neck. Lizzie tried to push past her.

'I said why didn't he come back and get me?!'

'He thought Felipe would bring you. That's why.' Lizzie tried to push past her again but Bee grabbed her wrist.

'Well he didn't, did he?'

'Let go of me! That hurts.'

Bee twisted her grip and Lizzie yelped.

'I waited *all* afternoon for you to come back. I sat here and waited and waited.'

'And?' Lizzie tried to pull her arm away but Bee yanked her closer.

'Why didn't he come back for me?'

Was her face still red from all the kisses? Did it show in her eyes what she'd been doing? Was the flame in her belly that obvious? A flare of rebellion rose up and she wrenched free.

'Maybe he was having such a good time with me he forgot all about you.'

Bee opened and closed her mouth. 'What do you mean?'

'I mean, maybe it's not *you* he likes.'

Bee leapt forward and grabbed a handful of Lizzie's hair. 'You're lying. He wouldn't go for a girl like you!'

Even though Bee had her twisted to her knees, Lizzie smiled. 'Wouldn't he?'

Bee pulled her hair tighter. 'It's *me* he likes not some ugly freako girl like you!'

Lizzie laughed even though her eyes stung.

'Couldn't wait, could you? You couldn't get your own boyfriend back in England so you thought you'd take mine here!'

'He wasn't your boyfriend!' Lizzie tried to shove Bee away but only ended up punching her accidentally in the stomach. Bee howled and wrenched Lizzie's shoulder so hard that both of them fell to the tiles.

'Get off me!'

Bee pushed her knees into Lizzie's arms and pinned her on the floor. Fighting from some primeval source, the same place that all the fire came from, Lizzie reared her head and tried to bite Bee's arms. Bee howled and jabbed her knee harder into Lizzie's biceps. Lizzie tried to bite her again. Both of them breathed hard and ragged.

'I bet Rafa doesn't know about you, does he? Not the *real* you.'

'At least there *is* a real me,' Lizzie spat.

'Am I interrupting something?'

Both girls looked up in surprise toward the doorway. Rafa leant against the frame, swathed in light, looking from Bee to Lizzie. In his hands he carried Lizzie's suntan lotion. He tossed it across the room. The bottle skimmed across the floor.

Lizzie squirmed under Bee and shoved her off. She flushed as she brushed the dirt off her clothes. Her heart thudded fast. How much had he heard?

Bee folded her arms and looked petulantly at Rafa. 'It's not true, is it?'

'What is not true?' Rafa stepped into the kitchen and moved toward them. Bee grabbed his arm and Lizzie almost snarled.

'That you're with *her*?' She pointed toward Lizzie.

There was a moment's silence in the room where the only

sound was the ticking of time. Lizzie held her breath.

'Yes,' he said looking pointedly from one girl to the other and finally resting his gaze on Lizzie. 'It is true.'

As Lizzie's heart soared in victory, Bee's face paled to that of a graveyard.

'You're with *Lizzie*?'

Rafa nodded.

Lizzie didn't even stop to wipe the smile off her face. She stepped forward and peeling Bee's fingers off his arm, she curled her own hand around his bicep.

Victory tasted sweeter than honey.

Bee's face caved in completely, like her world had been completely dismantled. But the moment was fleeting. From whatever place she was in, she crawled her way out of it and a cruel but familiar expression appeared. 'Have you told Rafa about your special *gift*?'

Lizzie felt her stomach churn. 'Shut up, Bee.'

'Why should I?' Bee smiled.

'Just because he doesn't want you doesn't mean you have to ruin it for me. That's why!'

'Why shouldn't I ruin it for you? You ruined my summer!'

'Exactly how have I ruined your summer?' Lizzie grabbed back hold of Rafa's arm for support, as if he were her statue, but somehow the feelings in the stomach wouldn't settle.

'I wouldn't even be here if it wasn't for you! It was your mum's idea to send me here.'

'You were the one who acted like a slut!'

The slap was sudden. A whoosh in the air and then a sudden sting on the side of Lizzie's face. She stumbled.

Rafa grabbed Bee by the shoulders. He swore at her in Spanish. God knows what he was saying but he shook her so hard she rattled.

'She's a freak, Rafa. She's a freak!'

'Rafa, let her go! Please!' Lizzie grabbed his arm.

Rafa reluctantly dropped her, but still glared at Bee. 'Why do you do that?'

Bee rubbed her shoulder. 'Ask her. *She's* the one who's got something to hide.'

'What do you mean?'

'She goes around pretending to be normal but she's not.'

'Bee! Don't!'

'Don't what? Don't tell him about you?'

Lizzie swallowed. Why did it have to be like this? Why couldn't she have just a *bit* longer with him?

'If you don't tell him, I will Lizzie Fisher.'

She covered her face with her hands but not before she saw Bee's smirk.

'There's something you don't know about me.'

'What do you mean?'

There was a long silence as Rafa stared at her. He shifted and she saw the moonlight glisten behind him. He spoke louder. 'What do you mean?'

She gulped. Her lips were cracked.

'A black mark,' she mumbled.

Rafa shook his head. 'I don't know what you are talking about.'

'I see black marks.' She pinched the top of her nose in an effort to stop her head going dizzy. 'Like Joopy. He had a black mark. So did Mrs Froust. And Hooper. They all had black marks.'

'What is a black mark?'

Bee snorted. 'Yeah, what *is* a black mark? I'm sure Rafa can't wait to find out.'

His fingers tightened on her wrist.

'It means…it means I can….'

'It means she can see when people are going to die.' All three heads snapped round. Ariadne stood in the hallway doorway with North curled up in her arms. She wore a purple, jewelled turban and an orange, floor-length gown. Her face was fully made-up with Cleopatra eyes and ruby red lips. She looked regally at each of them in turn and then drew a breath in to heighten herself.

'And that includes me.'

Chapter Twenty-nine

'You know?' Lizzie whispered.

Ariadne dropped North to the floor and took centre stage. 'Of course I know! I just wondered when *you* were going to see it too. That means it must be soon.'

'Saturday,' Lizzie murmured.

'Oh my God!' Bee screamed and grabbed the chair. 'You're going to die?'

'There's no need to be quite so dramatic, but yes, I am going to die.' Ariadne dropped North to the floor. 'In just a few days apparently if Lizzie's prediction is correct.'

'It's correct,' Lizzie said bitterly. 'It's *always* correct.'

'How?' Bee asked, her eyes bulging from their sockets. 'How's it going to happen?'

Ariadne frowned. 'As peacefully as possible, I'm hoping. A peaceful death is all one can hope for.'

'You are dying, *abuela*?'

Rafa stood still as a statue and had gone sheet white. Ariadne went up to him and rested a hand on his shoulder. She spoke to him in Spanish in a low soft voice, as if she were speaking to an animal, calming and soothing him. No matter. Rafa's face crumbled in seconds. The dark, angled lines literally lost their edges and his whole face became soft and immobile.

He looked broken.

'You knew this?' he turned to Lizzie. 'You knew this all afternoon? But you did not think to tell me as we lay on the beach that my grandmother is dying?'

Lizzie started. 'I....how could I have told you?'

'By telling the truth!' Rafa yelled so hard that Lizzie trembled. 'You tell me what is in here.' He jabbed her heart. 'You tell me what is in your heart! You do not hide things like this! Not from me. Not after this afternoon!'

Ariadne squeezed his shoulder. 'It's not her fault, Rafa.'

'You are joking, no?' he stared wildly at her. 'This is a sick joke.'

'No joke,' trilled Bee triumphantly 'All true. I told you she was unpopular at school. I told you we all called her freak. But you didn't listen to me. She saw when Mrs Froust was going to die and now this!' She stood up and pointed a finger toward Lizzie. 'Wherever you go, people die. What is it with you?'

'Bee!' Ariadne snapped.

'I don't care! She's a freak! I *hate* being around her.'

'Shut up Bee! Just shut up!' Lizzie ran to Rafa's side and took his arm. He roughly shook her off and glared at her. She had seen this exact same look before. It was the same look Nathan Parks had carried on his face that day in the playground when he had ruffled her hair for horns.

Her insides stiffened.

'Please Rafa!'

'Leave me alone!' he shouted. 'I thought you were brave. But you are not brave. Not here.' He touched his heart. 'Not where it is most important.'

'Rafa!' Lizzie heard her voice waver. 'I'm sorry.'

He punched the door frame so hard it rattled. Then he turned round and ran into the night. Lizzie went to follow him but Ariadne grabbed her shoulder.

'Leave him,' Ariadne said. 'Bee, you go.'

'Not her!'

Even Bee seemed surprised. 'Me? And what do I say to him?'

Ariadne squared up to Bee. 'Now is your chance to practice the art of compassion. That is all he needs right now.'

Bee hesitated.

'Just go!'

Lizzie tried to follow her but Ariadne held her back. 'No, Lizzie. Leave them.'

'But why her?' Lizzie cried.

'Because you lied to him, Lizzie.'

'I didn't lie! I just didn't tell him who I really was.'

Ariadne sighed sadly. 'Exactly.'

* * *

She didn't know how she got to her bedroom. There were vague memories of someone lifting her. Hauling her inside. Strong hands. Not Rafa's. The cool, sharp relief of a wet flannel pressed to her head. Some murmurs. This same person carried her to the bedroom. Laid her on the bed, gently closed the shutters and then sat with her whilst sleep came. Dreams drifted in and out of her like breath. Someone stood at the foot of the bed.

'Rafa.'

But the image disappeared and she knew it hadn't been Rafa at all. It had been that silver shadow thing. Except that thing wasn't scary any more. It felt safe. Just like her angel. Standing tall by the edge of her bed. Like a stone statue. Like an angel. A silver angel sparkling with a thousand twinkling lights. Filling her bedroom like the night sky.

'You know who you are,' he said. 'And you know what you have to do.'

Then he was gone. Like a wisp of air on an aisle seat.

And she told herself it was just a dream.

So she slept and she dreamt of London. It was a vivid dream of her house back home. She was in the kitchen watching Mum make lasagne. Mum was layering the egg pasta on the meat and she looked up and saw Lizzie watching. Instead of scolding her for staring at her, Mum started to cry. She opened her mouth and said her name.

'Lizzie?'

Lizzie wanted to run across the cool kitchen tiles and throw herself into her arms. But she couldn't move. She was glued to the floor. Mum kept staring at her whilst tears streamed down her cheeks.

'Hello, Lizzie.'

She woke up from the dream to see Ariadne sat next to the bed with a detective novel in her hands. She rubbed her eyes. The black mark was still there. Darker than ever before. She must have been staring because Ariadne ran a hand above her head.

'Tell me what it looks like.'

'The black mark?'

'Of course the black mark! What else could I possibly mean?'

'It looks like a bird,' Lizzie started.

'Go on.'

'You're not afraid?'

Ariadne laughed. 'Why should I be afraid?'

'Because you're going to die! That's why!'

Ariadne grasped her hand. 'And why should I be afraid of that?'

'Because *everyone's* afraid of dying!'

'Everyone?'

Lizzie tried to struggle upright. 'OK, most people then. Don't you think about what happens after?'

'Of course, but who can really know, Lizzie?' Ariadne plucked at the fabric of her skirt. 'I try not to question it too much.'

'But how can you not question it?!' Lizzie thought back to Milton Graveyard. The questions that used to run through her head. What happened when you died. Where you went. If anything existed afterward.

'If you question, you take away the mystery.'

'But I thought you loved mysteries!'

'Oh I do!' Ariadne grinned. 'And I can't wait to find out how this one ends.'

Lizzie slumped back down. How could Ariadne be so … matter of fact about it? Just the thought of losing her make her own heart weep. She brushed away the tears which threatened. 'I don't want you to die.'

'Oh, Lizzie,' Ariadne grasped Lizzie's hands in her own. Her skin was papery and dry. An old woman's clasp. 'It's my time and fighting time is always a losing battle.'

It didn't make her feel any better. It didn't take away the lump in her throat. It didn't take away the feeling she'd last had when Joopy had the black mark. Death hurt. It hurt a lot.

'The only people who are afraid of dying are those people who haven't lived.' Ariadne gazed around the room with a huge, infectious smile on her face. 'And Lizzie, have I lived! I've had the fullest life anyone could ever hope for.'

'How did you find out?'

'The *medico* told me in a check-up in March.'

'But what is it?'

'An aortic aneurism. Which basically means a swollen blood vessel in the heart which could burst at any time.'

'Can't they do anything about that? Surely there's operations?'

Ariadne nodded. 'Yes there are. But they caught it late and the operation is not without its own risks. I could choose to die on the operating table or I can choose to go peacefully here in the place where I love.' Ariadne nodded toward the open window. 'It's my time.'

'But you've only got days!'

'Well, I'd better make the most of them then.' She smiled cheekily. 'The irony of it being my heart that is failing is not lost on me. I rather suspect I have worn it out. But better that than not to have used it at all.'

Lizzie nodded. It didn't make the coil of anger go away but what was the point? If she had learnt one thing this summer, it was not to fight her emotions. It would be wiser to spend these last few days enjoying her time with her grandmother than battling against the inevitable.

Ariadne ran her hand above her head again. 'I can't feel it at all. Tell me again what it looks like so I can see it.'

'It's as black as ebony,' Lizzie said softly. 'And it moves too. Like it has its own dance.'

'Doesn't it ever change colour?'

'No, not that I've seen.'

'Pity.' Ariadne brushed her hand above her head again 'I rather think a multi-colored one would be more fun, don't you?'

Lizzie smiled despite herself. 'What are you going to do...?' she trailed off, not knowing how to answer.

'With my last few days, you mean?'

She nodded.

'Enjoy them!' Ariadne sprung to her feet. 'Spend time with the people I love in the place I love most of all.' She swept her hand toward the window. 'Here.'

'That's all? You don't want to go anywhere special?'

Ariadne shook her head. 'There's only one place for me now and that's home.'

'And have you thought about Saturday?'

'My death-day you mean?! Oh, I've been planning the party all summer, although I must be honest, I had no real idea of which day I would go.' She laughed. 'I have to say my timing is impeccable. Fingers crossed I last till the evening because that means we can have lunch with all my favourite foods and then in the afternoon Rafa can play for us and then I thought I would go up there.' She motioned toward the tree of life. 'That's a nice place to say goodbye to this world, don't you think?'

Lizzie gulped. 'It's perfect.'

'I think so too. It's a perfect death.'

'There's just one thing....'

Ariadne looked across.

'What about mum?'

The air thickened.

Ariadne sat back in her seat and said nothing for a few moments. 'I wrote to your mother a few months ago. It was the first letter I'd written in nearly five years.'

Lizzie remembered the unopened letter on the kitchen surface. Had mum thrown it away?

'I thought, at first, when you came out here it was because of that. Your mother's way of communicating with me. Perhaps even forgiving me. It was just a silly argument, have I told you that? But time has a way of building things up into something they're not.' Ariadne ran her fingers over the dresser. 'But when you came out I realized straight away you didn't know at all.'

'What did you tell her?'

'Just the medical terminology. When and how I got diagnosed, how long I had left, that kind of thing.'

'You have to invite her out!'

Ariadne sighed. 'She won't come, Lizzie.'

'If you phone her yourself and ask her, she will!'

Ariadne shook her head.

'But there's still time! You've got four more days.'

'Time is irrelevant. We've had *years*, Lizzie.' Ariadne shrugged. 'Enough of me. Tell me what happened with Rafa. Why didn't you tell him?'

Lizzie sunk back down on her pillow. 'How could I? He would have hated me!'

'And he doesn't now?' Ariadne raised an eyebrow. 'Oh Lizzie, why do you think I asked him to take you to the beach?'

'So that's why you arranged it! But why?'

'Because I didn't want to leave this planet without knowing he would look after you.' She sighed. 'Everyone needs someone to protect them and the Romero family do make rather good guardian angels.'

Lizzie pictured Gabriel's kind face and the way he fussed over Adriane. She blushed. 'I thought you just wanted us to ... you know, get together.'

Ariadne knitted her brows together. 'You've got all the time in the world for that! No I thought you might open up and tell him. I know Rafa.' Ariadne took Lizzie's hand. 'He wouldn't have turned you away. Not someone like him. If for one moment I thought he would, well I wouldn't have sent you there.'

'It's too late now.' Lizzie brushed away the tears that threatened. 'I've blown it.'

Ariadne sat in silence for such a long time, Lizzie thought she wouldn't speak. 'Not necessarily.'

Chapter Thirty

She waited by the wooden door where they'd first met. It wasn't just coincidence that she'd organised to meet him here. It was the only place she knew where Bee wouldn't interrupt them. She'd sent a message via Ariadne to Rafa to meet her here at midday. She had no idea if he would come or not.

How long ago it seemed, that day they'd first met. When she'd been trying to break into this door. He'd told her he wanted her then. Looking back, had she wanted him too? Not on the surface because she couldn't get past the smell of goat. But something inside had clicked. She'd had a strong physical reaction to him. So much so it was as if her body had a mind of its own.

She rubbed the top right panel with her forefinger.

'Lizzie.'

She jumped out of her skin. 'You're here!'

Rafa was wearing a black T-shirt and shorts. Did he ever wear anything other than black or red? Her breath caught in her throat.

'What do you want?'

'I want to tell you the truth,' she said in a small voice.

He knitted his brows even closer together. 'It is a bit late for the truth, no?'

'I'm sorry.'

'Sorry for what?'

'I'm sorry I didn't tell you about me before.'

'No?'

Against the bright glare of the sun he was a silhouette, she couldn't even see his face. So she imagined he was the stone statue. It made it easier to speak. To pour it all out. To pretend noone else was listening.

'I didn't know about Ariadne until the night of the party. I swear. I only found out that night about ... about her dying.'

'And?'

'And I never know what to do with the black marks, who to tell or who not to tell. I don't understand why I can see them. But I can see them and maybe I always will and…'

'You saw one of these black marks with Hooper, no?'

She nodded. 'Yes.'

'That's how you know that night that he is in the water.'

She nodded again.

'Why didn't you tell me the truth?' he sighed. 'Why could you not trust me? Why these lies?'

'They weren't lies!' she muttered.

'No, but you were not being *you*.'

Lizzie wiped her brow and wished she didn't feel so hot. 'I didn't want to tell you because I was afraid you wouldn't like me. Everyone in my school in England, well they, they didn't like me, ok? Not when they found out about my . . . ability. So when I came here I wanted to start again. I just wanted to be normal.'

'*You* normal?'

She nodded. 'I thought you might like me more…if I was normal.'

Was his voice softer or was she just hoping that it was? '*Inglesa*, you are never normal even when you pretend to be.'

Her heart contracted and squeezed and a chasm of light opened up.

'But…'

And then faded.

'But you see death, no?'

She hesitated. 'I see when people are *going* to die.'

Rafa stared at her and something in his eyes made her stomach flip. 'I wish you could trust me and tell me earlier.'

'You don't think I am a freak?'

'No. You have a gift like I have a gift for guitar. Like Ariadne has a gift for making friends. Even Bee, she have a gift because she is so pretty. We all have gifts in this life, Lizzie. It is just your gift is different and that is what makes you special.'

Lizzie held her breath. 'So?'

Rafa stared at her a long time. 'But I am sorry I cannot be with you.'

'Why not?' The words came out before she could stop it. She wished she hadn't sounded as wretched as she felt. 'Because I didn't tell you about Ariadne?'

'That I do not like, but I can forgive. I know why you did. Perhaps I would do the same.... but....'

'Is it because you don't believe in things like this?' She knew she was beginning to sound desperate but she didn't care. 'You said you didn't think there was a God or anything.'

'No. It is not that. Just because I believe one thing does not mean I cannot respect another.' He paused. 'It is you.'

'Me?' she whispered.

'Yes.'

'But *why*?'

He took her hands and squeezed them. 'You want to know?'

No. Yes. No.

'Tell me,' she whispered hoarsely.

'It is because you do not listen to the song in your heart.'

Whatever she was expecting she wasn't expecting that.

'What do you mean?' she stammered.

She could see him fighting for the right words. 'It is hard to explain it, but the heart of flamenco, you must understand, is that we feel things from here.' He patted his heart and then reclaimed her hands. 'This is where my music comes from. It comes direct from the truth in our hearts. You know that, *inglesa*. I teach you that. And so I ask myself since I find out . . . can I be with someone like you?' He gently took his hands back and she felt cold. 'And the answer is no. I cannot be with someone who is not honest to the song in their heart. I *cannot*. You understand?'

It was the longest speech she had ever heard him make.

The moment stilled to nothing.

'You don't want me?' she whispered, finally feeling the truth of herself seep into her soul.

He pulled away. 'I am sorry, *inglesa*. It is not that I don't want you. It is more I do not know you.'

* * *

After he had disappeared back into oleander, she sank to her knees. There were no tears left. Only bitter regrets. She wished many things but most of all she wished she could go back in time and reverse what she had said. Or *hadn't* said.

She sat like that for a long time.

It wasn't until a rare cloud passed in front of the sun that she realized she hadn't moved. Her knees were stiff and her heart was heavy. She wondered listlessly what she should do next. It was like she was losing everyone close to her.

For comfort, she drew an outline of an angel in the dirt.

'You were the only person I ever told the whole truth to,' she murmured. 'I felt safe around you.'

Ironically if she had told the whole truth to Rafa she'd still be with him. Her heart felt like it was breaking. Again. But as she looked at her clumsy angel sketch a feeling of strength entered her body and she realized with a shot that she couldn't let herself fall apart. Not now. If she fell apart, if she drowned in self pity about Rafa, if she cried out to the heavens, she'd miss out on the last week of Ariadne's life. And that would be another regret. No. She wasn't about to make another mistake. She pulled herself upright. It might be too late for Rafa but it wasn't too late for Ariadne.

She pushed the wooden door wide open so the sunlight flooded in. She rubbed her eyes and blinked. Once upon a time she'd been afraid of this hallway. But today, whatever spooky presence used to haunt it seemed to have disappeared. The hallway felt just like any other part of the house, albeit dusty and unused. Briefly, she wondered where *it* had gone, but then something caught her eye.

Her reflection.

For the first time in her life she properly looked at herself. Not just at the surface but if she were looking for gold.

She looked pale, like a moon. Ethereal almost. Something silvery, not quite human about her. Had she always looked like this? Like she didn't even belong to this world.

She looked at herself and saw herself for who she truly was.

'This is who I am.'

Was she really so bad?

Or was she perfect just the way she was? She had a gift, a very unusual gift, maybe it had come from the angels and maybe not. But regardless of how it had got to her, it was waiting to be used. She pulled her shoulders back and stood tall. She would make a vow to herself. Yes. Whatever happened from this point onwards, she would always listen to the truth in her heart and use her gift, no matter what people thought of her. Especially people like Bee.

Now she had decided who to be, what to do was easy.

One by one she unhooked the mirrors off the wall and carried them outside in the afternoon sun. Once they were all stacked up neatly against the wall, she grabbed some cloth and some cleaning fluid from the kitchen and polished every single one until they shone.

It took hours.

Once she had finished with the last mirror, the sun was already setting and each mirror radiated the dying embers of the sky.

Tomorrow she would put them up around the house where they truly belonged. Ariadne could look in each reflection and remember the man who had made them for her. The man who had loved her so much he'd wanted to capture her face a million times. The man she had never forgotten.

But for now there was one more task to do. Whether Ariadne liked it or not, she *had* to do it.

In her hand the phone felt heavy.

She climbed the hill and in the dusk stood under the olive tree and dialled the number.

'Hello?'

'Mum?'

'Lizzie!'

Neither of them said anything for a few seconds. Then predictably Mum moved on to safe topics like the weather and the food. She talked about school and homework. Things Lizzie hadn't thought about for weeks. Then there was a silence. Lizzie cleared her throat.

'I think you should come out.'

Mum acted like she hadn't heard and started talking about the Buckinghams and Bee. Apparently they were planning on sending her to a different school next term. A private school. They hoped it would sort her out.

It was the first piece of good news Lizzie had heard all day. She found herself smiling. No more Bee Buckingham at school! Then she remembered why she was phoning.

'No, mum, listen to me. You have to come out. Now.'

Mum stopped talking. In the background, Lizzie could hear the television.

'You know I'm different, don't you?'

'Lizzie, please don't start…'

'No, mum, listen! You've always known I was different. You always said I looked at you funny. You hated it.'

Mum took a sharp intake of breath. 'That's not true.'

'It is true. But it doesn't matter any more.'

'What doesn't matter, Lizzie? You aren't making sense.'

Lizzie took a massive deep breath. 'I'm psychic, mum. I can see when people are about to die.'

The phone felt hot in her hand. She changed hands. She could hear her mum breathing, the hot air blowing down the phone like bubbles.

'I knew about Joopy, didn't I? I knew he was going to die. That's why I didn't want to go to school. That's why I didn't want to let him out of my sight. You remember that, don't you?'

'Lizzie, *please*.'

'I *knew*, mum. I knew he was going to die. He had a black mark above his head.'

No, you didn't, Lizzie. You were sick with grief and unwell after Mrs Froust had died.'

'I wasn't! I saw that she was going to die too! I just didn't tell you because I knew you wouldn't understand! You never understand.'

'That's not true.'

'It is true! We never talk about things. Not *real* things. I never tell you what I'm doing because you never care.'

'Don't be stupid, Lizzie. Of course I care.'

'You care more about Bee than me!'

'How can you say that?'

'Because it's true! Because she's normal and pretty and I'm not.' Lizzie bit on her lip. 'I don't like wearing pretty clothes. Boys don't like me like, they like her. You know I'm different. You've always said so yourself!'

Her mum didn't say anything for a long time. For so long Lizzie thought she'd hung up the phone.

Her own breathing was ragged.

'I'm psychic mum.' She took a deep breath. 'And Ariadne's dying.'

'Don't say that, Lizzie!' Mum whispered. 'Just don't say it!'

'But it's true, mum, she has a black mark above her head. She's going to die on Saturday.'

The silence was so long this time that Lizzie was able to take the phone, rub the perspiration off it, and then replace it to her ear. She couldn't even hear her mum breathing this time.

'Mum? Are you still there?'

'Yes,' mum said quietly. 'I'm still here.'

'She's going to die, mum.'

Another long, flat silence.

'I know.'

Chapter Thirty-one

Lizzie woke when dawn was just breaking. The bedroom was stuffy so she stumbled out of bed and opened the shutters.

She almost missed her. Emerging from the thicket of oleander. Her hair was tousled and even from this distance, her mascara was smudged into two huge panda eyes. She zigzagged across the garden, unsteady on her bare feet. In one hand she carried her heels.

Bee.

Where had she been? Lizzie's heart kicked against her chest and she pressed her hand against it.

Bee paused. She'd dropped one of her shoes and bent over to pick it up. As she did, her dress fell open to reveal a pink balcony bra. She shoved the dress together again but still it flapped. Lizzie saw why. Because it was torn. She thought back to how hungry Rafa had been with her. How intense. How full of desire he'd been.

Lizzie closed the shutter.

She'd seen enough.

* * *

'Do you like them?' Lizzie asked shyly.

Ariadne's gaze spread around the kitchen like fire. On every spare surface of wall a reflection of her face stared back from the sun mirrors. She tip-toed up to one, as if in a dream, and tentatively stroked it with her fingertips. A long, low sigh escaped from her mouth.

'I don't just like them. I *love* them.' She spun round and clasped Lizzie by the shoulders. 'You did all this? By yourself?'

Lizzie nodded. She hadn't been able to get back to sleep, not after seeing Bee in that dishevelled state, so she'd gone back to the mirrors and brought them into the house. It hadn't been easy hanging them all up in the dim dawn light but it had been worth it just to see the look on Ariadne's face.

Ariadne clapped her hands in delight. 'I love them! Thank you!'

A surge of joy ran through her. She had done the right thing.

'What made you do this? Why now?'

Lizzie thought about her words carefully. 'I just wanted you to enjoy your last few days, that's all.'

Ariadne beamed.

'Now come out here! Close your eyes, here hold onto my arm for support.'

'Another surprise?'

Lizzie grinned. She guided Ariadne out of the back door, across the courtyard and into the shady inner den of the orchard. A small circular hollow in the midst of all the trees. This was where Ariadne had decided to hold her party.

'You can open them now.'

At first Ariadne didn't see it. It fitted so well into its surroundings that it almost seemed invisible. But then she caught sight of it and gasped.

'An angel!'

This had been much harder to do but luckily Gabriel had materialized from no-where before breakfast and helped Lizzie carry the cherub angel to the hollow.

'You can't have a death party without an angel,' Lizzie said.

Ariadne said nothing. It looked like she might cry but Ariadne didn't cry did she? Instead she rubbed her eyes. 'I'd forgotten all about him.'

'He was in the hallway covered in cobwebs.'

'Thank you, Lizzie.'

She grasped Lizzie in a tight hug and for a moment it was like that first day at the airport. She breathed in her grandmother's smell. It no longer smelt of lavender. It smelt like home.

'It's going to be a perfect day.' Ariadne pulled away and swept her hand around the hollow and then up toward the top of the hill.

'Are you sure you want .... it to happen up there?'

'Why not?' Ariadne fingered her necklace. 'I can't think of a more symbolic place.'

'I suppose not.'

'Shall we go up there now and take a look?' Ariadne didn't wait for answer and already strode on ahead.

Lizzie followed. She was fitter than she had been the first time she'd climbed this hill. Either that or Ariadne had got weaker. She slowed her pace so she wouldn't overtake.

At the top, Ariadne stopped to catch her breath. 'Walk the light, do you remember me telling you that, Lizzie?' She took her seat on the olive tree roots. 'The day is going to be just perfect.'

Was there such a thing as a perfect death? Ariadne seemed to think so. And if there was such a thing, then surely the days leading up to the moment itself also played a part. Lizzie thought about the role she had been cast.

'You've done well.' Ariadne didn't take her gaze from the horizon. 'Your gift has served you. Or perhaps you are serving your gift.'

Lizzie muddled this one over.

'I think I...'

Lizzie's mobile rang. She stared at the number.

'Go on, answer it then!'

She hesitated just a fraction before hitting the green button. '*Mum*?'

* * *

She ran down the hill. Neither time nor the hot thud of the sun could stop her. Clods of dirt skirted up under her feet. She slipped a little and scraped her hand on a rock. No matter.

The blue Nissan sat at the end of the track. Shimmering in the haze like a mirage.

'Mum?'

She stopped and shouted her name and her voice echoed around the valley like gunshot. One of the car doors opened and the dark glossy hair of her mum appeared. She looked up.

'MUM!' She screamed and skidded across the rutted dirt track and raced the last hundred yards before skidding to a halt just yards from where mum stood woodenly against the car.

They faced each other and suddenly everything felt awkward.

'You've changed,' mum said at last.

'Have I?' She peered up at her. *She* looked exactly the same as ever. Lizzie twirled a strand of hair around her finger. 'I suppose my hair is different.'

'It's not just your hair.' Her mum narrowed her eyes. 'It's you.'

'That's a good thing, no?' She caught herself using the inflection Rafa always used. She *had* changed, even down to her language.

'Yes,' mum said. 'I suppose so.'

'I'm glad you came.'

A faint sheen of perspiration beaded mum's forehead and her crisp white blouse stuck to her chest.

She noticed then there weren't any suitcases.

Her stomach clenched into a tight knot and she took an instinctive pace backward. 'No!'

'Lizzie, I'm not here to discuss this with you, I'm here to bring you *and* Bee home.'

'Are you joking?' Lizzie spluttered.

'Why would I joke? After your last phone call… what did you expect?'

'That you might come out to see your mum before she dies on Saturday?'

Her mum turned to her and she flinched at the intensity in her cocoa coloured eyes. She hadn't seen her look like since the day

Joopy died. 'Lizzie, listen to me. Noone can predict the exact day people are going to die, except doctors maybe, and even they get it wrong.'

'*I* know. *I* can tell.'

'I don't know why you suddenly think you have this … ability…. but drop it now.'

'And what if I don't want to?' She bit down the urge to yell. She took a deep breath instead. 'What if I want to stay here until after Saturday? What if I want to stay here for good.'

Mum looked as though she had had the air sucked out of her. 'For good?'

'I *belong* here. This is my home now.'

Mum took a sharp intake of breath. 'London is your home, Lizzie. Not this . . . place.'

'What's wrong with this place? *You* grew up here. Why can't I?'

Her mum winced. 'You're leaving with me and that's final.'

Lizzie walked away a few steps and took a couple of deep gulps of air. Stay calm. She placed her hand against the bark of an olive tree and felt the coarse wood under her fingers. 'You can't speak to me like that any more.'

'I'm not speaking to you like anything.'

'Yes you are. You're speaking to me as though I don't have a say in all this. But I do, mum.' She dropped her hand. 'You were right. I *have* changed. I can't leave Ariadne. Not now.'

'You don't know that she's going to die on Saturday.'

'Oh yes she does.'

Mum spun round. Ariadne stood resplendent in her long purple dress. In one hand she held a clump of fresh lavender and she held out the other. 'Rachel? How very lovely to see you again.'

Mum's brown eyes widened so much Lizzie thought they would fall out. 'Ariadne?'

'Who else?' She smiled. 'I realize it's been a few years but I trust I have not aged that badly.'

Mum and Ariadne stared at each other for so long that the sun shifted in the sky and the trees murmured in discontent.

'I …' mum stuttered.

'You had hoped not to see me.' Ariadne interrupted. 'I know.'

Mum looked away. Her eyes scanning the vista as if for the first time. 'It's as I remember it.'

'But of course. Nature does not change that much. Only we do.'

Mum snapped her gaze away and pulled herself upright. 'Let's not waste time on niceties. I'm here to take Lizzie home.'

Ariadne raised an eyebrow. 'I rather think that's up to Lizzie. She's perfectly capable of making that decision by herself.'

'She's only fifteen!'

'And?' Ariadne cocked her head to one side. 'You were fifteen when you decided you wanted to leave here.'

'That's got nothing to do with this!'

'Hasn't it?' Ariadne asked. 'I rather thought it had.'

The furrows in mum's face deepened. 'I want Lizzie to come home.'

'Well, let's leave it up to Lizzie, shall we?'

Lizzie stared from her mum back to her grandmother. Now they were side by side, she searched for any family resemblance. But it was as if they had been carved from two totally separate blocks of wood. The only similarity was the way they both looked at her imploringly. She gulped.

'Well?' her mum asked.

Lizzie faced her mum and they locked eyes. She willed her to back down. But she continued to stare back and her lips thinned to an invisible line.

'I . . . I want to stay here.'

Mum frowned and in the background, Ariadne coughed.

'I would give in now, Rachel, whilst you still can. Lizzie has a formidable spirit, just like you did at her age. It's admirable you've come all this way to take her home but short of forcing her on that plane, what can you do?' She held the lavender to her nostrils and inhaled deeply. 'But by all means, do take the other one.'

As Ariadne's eyes glittered with mischief, mum dropped her chin.

'I take it Lizzie has told you about the party?'

'You're having a party?'

'We have a birthday and we have a deathday. Why not celebrate both?'

'Because I don't see much to celebrate about death.' Mum's jaw tightened. 'I cannot believe you think this is appropriate.'

'Appropriate or not, this is what I have chosen to do and Lizzie has made her choice. Here, take this, it's good for nerves.' Ariadne handed her the lavender. 'So, are you staying here?'

'I have a room booked at the hotel in San Juan.'

'Don't be such a stubborn fool, Rachel. We have space, don't we, Lizzie?'

Lizzie nodded and waited for her mum's answer. So intent was she on her response, she almost didn't notice the looming shadow on the ground.

'Kala?'

Everything about him was dark and brooding. And yet so magnetic. At least to her. He wore black shorts and a black T-shirt. She shuddered. Even though he had said he didn't want her, every cell in her body leant toward him, wanted to curl up against his hot skin and feel the saltiness of his lips pressed against hers once again. She dug her fingernails into her palms to stop herself going over.

She wanted to tell him she had changed. That she had accepted her gift at last. But what was the point. He'd made it clear he didn't want her. Not now. But that didn't stop the hammering of her heart.

Beside her, mum bristled.

Ariadne stepped forward. 'Rachel, may I present my grandson, Rafael.'

Lizzie had never heard Ariadne call him by his real name before. It sounded strange.

'Your grandson?'

'Not her real grandson,' Lizzie explained hurriedly. 'But she's been *like* a grandmother to him.'

Rafa stabbed over a sudden look at Lizzie and all sorts of emotions rushed through her belly. The hot knife of desire, the rough memory of his kiss, the taste of his skin. She shivered.

Mum looked between Rafa and Lizzie. And she knew that she knew.

She let out a long, slow sigh. 'Maybe I should stay here tonight.

* * *

How could she forget the mirrors?

As soon as they stepped in the kitchen, her mum's frown stared back at her in multiple forms. It was not a good look. And it was only when she saw their reflections side by side that Lizzie saw how tanned she had become and how pasty her mum seemed. Had she really looked that white too, once upon a time?

Her mum muttered something under her breath and went straight to the sink to pour herself a glass of water. She had to rinse the glass twice before she was happy.

'It's so dirty here,' she muttered. 'I might as well live in a pigsty.'

Lizzie groaned. 'It's not that bad.'

Her mum tutted loudly. 'I hate to think how many germs are in this kitchen. Lizzie we cannot stay here. I'll book you into a room in the hotel too.'

'No,' Lizzie said. 'I said I'm not leaving!'

Just as she said this Rafa entered the kitchen and looked at her strangely.

Standing in the same small space as him made her feel claustrophobic. Like her breath had been squeezed out of her chest. It didn't matter that he sometimes smelled goaty, it didn't matter that his hair stuck up like a brush, all that mattered was the molten want that ran through her veins. It didn't even matter that he didn't want her.

She couldn't turn desire off.

'Let's go for a tour of the house. It's cleaner through there.' She grabbed her mum's arm and pushed her through the internal door and as they did, they came face to face with Bee.

'Mrs Fisher?' She paled. 'What .... are you doing here?'

'Taking you girls home as soon as I can get blasted reception on this phone.' She shook her mobile uselessly.

'There is no reception. We have to stay here.' Bee darted a look toward the kitchen where Rafa stood. 'Besides it's not the end of summer yet.'

'I take it you don't wish to leave either,' Lizzie's mum muttered. 'What is it with this place?'

Both Lizzie and Bee were unable to stop themselves looking back into the kitchen. Lizzie's mum followed their gaze – toward the dark, brooding presence of Rafa who filled the kitchen with all the cheery energy of a black mark.

'I thought you hated it here,' Lizzie said tearing her eyes away.

'Not any more,' Bee said pointedly as she edged past her and made her way into the kitchen. She smiled and then pushed shut the door in Lizzie's face.

Mum frowned at the closed door. 'Let's get your clothes and get you out of here.'

'Mum. I told you I'm not leaving. Why can't you just accept that?'

'You can't stay here,' Mum hissed. 'Let alone the fact how unhygienic it is, it is not appropriate for a fifteen year old to be around someone who is dying.'

'So you believe me then do you?'

Mum sighed. 'I read the letter, Lizzie. I know all about Ariadne's aneurism.'

Lizzie started. 'Why didn't you come out earlier then?'

Her mum pushed a hand through her hair in a gesture that reminded Lizzie of herself. It was what *she* did when she was nervous.

'Well?'

'Well nothing. I don't have to tell you everything do I? You don't tell me anything.'

Lizzie blinked at the bitterness in her voice. Mum pushed on through the house and paused by Lizzie's bedroom. 'You chose this one, didn't you?'

'How did you guess?'

'Because this was *my* bedroom. May I?'

Lizzie nodded and her mum opened the door. They both stood on the threshold and looked in. The light spread out across the room like a mosaic. Particles of dust floated in the air. Lizzie was glad she had remembered to make the bed this morning.

'Why don't you keep your room at home this tidy?' Mum looked around.

Lizzie shrugged. She wasn't about to admit she'd got used to being tidier and that it wasn't so bad.

Mum walked straight to the open window and gazed down over the oleandar. 'Even the view is the same.'

Lizzie hesitated before joining her. 'I love this view,' she admitted. 'It's so wild.'

'Is the dip-pool still there?'

Lizzie flushed. 'Yes.'

'You know your grandfather and I made that. Well, *he* made it, I just watched.' She smiled for the first time since she'd arrived. 'I used to love going there.'

Lizzie looked at her mum and could not imagine her mum

ever being relaxed enough to hang out in the dip-pool. With a stab, she realized she wished she had known the person who was her mother back then. What would her mum have become if she had stayed here? What would their relationship be like then?

Lizzie fished around for her voice. It seemed to come from a long way away. 'Why did you come?'

Mum's voice sounded as distant as her own. 'Because I found this.'

The room dipped in temperature. She knew with a punch to her stomach exactly what was coming as her mum unclasped her handbag and pulled out a sheaf of paper. It was the list of names with Bee heading the top.

She remembered the day she had buried it next to the angel and felt her skin whiten. *How*?

'It came through the letterbox one day.' She paused. 'I never knew . . . I didn't know this was happening. All these names and Bee too. Why didn't you tell me?'

Lizzie shook her head wordlessly.

'Liz?' Her mum touched her shoulder softly.

'Because I couldn't, ok?' Lizzie said. 'I couldn't tell anyone.'

'Not even your own mother?'

They stood in the light of the window and Lizzie tried to speak but she couldn't. The whole scene was like something out of a dream.

'I'm sorry,' her mum said.

Lizzie pulled away and stared at her mum until she looked uncomfortable. 'Anyway, I'm staying for the party.'

Chapter Thirty-two

It was a party to beat all parties.

And it started from the very moment Lizzie opened her eyes on Saturday. As she looked around her bedroom even the air looked different. Had the tiny particles of dust always danced in the light? Had the air always kissed her skin in this cool way? Had each minute always seemed eternal?

This was death's gift.

She remembered it from last time, when Hooper died. Death's shadow hung over life. And by doing so, it breathed vitality into every single moment.

She wriggled her fingers. Funny how such a tiny movement could be so magical and yet at the same time so commonplace it was taken for granted. This time tomorrow Ariadne would never be able to wriggle her fingers again. Nor would she see the particles of dust dancing in the light or feel the kiss of the air on her skin.

Life had many gifts.

Lizzie slung over her legs over the edge of the bed and smiled as she heard the distant strain of music drift up from the kitchen.

In fact, for the past three days the music hadn't even stopped because Ariadne had decided to start the party early. From Wednesday night people had been coming and going. Faces Lizzie had never seen before. They'd come from various corners in Spain, and many more from beyond. Ariadne, after all, was a woman of the world for whom making friends was easy. This was her gift and so when she wanted to throw a party, people attended.

'It's a living wake.' She joked on Thursday. 'At least I get to have fun with it.'

She'd been organising this week all summer. The invitations had gone long ago and Lizzie could only gaze in wonder at the assortment of people who tripped in and out of *Casa del Sol* during the past three days. She laughed when she looked back and remembered asking Ariadne if she wanted to go anywhere else during her last week.

Why? The world and all its wonders had come to her.

Only Ariadne could have friends like these. Everyone who walked in the door seemed to be an odd-bod of some sort. The kind of person who hung on the fringes of life, destined never to fit in or conform. But none of them seemed to care much about it either. Each of them alone would stand out in a crowd, but together, it was like a circus.

Lizzie was positively normal compared to the others and never had she felt so comfortable in her own skin. Not only that, they all seemed to find her fascinating.

'I hope you don't mind,' Ariadne confessed. 'But I told them all about you.'

She was the girl who could predict death and everyone who walked in the door begged to know more. And not one person was repulsed or horrified or thought she was a freak.

'Why should they be?' Ariadne asked.

Lizzie shrugged. There really was no answer for it anymore. She was different, and so what?

'I knew you would like my friends!' Ariadne beamed. 'I do pick the most interesting of friends. Did I not tell you I look for gold?' She swung her arm around the kitchen where an incredibly tall, thin man stood by the sink wearing a check suit and a bowler hat talking animatedly to a tiny Russian mime artist by the name of Serka.

'Those two have been married for nearly twenty-years. Sun and moon, Lizzie. Not everything is as it seems.'

When the Dutch juggler called Robb arrived on Thursday in the middle of the night, Lizzie was woken by Ariadne's screams of delight.

As was the rest of the house.

That was everyone except for Bee and her mum.

She'd not seen Bee since the guests had started to arrive. It was strange, but seeing so many *different* people in the same place made Bee the odd one out. Her normality suddenly seemed freakish. Bee had taken one look around, grabbed some clothes and ran.

Lizzie presumed to Rafa's.

The other person who didn't hang around was mum. After the first night in which mum claimed she hadn't slept a wink because of bed bugs, she'd left without saying a word at the crack of dawn and checked herself into the hotel. She'd been back only once and that was to invite Lizzie for a visit to the Botanical Gardens in Malaga.

Lizzie refused.

But Ariadne had urged her to change her mind so reluctantly as Ariadne entertained the Dutch juggler in peals of laughter, she and mum had spent the afternoon together in Malaga. The day was strained with all the things that were unsaid.

'It's just not something I wish to talk about.'

'But what about Saturday?'

'What about it?' Her mum had snapped.

'Are you going to come to the party?'

'Unlikely.'

They had stopped off at Malaga port on the way home to admire a huge cruise ship slip elegantly into dock. A bright shiny vessel full of promise. Neither spoke as the water churned.

'Why would I want to go?'

Lizzie shook her head incredulously. 'You're not even going to say goodbye to her?'

'Don't be so dramatic, Lizzie. You make it sound as though we're living on a film set.'

The ship's fog horn blew and both of them jumped.

'But don't you want to make up with her? You know, before she dies?'

Her mum turned back to the sea and didn't reply.

* * *

Now Saturday had come.

She wriggled her fingers, then her toes, and stood up.

'Today's the day.' She said out loud and closed her eyes. 'Please angel, make it be the most beautiful day of Ariadne's life.'

It wasn't the first time she'd prayed to the angel this week. She couldn't visit him, but she could picture his face and remember the coolness of his stone on her cheek. It was funny to think that once upon a time she'd had a crush on him.

But maybe it was safer that way. You didn't lose.

The shutter creaked in the breeze.

Lizzie shivered and with the sheet wrapped around her stood by the open window. In the herb garden, Ariadne was pulling up weeds. She wore the tatty straw hat and an old white shirt. As if she knew she was being watched, she paused and looked directly up at Lizzie's window. A cloud passed across the sun.

Death was still heartbreaking no matter how you dressed it up.

* * *

Most of Ariadne's out of town friends had come and gone. Their visits were short and sweet, trailing through like a comet and then trailing out again.

The Dutch juggler left after breakfast taking a sack of sweet figs with him.

Lizzie had made breakfast. Eggs, figs, crème fresh, nectarines, peaches, fresh orange juice, homemade bread, *jamon*, everything and anything Ariadne desired was on the table. Lizze had even laid out a battered detective novel on the table just in case her grandmother wanted one last mystery.

'It's a feast!' Ariadne exclaimed when she clapped eyes on the mini-banquet.

'It's all your favourites.'

Ariadne shoved a slice of *jamon* in her mouth. 'You really have thought of everything, haven't you?'

'Well, I've tried.'

'You haven't just tried, Lizzie, you've been incredible these past few days. I can't thank you enough.'

Lizzie laughed. 'Yes you can. You haven't stopped thanking me! Now eat your food.'

They ate until they could eat no more, each mouthful tasting richer than the last, and then they sat quietly with the remains sprawled around them. Ariadne ran her fingers down the spine of the novel.

'I've read this one before.'

Lizzie offered a half-smile. 'There was no point choosing you a new one.'

'True. Not unless where I'm going has a library.'

'Do you think ... do you think there is a somewhere?'

Ariadne picked up a knife and looked at her reflection. 'I'm not sure if a somewhere exists. Not in the real, earthly sense.' She put the knife down and paused. 'Do you think there's a someone?'

Lizzie was lost for words. 'Like who? *Seth*?'

Ariadne blushed. Lizzie had never seen her blush before. 'It's a long time to wait, even for someone like me.' She attempted a laugh but it came out all wrong. Instead she cleared her throat and stared down at her hands. They were spotted with age.

Lizzie leant forward. 'I'm sure he will be there.' Never had Lizzie seen Ariadne look quite so vulnerable. '*I'm sure*.'

There was a sound outside and Ariadne looked up sharply.

'Do you think mum will come?' Lizzie asked.

Ariadne sighed. 'I'm not sure.'

'What did you do?'

Time ticked as Lizzie waited for the answer. Her mouth was dry. 'You told me before that mum thinks it's your fault that Seth died. Was it?'

Ariadne's face darkened.

'But how?'

Ariadne touched her necklace in an unconscious gesture.

'I want to know,' Lizzie said. '*Please*. I want to hear it from you. Before it's too late.'

'There is not much to tell truth be known.' Ariadne coughed. 'Seth wanted to sell the mirrors because we needed the money and I wanted to keep them because he said he had made them for me.'

'And you argued about it?'

'For hours. It was one of those arguments. Unfortunately, your mother overheard some of it.' Her next words were so soft Lizzie barely heard them. 'She heard me tell your grandfather that I wished he would die.'

'But you didn't mean it?'

'Of course I didn't! It was just something foolish I said in the heat of the moment. But it was the last thing I said to him.' Ariadne paused and a thousand different emotions criss-crossed her face and reflected in the suns. She dropped her fingers to her lap and lowered her head. 'That's why I have kept them hidden for all these years. They remind me of my vanity.'

Lizzie reached out and grabbed her grandmother's hand. 'And now?'

'And now I am happy to see them because they remind me of him.'

'But it wasn't your fault anyway!'

'She thinks he died because of me.'

'It was an accident!'

'The surfboard hit him on the head and knocked him unconscious and that's why he drowned. Who knows – if we hadn't have argued he might have been paying more attention.'

Lizzie didn't know what to say.

'That's just speculation,' she said at last.

'Yes. Or it might be the truth.'

Lizzie put her arms around Ariadne's frail shoulders. 'I'm sure he forgives you.'

'I shall find out soon enough, I dare say,' Ariadne said. 'Anyway, now you know what happened, let's change the subject.' She smiled brightly. 'I've decided to wear my purple ball gown. What do you think?'

Lizzie nodded. Ariadne's choice of dress had been a hot topic all week. She herself had chosen to wear the blue dress she'd worn to the dip pool that day. It evoked memories. Mostly good.

'One more thing Ariadne.'

'Yes?'

'How did you ever move on from what happened? You know, from the hurt.' Lizzie touched her own heart. The place which still stung from Rafa's rejection and her own stupid mistakes.

Ariadne jumped up from her chair and pressed play on the stereo. At once the kitchen was filled with Rafa's music 'It's simple. You just keep on living!'

She held out her palm, and her wrist jangled with bracelets. 'Want to try it?'

'Try what?'

'Living. Let's dance.'

'What, now?'

'Lizzie, there's only ever now.' She hitched up the ends of her skirt and hoisted herself onto the kitchen table.

'But, the breakfast?' Lizzie bit her lip and wished she didn't sound so much like her mum.

'And do I care about the breakfast today? I want to *show* you something.'

Ariadne grinned and it was that total lack of anything else but this moment that inspired Lizzie. As if it were *her* last day on earth. One of the cats mewed, as if in approval and before she knew it, Lizzie was up on the table, face to face with Ariadne.

She felt absurdly tall and silly for a moment but Ariadne clutched both of her hands within her own and swayed them from side to side.

'Let's dance!'

She shuffled her feet in minute movements, trying to avoid the open jar of marmalade and the plate of *jamon,* keeping her eyes open to make sure her feet fell in the right places. She opened her mouth to warn Ariadne that her left foot was dangerously close to the butter, but Ariadne had thrown her head back, her hair hanging loose down her back, her mouth parted.

She had become the music.

Lizzie felt a stab of envy. She wished she could lose herself to that degree that nothing else in the world mattered. Instead she stood woodenly on the table and had a desperate urge to climb down and be sensible.

'Feel it,' Ariadne murmured. 'Forget everything else. Forget me, forget the table, forget where we are. Close your eyes, if that helps.'

Lizzie nodded and shut her eyes. For a moment she stood stiff, feeling like a girl standing on a kitchen table.

'Go deeper,' whispered Ariadne.

She tried to imagine how she felt in the plaza, the first time she heard Rafa's music. How had she been then? She'd been turned on by the music, hadn't she? It had coursed through her veins and woken up her up. Ever since that moment, she had wanted Rafa with a burning passion.

Wanting him to touch her everywhere - her shoulders, her neck, her torso, her hands, her feet, her lips....

And now! Now she could hear the music.

'That's it. Let it go deeper still. Go as deep as it can. Let it into your heart, Lizzie.'

And the music burrowed its way into her, until she started to sway and she felt her fingers flutter, her lips part, and behind her eyelids music painted pictures. They moved together, and there was a clash as something fell of the table. What was it?

'Don't open your eyes,' Ariadne whispered. 'It doesn't matter. Move your feet, it's ok.'

She took a tentative step, realised she wouldn't fall, and then the music shot into her heart and they were dancing and what kind of dance was it?

'It's love and longing and parting.'

And another plate crashed, as if in symphony.

And another. And it was as if the cat howled. But not the cat. Something, someone in pain. From where? From the gut? Ariadne's fingers dug into her shoulders and Lizzie felt her own head tip back, her own hair fall down her back, and the music and she were one. She threw up her arms.

'Yes, that's it! Dance, Lizzie. Dance with the music.'

How long it lasted like this, this complete union. Seconds? A minute? A lifetime? And then the moment passed as the song ebbed away. And she felt her toe was wet and smeared. She opened her eyes to see that she had trodden in the butter.

Ariadne didn't notice. She was gazing over Lizzie's shoulder with a beam splintered across her face.

'Rafa! You're here!'

She jumped off the table, like a cat, and ran toward the open back door.

Lizzie turned round slowly, running a hand through her hair. She caught a flash of Rafa's surprised face as Ariadne hurtled herself into his embrace.

Chapter Thirty-three

The first guest, a Spanish woman around the same age as Ariadne who had lived in San Juan since birth, arrived at noon. She carried with her a huge dish of *paella* and a carton of the local sweet wine. For the next few hours, a steady stream of local friends flowed to the house and brought with them plentiful gifts of food and wine. Lizzie recognised a few faces from the village, some she had seen at Rafa's party on the beach, others from the concert on the square. There were the familiar faces of Felipe, Jesus, Antonio, Oscar and Ana.

Most of the other guests might have been friends with Ariadne but they were strangers to Lizzie. Where had they all come from? She marvelled at how many people had turned up and how Ariadne welcomed each one like a long lost friend. There must have been well over a hundred people crammed into the orchard and the noise levels kept rising higher and higher.

As Ariadne had once said, the Spanish liked to party.

And so did Bee. Now Ariadne's out of town friends had disappeared, Bee had reinstated herself at the house. For today's party, she wore little more than her white bikini. She turned heads everywhere she went. And everywhere she did go, Carlos the waiter was about two foot behind.

'She's just so obvious,' Lizzie muttered, biting into a chicken drumstick and feeling overshadowed by Bee's allure. Her own blue dress was short and sexy but was it a jaw-stopper? Not compared to Bee's nakedness obviously. Unfortunately no-one was there to listen to her apart from Gabriel and as he didn't speak English, he couldn't answer. Nevertheless she liked to believe he understood her because every time he looked Bee's way he glared.

She'd ended up sitting next to him in the orchard over lunch. For once she didn't mind the smell. In fact she felt a certain fondness for him. He was Rafa's grandfather wasn't he? And she rather liked the way his eyes sparkled when they saw her. It was as if he knew something she did not. As if he saw her in a way no-one else could. She wondered if he knew. If Rafa had told him. But Ariadne said no-one knew here today that she was dying. She needed no excuse to throw a party in Spain.

And no-one remarked on the angel statue either.

She'd caught sight of Rafa a few times. It was hard to miss him in his bright red shirt. Each time she'd seen him her heart missed a beat. Not only that but her palms went sweaty and a flush rose to her cheeks. She wished she could turn her body off. But she couldn't. It didn't matter that they had finished even before they had ever really got started. Something had been ignited and it was impossible to dampen it.

But ever since breakfast when he'd seen her dancing on the table he'd not come near her and she'd not gone near him. The only consolation was she hadn't seen him with Bee either. Although, to be frank it was hard to get near her with the swarm of guys buzzing around her perpetually. Even now, her laugh trilled out across the orchard.

She put down the chicken. Her appetite had gone.

Looking around for Ariadne she saw that her grandmother had started to gather people to form a circle in the orchard. When she saw Lizzie, she waved and strode over. Wearing her purple ball gown *and* a sparkly tiara on her head, she looked resplendent.

'I think it's time for the music, don't you?'

'It's still early.' The day had been hot and the heat hadn't worn off yet.

'I know,' Ariadne looked bashful. 'But I don't want to miss him, you understand?'

Lizzie bit her lip. 'Of course.'

'Just a few songs.' Ariadne said. 'That's all I want.'

'Do you feel sad?'

Ariadne pulled the purple shawl round herself 'It would unnatural if I didn't.'

Lizzie nodded, not trusting herself to speak.

'You'll be ok won't you, Lizzie?' Ariadne asked looking directly at Bee who had swanned into view.

Lizzie's throat tightened but she nodded anyway. Although she hadn't spoken to Rafa, she'd caught him looking at her more than once today. She didn't even have to be looking at him to know. She could *feel* the intensity of his gaze boring into her.

On the other side of the circle Bee plopped herself down on her tummy. To her side, immediately, appeared Carlos. But Bee only had eyes for the person striding into the circle with a guitar under his arm. Rafa.

Lizzie's mouth felt dry.

'If he wants her....' Her voice trailed off. Why wouldn't the pain in her heart just go? She swallowed. 'If he wants her then he's not the one for me.'

Ariadne patted her hand. 'You will win him back, trust me.'

'I doubt it.'

It was then that Rafa started to play. At which point a hush fell over the circle. The Spanish had a reverence for flamenco which was like being in church. Rafa played slowly at first, plucking each chord like he was plucking flowers, touching the guitar like he had once touched her, and then gradually getting faster, until his fingers danced across the strings and the magic of the music echoed not just in this small clearing, but over the entire valley.

As the sun set in shades of gold, Rafa played song after song after song. He played with such an intensity that Lizzie could tune out the people, tune out the orchard, tune out the sky, and feel only the haunting world of Rafa. He had said that flamenco came from the heart and that's why it touched other people so effortlessly. His music slid into her heart and poured through every vein in her body.

She watched him, knowing she was staring, but unable to tear her eyes away. He must have felt her gaze too, because he looked up only once during the whole set, and he looked straight at her. They locked eyes and the fire danced between them and the flame in her belly reared up like a firework. She wanted to sprint across the circle and throw her arms around him so tightly that he would never let go. She wanted him to run his hands up and down her again. She wanted to taste the salt on his lips.

He missed a chord. And she was aware that other people in the circle were watching too. She heard herself gulp. Then he lowered his head once more and picked up the music.

Beside her, Ariadne chuckled. 'Do a dying woman a favour will you, just go to him.'

'What?'

'You heard.'

'I can't just go to him! He's playing.' Lizzie hissed.

Ariadne raised an eyebrow. 'And?'

'*And* he doesn't want me.'

'Are you mad? That boy is crazy about you!'

Lizzie saw Bee looking over at her across the circle. She edged closer to Ariadne. 'But what about Bee?'

'What about her? I'm serious, Lizzie.' She pointed to the sky towards the stars which hadn't come out yet. 'That's my wish. My *dying* wish. To see you get together before I go.'

'You can't say that!'

Ariadne grinned smugly. 'Yes I can. I can say anything I want today. And I want to see you walk across that circle and give that boy the kiss of his life. And then after that, I want to see the look on Bee's face.'

Lizzie's heart fluttered.

Ariadne lowered her voice. 'I want to know that he'll look after you . . . after I've gone. Please Lizzie. For me?'

Lizzie hesitated. 'But what if, what if he says no?'

Ariadne touched her necklace. 'If you're his moon, he won't

say no.'

On the other side of her, Gabriel clapped his hands, as if in agreement.

Rafa was coming to the end of another song. He had his head dipped and a lock of curly, wild hair fell over his forehead. Her legs felt shaky as she stood. They wobbled and wanted to collapse under her.

'I can't do this!' She tried to sit back down but Ariadne shoved her up. Across the circle, Bee widened her eyes in surprise and jabbed Carlos in the ribs to look up. Both of them leered and Lizzie felt like she was back in the classroom.

'Frizzo?' Bee called out. 'Frizzo Fisher, what *are* you doing?'

Lizzie turned to her briefly. 'I'm going to claim what is mine and you're going to stay there and watch.' She held up her palm. '*Enjoy.*'

Bee's mouth fell open in shock but Lizzie didn't stop to hear a response because now she was only feet away from Rafa.

Her mouth was dry and her tongue stuck to her teeth. She was clenching and unclenching her hands. Rafa hadn't noticed her yet. And yet she was so close she could see his fingers on the strings. See the veins in his hands. The muscles in his arms. The pulse throbbing in his neck.

'Rafa?' Her voice was shaky. She cleared her throat. 'Rafa?'

He looked up and their eyes collided. He stopped playing and now everyone in the circle was staring at them both. The tension crackled between them and standing so close she was aware of how every cell of her body craved him. Wanted him. He looked from her to the guitar and then back again. There was a long moment where Lizzie held her breath and then he placed the guitar down and stood up so they were face to face.

'Inglesa? Que pasa?'

He stepped closer and someone in the circle whistled. She placed one of his hands on her heart. It was hammering like mad.

'You feel it?' she murmured.

Rafa nodded staring at her like she had gone mad. Maybe she had.

'It's my song.' She blushed. 'My gift to life.'

They stood like that for what seemed like eternity. Rafa's expression was inscrutable. Oh God.

She took a deep breath. 'I'm a girl who can see when people die and this is who I am.' She paused. 'And I'm proud of it.'

There, she had said it. Now what? Had she done enough? Because there was just one last thing she could do. The very thing she'd been wanting to do ever since their souls first connected.

She placed one hand against his chest, his heart was beating wildly, and leant up on tiptoe and kissed him lightly on the lips. He tasted of wood smoke and salt and up close she could feel the heat radiating out from him. He groaned softly and someone in the circle whistled followed by another.

She looked him in the eyes. 'And ...'

'And?' He raised an eyebrow.

'And I love you.'

A moment passed. It felt like eternity.

And then he crushed his arms around her and kissed her back. It wasn't the kind of kiss that she ought to do in front of her grandmother. But so what? His arms wrapped tightly around her and he pulled her closer so she felt the full length of his body pressed against hers. Their tongues and lips collided and her belly lit up as she curled her hands around his neck.

He breathed into her ear. 'And I love you, *inglesa,* always and forever but especially right now.'

Over his shoulder she had the perfect view of Bee. It was as if someone had punched her in the face. She was open mouthed in shock and this made Lizzie enjoy the moment even more. Carlos was cheering and Bee elbowed him in the stomach before getting up and flouncing off.

Someone whooped, someone sounding suspiciously like Ariadne, but it didn't stop her from kissing him. Eventually, Rafa pulled back slightly, holding her still in his arms and gazing at her.

'You always surprise me.'

She nodded. 'I surprise me too.'

'Come with me.' He pulled her out of the circle and as he did she saw that Ariadne was on her feet and Gabriel was talking to her animatedly. But she didn't have time to ponder it because Rafa pulled her away and pressed her up against the rough bark of an orange tree. He kissed her again. Then again. She wrapped her arms around his neck and curled one of her legs around him. He pulled away again.

'Lizzie.'

'What?'

'We must be sensible.' He breathed into her ear. 'At least in public.'

She stroked his cheek and sighed. 'I know.'

He rested his forehead against hers. 'You are crazy.'

'Maybe.' She leant forward. 'So, am I forgiven?''

He laughed gently and cupped her cheek with one calloused palm. 'What do you think?'

'It doesn't matter who I am, does it? Not to you,' she said almost incredulously.

'Not really. I care only that you are happy in here.' He tapped her heart. 'And you are happy in here because you have a gift.'

'I'm happy because I have you too.'

Rafa smiled. 'And I am happy too, *inglesa*.'

Lizzie whispered. 'You're my angel.'

'I will be your dark angel,' Rafa teased.

'Yes, that's more apt.' She kissed him hard on the lips. 'And Bee?'

'There is nothing with her.' He shrugged. 'I have not seen her for days.'

'But that night?' Lizzie thought back to the night she'd seen Bee come in late with her clothes torn. 'She stayed with you?'

'No! I have not seen Bee since that night I tell you about that before. When she try to lie about you. But I say no thanks and she starts to cry. What can I do? So she phones Carlos to pick her up. I think she is with him, no?'

'Carlos the waiter?' *Of course.* 'But I thought she liked you?'

'She does like me,' Rafa said. 'But she cannot always get what she wants, no?'

She grinned.

'Besides, why do I want a girl like that? She has no passion. When I see you dance on the table I know you live with passion through all your body. You are true Andalucian.'

It was his turn to kiss her hard. He pulled her closer and she melted against his chest feeling every beat of his heart pressed against hers. If this was heaven, please let it last forever. The kaleidoscope of feelings swirled around her entire body and she . . .

'Lizzie? LIZZIE?'

Lizzie jumped a mile in the air, her whole body in shock.

'Mum!'

Her mum had appeared from nowhere, panting, out of breath, her hair uncharacteristically tangled around her flushed face.

'Mum?'

She peeled herself away from Rafa, brushed the dirt off her top and smoothed her hand through her hair quickly. 'Mum, meet Rafa, Rafa meet mum.'

Mum barely glanced at him. Her forehead was covered in a sheen of sweat. 'Where's your grandmother?'

'In the circle.' Lizzie waved toward the orchard.

'She's not there. I've looked.' Mum's jaw tensed. 'Nobody's seen her for about ten minutes.'

Lizzie's whole body froze.

'What is it?' Rafa paled.

'It's Ariadne.'

And then she ran.

Chapter Thirty-four

The three of them ran past the orchard and raced up the hill. She was surprised at how nimble mum was. She kicked her heels off along the way, thrust off her jacket, and clawed her way up the hill like a goat. They ran shoulder to shoulder, panting, shoving, pawing to get up. Just behind them was Rafa and behind him was Gabriel who they had picked up along the way.

Finally they got to the top of the hill and Lizzie skidded to a halt.

'Oh my God,' her hand flew to her mouth. 'Ariadne!'

Ariadne was lying motionless on the ground by the roots of the olive tree, curled up in the foetal position, with her gown spread under her like a puddle of purple blood.

'Ariadne? Please?' she heard the choke in her voice. '*Please*?'

She half ran, half stumbled over and slid to the ground next to her grandmother. Her eyes were closed and her face was still. Like a statue.

Her mum let out a sound that Lizzie had never heard before. She sank to her knees on the other side of her.

Lizzie picked up Ariadne's wrist. It was cool, limp and lifeless.

'Help her, mum! Do something!'

Her mum picked up the other wrist. 'I ... I can't feel a pulse.'

Lizzie's stomach clenched. 'No! She can't just die. Not like this.'

Her mum bowed her head over Ariadne's body and her shoulders shook.

Lizzie looked back down. Ariadne's face was pale and still. 'She can't be dead!' She scrabbled around, searching for a pulse on her other wrist. 'Rafa! Do something. Please!'

Rafa checked the pulse in her neck whilst Gabriel crossed himself. Somewhere in the distance a dog howled. It sounded like Joopy but of course, it couldn't be. Joopy was dead.

'She's still alive, isn't she?' Lizzie pleaded. 'Tell me she's still alive! I've still got to say goodbye.'

Rafa pressed his fingers against her neck for a long time. He shook his head.

'No! You're lying! She can't be!' Lizzie pushed his hand away and felt for Ariadne's pulse. Her skin was still warm. She dug her fingers in to feel for even the faintest murmur. There was nothing.

She was dead.

There was no blood, no broken limbs, no sign of life. Ariadne's face had fallen into its last ever expression but even in death, Lizzie couldn't read it. Surprise? Pleasure? Pain?

She would never know.

The pain rose up like a wave. She hadn't been here. Ariadne had died alone. Up here on the hill. Mum had come but *why* did she come so late? She squeezed her eyes shut. Oh God, the pain. That pain of death. The way it seared through her like a poker. Just like Joopy. That clamping, clawing, shuddering pain that gripped her stomach.

She stood up and turned away, toward the sea, away from Ariadne, away from everyone and she stood like that for a long time looking at an invisible horizon and a continent out of reach.

It didn't get any easier. Even when death was forecast, it didn't help. It still happened.

'Lizzie?'

She turned round. Rafa faced her. His eyes were bloodshot. 'We have to go down now. There is nothing more we can do.' He glanced toward the body and took a deep breath. 'We must call the undertaker.'

'No! Don't take her. Not yet.'

'The undertaker will need to take her, Lizzie. She can't stay here.... not in this heat.'

She nodded. 'I know. But please just let me stay with her for ten minutes. Just ten minutes with her.'

Rafa hesitated. His eyes were dark with grief and their kiss seemed a long way away. 'Are you sure?'

'Yes. I want to be with her.'

He squeezed her shoulder.

'I wasn't even here,' she replied flatly. 'I said I was going to be here and I wasn't.'

'Maybe she prefer it that way.'

'How can anyone prefer to die alone? Up here?!'

'This is what she chose,' Rafa said softly. 'She want to be by herself.'

Lizzie pressed her fingers to her eyes. 'But that's what hurts the most.'

Rafa nodded. They stood in silence as the stars around them started to sparkle. He touched the end of her fingertips.

'I take your mum down if you want.'

Lizzie looked across. Her mum was slumped against the olive tree. All the life had gone from her and she couldn't say anything that would ever make her feel better.

'Leave her with me.'

Rafa stroked her cheek. 'I go now, *inglesa*.'

He cupped her jaw and she pressed into his hand like a cat. The look between them spoke of the past and the future wrapped into one present moment which could last forever if you wanted it to. It was a look that seeped into her soul.

She swallowed the lump in her throat. Right now she loved him and he loved her. He was her sun and she was his moon. He burned for her just as she burned for him. He had chosen her over Bee and he had helped her find herself. She was Lizzie Fisher.

And she liked it.

Such a moment passed in an instant. The time it took for a star to shoot across the sky. The time it took for the boughs of the olive tree to whisper in the wind. The time it took for one long look which spoke of the mysteries of life and of death. The time it took to say goodbye.

Rafa crouched down next to Ariadne, swept the feathery hair away from her forehead and murmured something in Spanish to her. Lizzie turned away. Goodbyes were sacred things so she let Rafa and Gabriel each say their own private goodbye.

A few steps away stood mum. Her shoulders were shaking. Lizzie wanted to cross the short distance between them but her feet were rooted to the ground.

Rafa touched her shoulder and she jumped.

'You're going?'

'Yes. I take my grandfather. We will wait at the bottom of the hill for you.' He stroked her hair.

'She had a beautiful day, didn't she?' Lizzie buried her face in his shoulder.

'She had a beautiful *few* days thanks to you. She told me how much you did for her this week.'

'It's my gift.' Lizzie attempted a smile.

Yes, it is your gift.' He pulled her tighter. 'Your heart is my heart. I see you soon, *inglesa*.'

They stood like that for a moment until Lizzie peeled herself away. She watched as Rafa took his grandfather's elbow and guided him down the hill. At some point they would phone the ambulance and the undertaker would come.

At some point.

She watched until they were specks and then she took a deep breath and tentatively faced her mother again.

'It's time,' Lizzie said.

Her mum looked over and in that look Lizzie found the courage to cross the few steps between them. It was easy. Without thinking she threw herself into her mum's arms.

'Oh, mum.'

Mum held her awkwardly at first. But then she hugged her back. She didn't want to cry but the lump burst out of her throat, the place where she'd been holding it, and she pressed her face against her chest and sobbed. They stood there for ages whilst her mum stroked her hair with her smooth, cool hand and she breathed in her perfumed smell.

'You haven't hugged for me ages.'

Her mum prised himself away and gazed at her. 'I haven't done a lot of things for ages.' And nothing more was said because sometimes, Lizzie had learnt, words just weren't enough.

Hand in hand they walked over to Ariadne's body. The air shifted and became noticeably cooler. In the sky, the stars sparkled like diamonds whilst the branches of the olive tree whispered.

The pain hit Lizzie again in her stomach and she sat doubled over her grandmother, pressing her fingers to her eyes. It hurt. When she opened them, everything was the same.

Except that mum held her hand open and in the centre of her palm sat a shiny half moon. The other half to the necklace. Lizzie's mouth opened in surprise.

'You had it all this time?'

'After dad died I kept it. It was my way of remembering him, except I've kept it locked in a draw all these years.' She held out her palm. 'You do it, Liz.'

'Me?'

Her mum nodded.

'Are you sure?'

'Yes. It has to be you.'

Lizzie took the half moon and gently placed it into the necklace so it clicked onto the sun. They joined together perfectly. It sat in the pool of Ariadne's throat and Lizzie touched it with her fingertips.

'She had it all planned, didn't she? Right down to the final moment,' Lizzie sighed. 'She didn't want me here at all. Not at the end.'

Mum tried to smile and failed. 'She always did things her way.'

Lizzie looked up. 'It wasn't her fault you know. She never wanted him to die.'

Her mum spoke so softly Lizzie almost missed it. 'I know.'

Lizzie reached out and touched her mum's hand. It was too late to make the peace with Ariadne for her mum, but it wasn't too late for her.

'I will come home, mum. After the funeral.'

Mum's face collapsed in such relief that Lizzie knew she was doing the right thing. And strangely, school didn't scare her so much anymore. She was Lizzie Fisher, *la inglesa,* she was brave and she was different.

And she was loved!

'You are so much like your grandfather,' mum murmured.

'Ariadne always said that too.'

'You are. One day you must go and to meet his family.'

Lizzie smiled. 'I'd love that.'

Instinctively, they both quietened at the same moment and turned to face the woman who lay between them. The only noise was the sound of a wind picking up. She might have left this life and yet around her, Lizzie felt a sense of peace. Perhaps that was Ariadne's last expression – one of peace. As if she were now a stone angel.

'She wanted to be with him, didn't she?' Lizzie whispered. 'Right at the end, she just wanted to be with him.'

Her mum stroked Ariadne's hair from her face. 'They loved each other very much.'

'Did he come back for her, do you think?' She looked back at Ariadne's peaceful face. 'Do you think they're together somewhere now?'

Her mum paused and then smiled. 'I think so, yes.'

Somewhere in the distance a dog barked. Really, it sounded so like Joopy. She cocked her head to listen. Nothing. Just the emptiness of the land around her and the vastness of the night. The sky was like one giant black mark. The dog barked again.

And all the way from Africa, the wind blew. Bringing in sand from the Sahara and as it did, it carried something on the breeze.

Infinity.

About the Author

Hannah M Davis lives in a white-washed village in Andalusia in southern Spain and is head over heels in love with tapas, fiestas and the occasional siesta.

With a background in film, Hannah brings over 10 years of editorial experience to her writing and has professionally critiqued scripts for many leading people in film and theatre. In fact, somewhere in the bowels of the London Film Industry a dusty film script of hers still awaits production. Above everything however, her heart is in writing transformational and entertaining books that help people, particularly teenagers, believe in themselves just that little bit more.

She is currently having lots of fun living by the sea and writing the sequel to *Voices of Angels*.

Come say hi on my blog and get yourself a free gift in the process!
www.hannahmdavis.com

Or connect with me via social media!
http://twitter.com/#!/Hannah_Author
http://www.facebook.com/#!/pages/Hannah-M-Davis

Soul Rocks, is a fresh list that takes the search for soul and spirit mainstream. Chick-lit, young adult, cult, fashionable fiction & non-fiction with a fierce twist.